Love's Dangerous Game

"I am certainly not m[...]
you have any secret[...]
end up, Francis, for[...]

"There is nothing to forget," Lord Francis said. "It will be all charade, Soph. All panting and pretended passion. A counterfeit passion. I rather fancy it. Life has been tedious lately. What do you say, Lady Sophia?"

"I say yes," Sophia said, lifting her chin and looking indignantly at Lord Francis's lazy and very white grin. "But I am not marrying you, mind, Francis."

"Good," he said. "But remember, if you fall in love with me in earnest, Soph, you may be doomed to a terrible disappointment . . ."

A
Counterfeit
Betrothal

—◆◆◆—

by
Mary Balogh

Ⓢ
A SIGNET BOOK

SIGNET
Published by the Penguin Group
Penguin Books USA Inc., 375 Hudson Street,
New York, New York, 10014, U.S.A.
Penguin Books Ltd, 27 Wrights Lane, London W8 5TZ, England
Penguin Books Australia Ltd, Ringwood, Victoria, Australia
Penguin Books Canada Ltd, 10 Alcorn Avenue, Toronto, Ontario, Canada M4V 3B2
Penguin Books (N.Z.) Ltd, 182-190 Wairau Road,
Auckland 10, New Zealand

Penguin Books Ltd, Registered Offices:
Harmondsworth, Middlesex, England

First published by Signet, an imprint of New American Library,
a division of Penguin Books USA Inc.

First Printing, June, 1992

10 9 8 7 6 5 4 3 2 1

1

"Anyway," Lady Sophia Bryant said, "I have no intention of marrying anyone. Ever." She gave her yellow parasol a twirl above her head and looked into the flowing waters of the River Thames, which sparkled in the May sunshine.

It was a rash statement to make considering the fact that there were three perfectly eligible gentlemen in the group that adorned the grass on the riverbank at Lady Pinkerton's garden party in Richmond. There were two other young ladies there too, one Lady Sophia's close friend and the other one of the greatest gossips of the younger generation. By nightfall the whole of London would know what she had just said, including her papa, who had brought her to London for the Season, doubtless with the intention of finding her a husband despite the fact that she had not quite reached her eighteenth birthday.

But she had meant the words.

"Then there will be no further point in being in town," Mr. Peter Hathaway said. "We gentlemen might as well pack our trunks and retire to the country, Lady Sophia." He caught the eye of Lord Francis Sutton, who was sprawled on his side, propped on one elbow, his chin on his hand. He was sucking on a blade of grass. He raised one expressive eyebrow and Mr. Hathaway grimaced. "Were it not for the presence of Miss Maxwell and Miss Brooks-Hyde, of course," he added hastily.

"But why, Lady Sophia?" Miss Dorothy Brooks-Hyde asked. "Would you prefer to be a spinster dependent upon your male relatives for the rest of your life? You do not even have any brothers."

"I shall not be dependent," Lady Sophia said. "When I am one-and-twenty I shall come into my fortune and set up my own establishment. I shall cultivate the best of company about me, and all the married ladies will envy me."

"And you will cultivate the label of bluestocking into the bargain, Soph," Lord Francis said, first removing the blade of grass from his mouth. "It won't suit you."

"Nonsense," she said. "You are going to be horribly covered with grass, Francis."

"Then you can brush me down," he said, winking at her and returning the blade of grass to his mouth.

"I do not wonder that the name of rake has sometimes been attached to you in the past few years, Francis," Lady Sophia said severely.

"Sophia!" Miss Cynthia Maxwell said reproachfully, dipping her parasol in front of her face to hide her blushes from the gentlemen.

Sir Marmaduke Lane entered the conversation. "Seriously, Lady Sophia," he said, "it is neither easy nor advisable to avoid matrimony. Our society and the whole future of the human race depends upon our making eligible connections. Indeed, one might even say it is our duty to enter the married state."

"Fiddle!" was Lady Sophia's reaction to this rather pompous speech. "Why would one give up one's freedom and the whole of one's future happiness just out of a sense of duty?"

"I would rather have said that happiness comes from marriage and the bearing of children," Dorothy said. "What else is there for a woman after all?" She glanced at Lord Francis for approval but he was occupied with the absorbing task of selecting another blade of grass to suck upon.

"Marriage brings nothing but unhappiness," Lady Sophia said hotly. "Once the first flush of romance has worn off, there is nothing left. Nothing at all. The husband can return to his old way of life while the wife is left with nothing and no means of making anything meaningful out of what remains of her life. And there is no getting out of marriage once one is in, beyond praying every night for the demise of one's partner. I have no intention of allowing any such thing to happen to me, thank you very much."

"But not all marriages are so unfortunate, Sophia," Cynthia said soothingly. "Most couples get along tolerably well together."

"Well, my parents' marriage is a disaster," Sophia said, twirling her parasol angrily and glaring out across the water. "My mother has not left Rushton in almost fourteen years and my father has not set foot there in all that time. Don't talk to me of getting along together."

"Sheer stubbornness is the cause, I would guess," Mr. Hathaway said. "I am not acquainted with your mama, Lady Sophia, but I can imagine that your papa is stubborn to a fault. They ought not to have carried on a quarrel for that long, though. Were they always unhappy together?"

"How would I know?" Sophia said. "I was only four years old when they separated. I scarcely remember their being together."

"They should make up their differences," Sir Marmaduke said. "They should find comfort in each other in their old age."

Mr. Hathaway snorted while Sir Francis grinned. "I don't know the countess, Lane," the former said, "but I would wager that Clifton would not enjoy being informed that he is in his dotage. You cannot find some way of bringing them together, Lady Sophia?"

"Why?" she said. 'So that they may quarrel and part again?"

"Perhaps they would not, either," he said. "Perhaps they would be delighted to see each other again."

"Of course," Dorothy said, "ladies do lose their looks faster than men. Perhaps he would be shocked to see her aged."

"Mama is beautiful!" Sophia said. "Far lovelier than . . ." But she would not complete the comparison. Lady Mornington was undoubtedly Papa's mistress, discreet as they both were about their relationship. But Mama was lovelier for all that. Ten times—a hundred times—lovelier.

"Then you should bring them together," Mr. Hathaway said. "It was probably a foolish quarrel, anyway."

"Oh, how could I possibly accomplish such a thing?" Sophia said irritably.

"Say you want your mama here for the Season, Sophia," Cynthia said. "It is perfectly understandable that you would wish her to be here for your come-out."

"Papa asked me if I wanted her or him to bring me out," Sophia said. "If I had said Mama, then he would have stayed away. I would not choose. I refused. Anyway, I do not believe Mama would have come. She has been in the country for too long."

"You will have to get yourself involved in some scandal, Soph," Lord Francis said after working the blade of grass to the side of his mouth. "That will bring her at a trot. Find someone quite ineligible to elope with."

"Oh, do be serious, Francis," she said crossly. "Why would I want to elope with anyone? I would be forced to marry him and probably would not bring Mama and Papa together after all. That is the silliest idea I ever heard."

"Conceive a grand passion for someone ineligible, then," he said. "Refuse to listen to reason. Threaten to elope if your father will not consent. Be as difficult as you girls know how to be. He will send for your mother out of exasperation before you know it."

"He would be more likely to pack me off to Rushton," Sophia said. "I do wish someone would change the subject. How did we get started on this, anyway?"

"By trying to guess who would be betrothed or married to whom by the end of the Season," Mr. Hathaway said. "Could you not betroth yourself to someone your papa will disapprove of, yet would not like to reject out of hand, Lady Sophia? Can you not present him with a problem that he would need your mama to help solve?"

She tutted. "One of the royal dukes, perhaps?" she said.

"One of your papa's friends, perhaps," he said, his brow furrowed in thought. "Or the son of one of his friends. Someone he would not quite want for his daughter, and yet someone he would not like to send packing because of his friend. A younger son, perhaps—with something of a shady reputation."

"Did someone mention my name?" Lord Francis asked. "You should conceive a grand passion for me, Soph. My father would be delighted and my mother would not stop hugging me from now until doomsday. Clifton would have an apoplexy."

"What a ridiculous idea," Sophia said.

"Not necessarily," Mr. Hathaway said thoughtfully. "Clifton and the Duke of Weymouth have about as close a friendship as they come, do they not? And Sutton is certainly the type of man I was just describing."

"Thank you," Lord Francis said dryly. "Don't forget, Hathaway, that there are only three older brothers and four nephews between me and the dukedom."

"But you are something of a rake, Francis, you must admit," Sophia said. "And what Papa calls a hellion into the bargain."

He grinned at her and winked again. "Fancy me, do you, Soph?" he said while Cynthia dipped her parasol again, and Dorothy was almost visibly storing up details to share with her mama as soon as she decently might. "It would work too, by Jove. I'll wager Clifton would send his most bruising rider tearing off on his fastest mount for your mama if you just whispered your intention of making yourself into Mrs. Lord Francis."

"How stupid," she said. "As if I would ever in my wildest moment consider marrying you, Francis."

He shuddered theatrically. "It is as well, then," he said, "that I would never in the deepest of my cups consider asking you, Soph. Don't glare. You started the insults."

"Besides," Sir Marmaduke said, "it would not be fitting to use the institution of holy matrimony as a charade to accomplish another goal entirely."

"But Sophia," Cynthia said, "do you not think it worth a try? Wouldn't your papa really be in a dreadful dilemma?"

"I believe," Sophia said unwillingly, "that he and his grace once expressed a wish that their families be united by marriage. But unfortunately for them, Papa had only me and I was too young. Francis is the only son still unmarried."

"And the black sheep into the bargain," that young man said. "Clifton has been ominously silent on the old topic since Claude, my last respectable brother, married Henrietta two years ago."

"The question is," Mr. Hathaway said, "are you willing to try it, you two?"

"Enter into a passion with Soph?" Lord Francis said. "The idea has its appeal, I must admit." His eyes laughed at Sophia as they traveled over her seated figure in its flimsy sprigged muslin dress.

"How stupid," she said. "Stop looking at me like that."

"But do you think your papa might send for your mama if you announced your intention of marrying Lord Francis, Sophia?" Cynthia asked.

"If I got into what Papa calls one of my stubborn moods and insisted that she be consulted, perhaps," Sophia admitted. "But perhaps not, too. They have managed to solve all problems for the past fourteen years without once meeting face to face."

"But are you willing to try?" Mr. Hathaway asked. "That is the question now. Sutton?"

Lord Francis was grinning at Sophia. "Soph?" he asked.

"I certainly am not marrying you," she said. "If you have any secret hope that that is how it will end up, Francis, forget it."

"There is nothing to forget," he said. "It will be all charade, Soph. All panting and pretended passion. A counterfeit passion. I rather fancy it. Life has been tedious lately."

"What do you say, Lady Sophia?" Dorothy asked, a note of suppressed excitement in her voice.

"Sophia twirled her parasol and prepared to say one more time that the whole idea was ridiculous and that she would not, even in pretense, show a romantic interest in her old childhood tormentor. There was no bringing Mama and Papa together anyway. If they had remained irrevocably apart for fourteen years, there was doubtless no way of changing things now.

"I would strongly advise against it, Lady Sophia," Sir Marmaduke said. "The holy institution of matrimony is not to be taken in jest."

That did it. "I say yes," Sophia said, lifting her chin and looking indignantly at Lord Francis's lazy and very white grin. "I say let's try it. But I am not marrying you, mind, Francis."

"Good," he said. "You had better be careful not to fall

in love with me in earnest, Soph, or you will be doomed to a terrible disappointment, you know. And if you puff up like that, my girl, you might explode. You gave the first set down. I merely took my cue from you.''

"This will not work," she said. "It is a remarkably foolish idea.''

"It might too," Mr. Hathaway said hastily. "But one thing we must all do is swear secrecy. Not a word or a hint. Miss Brooks-Hyde?''

Dorothy looked to be in an agony. She would fairly burst with the story. "Oh, very well," she said. "But I hope for your sake that this charade will not go for too long, Lady Sophia. It will do your reputation no good at all.''

"Thank you," Lord Francis said.

"I mean when she breaks off the betrothal," Dorothy said, coloring. "Or the connection, if it does not quite come to a betrothal.''

"I do hope the scheme works for you, Sophia," Cynthia said. "I know how you adore both your mama and your papa. And it is not as if you do not know Lord Francis at all. You have known each other forever, have you not?''

"For at least that long," Lord Francis said. "Or is it longer, Soph? I can remember outrunning you when you could scarcely walk.''

"Lane?" Mr. Hathaway asked.

"You may depend upon me," Sir Marmaduke said. "I can only applaud your efforts to effect a reconciliation between your parents, Lady Sophia, even if I must frown upon your methods. But I shall say nothing.''

"And I shan't, of course," Mr. Hathaway said. "So all is settled. And since the Earl of Clifton is at this garden party, I would suggest that the two of you link arms and stroll off and start falling desperately in love.''

"Done," Lord Francis said, getting unhastily to his feet and stretching out a hand to help Sophia to hers. "You will be able to brush me off after all, Soph.''

"I absolutely will not," she said indignantly. "You may brush yourself off.''

"You see?" he said, appealing to the rest of the group.

''She is afraid that if she once lays hands on me, she will not be able to remove them again.''

Miss Cynthia Maxwell tipped her parasol once more to hide her blushes.

She leaned forward in her seat the better to see out of the carriage window. It looked amazingly the same, the village of Clifton, though she had not seen it for well over fourteen years. She looked half eagerly, half unwillingly at the parish church with its tall, elegant spire and its cobbled path that wound through a sleepy churchyard.

They had run along it after their wedding, hand in hand, laughing, eager to escape from the boisterous greetings of family and friends and villagers, eager to reach the carriage outside the gate, eager to be behind the curtains where they had found the privacy in which to kiss lingeringly and gaze into each other's eyes and smile with the novel and incredible knowledge that they were man and wife, that she was his viscountess.

Almost nineteen years before. She had been seventeen, he twenty-one. Their parents on both sides had been reluctant to consent to the match on account of their youth, but they had persisted. They had been caught up in all the wonder of young love.

Olivia Bryant, Countess of Clifton, leaned back in her seat and closed her eyes. She did not want to view the ghosts of those young lovers rushing from their wedding to a happily ever after world—a world that had lasted not quite five years. She did not want to think of it. She had stopped thinking of it a long time before.

The carriage proceeded on its way through the village and to the gates leading to Clifton Court half a mile beyond. Her father-in-law's home when they were married, now her husband's.

Despite herself she felt her stomach churning with apprehension. What would he look like now? Would she recognize him? He had been tall and slim when she last saw him, his dark hair thick and always overlong, his face handsome and boyish and ever alight with eagerness and a zest for life—except the last time she saw him, of course. He had been twenty-six years old at that time. He was forty now. He had turned forty in May, two months before.

Forty! He was middle-aged. She was middle-aged. She would be thirty-seven in September. They had an eighteen-year-old daughter. Sophia had celebrated her eighteenth birthday in London one day after her father's birthday. Although in labor all through his birthday eighteen years before, the countess had been unable to give birth until two hours into a new day. They had laughed about it, gazing fondly and triumphantly into each other's eyes after he had been allowed into her bedchamber to view his new daughter.

She would give him a son the next time, she had promised him. But there had been no next time. She had not conceived in four years, and after four years he had left, never to return.

Would she recognize him? She felt rather sick.

Sophia's letter had been abject and pleading, Marc's cool and formal and to the point. But both had made her see that it was necessary for her to come. She had shown both letters to her friend Clarence—Sir Clarence Wickham—and he had agreed with her. She should go, he had advised. Clearly a family decision must be made, and it was the kind of decision that could not be discussed by letter.

Sophia was deeply in love with Lord Francis Sutton, youngest son of Marc's friend, the Duke of Weymouth. Deeply, head over ears, forever in love, according to her letter. He was handsome and charming and intelligent and kind and everything that was wonderful. And if ever he had given in to a youthful wildness, it was all behind him now. He worshiped her and was going to love her and care for her for the rest of their lives. And though he was a younger son and had lived somewhat extravagantly for some years, he was not without prospects. Apart from the settlement his father would make on him when he married, he was the favorite and heir of an elderly great-aunt, who was very wealthy indeed. Please, would Mama come and see for herself just what an eligible husband he would be for her, and persuade Papa that his wild days were at an end? Please would she come? *Please?*

Their daughter had conceived a quite ineligible passion, the earl had written, and had declared her intention of marrying the young man or running away with him. Lord Francis Sutton was a hellion, no less, an irresponsible puppy who would lead Sophia a merry dance if they were wed. Besides, she was far too young to be thinking of marriage. And yet the situation was awkward. The young people had been unfortunately vocal in their intentions, and Weymouth and his wife were delighted at the proposed connection. He had been forced to invite them and the young man to Clifton with a few other guests, hoping that somehow the betrothal could be avoided. Weymouth, on the other hand, seemed to believe that it was a betrothal party that was in the making. Would Olivia please come to Clifton to help talk sense into their daughter?

"You always seem to have had more influence over her than I," he had written graciously.

And so she was coming. She felt the carriage rumble over the humpbacked stone bridge and knew that the house would be visible out of the left window. She turned her hands palm up and examined them closely.

Surely there must have been some other way. But there had not, she knew. Sophia must be dissuaded from making a disastrous marriage. The countess could remember Lord Francis only as a young and mischievous little boy, three or four years older than Sophia. But Marc had said in his letter that the young man was wild. That would mean that he was a daredevil, a gambler and drinker, a rake. A womanizer.

Not that for Sophia. Anything but that. If they were in love now, it would not last. He would return to his old ways once the gloss had worn off their marriage. Sophia would end up with a lifetime of misery, an unfaithful rake for a husband.

Not that for Sophia. Please not that, she begged an unseen power silently. Please not that. Sophia was all she had. If she had to live to see Sophia rejected and desperately unhappy, she would not be able to bear it.

When finally she could ignore the approach of the house no longer, she saw that the front doors to the house were open. And Sophia herself was eagerly rushing down the marble steps, looking pretty and fashionable with her dark hair cut short and curled—very like her father as the countess remembered him. She had a young man by the hand and was dragging him after her—a tall and slender young man with fair hair and a laughing handsome face.

"Mama!" Sophia stood beside the carriage almost bouncing on the spot in her impatience, waiting for a footman to open the door and lower the steps. She continued speaking as soon as the door was opened. "I thought you would never get here. I said you would be here yesterday, but Papa said no, that you could not possibly come all the way from Lincolnshire to Gloucestershire before today at the very earliest. Perhaps even tomorrow, he said. But I knew it would be today once it became obvious that it would not be yesterday."

She hurled herself into her mother's arms as the latter descended the steps.

"It seems forever," she said. "I wish you had come to London, Mama. It is so splendid there. This is Francis." She turned to smile dazzlingly at the fair young man and to link her arm through his. "Do you remember him?"

"Only as a very young boy who had a gift for getting into mischief," the countess said, smiling and extending a hand to him. She noted with a sinking of her heart his very attractive grin. "I am pleased to meet you again, Lord Francis."

"I do not wonder that you have kept yourself in the country, ma'am, rather than come to London," he said, taking her hand in a firm clasp. "I see that you have been keeping yourself close to the fountain of eternal youth."

The Countess of Clifton was far from pleased by the young man's flattery. If he used it on Sophia, it was no wonder that he had turned the girl's head. And he was far too handsome. But such thoughts fled from her mind as she became aware without looking—without daring to look—of someone else coming out onto the steps of the house and beginning to descend them.

Was it? she thought in some panic when it was no longer possible to keep her eyes from straying beyond Lord Francis's shoulder. Could it be? Her heart was beating so painfully that she thought she might completely disgrace herself and faint.

He was broader. Not fat—there was not one spare ounce of fat on his body as far as the eye could tell. But broad and powerful of shoulders and chest. He looked fit, well-muscled, strong. He was taller than she remembered. His hair was still thick—he had not lost any of it, as she had expected he might. It was still dark, but liberally flecked with silver. Oddly enough, the silver hairs added to rather than detracted from the overall impression of virility that he gave.

His face was different. Just as handsome—more so, in fact. It was a man's face now, not an eager boy's. But there was a hardness there, about the jaw and in the dark eyes, a cynicism that had been totally absent before.

It was him. Of course it was him. So very different. So very much the same.

"Olivia," he said, stretching out a hand. She remembered his hands, the long strong fingers, the short, well-manicured nails. "Welcome home."

"Marcus," she said, placing her hand in his, watching it close about hers, feeling with some shock its warmth and its firmness, almost as if she had expected to watch but not feel.

And she watched and felt more shock as he raised her hand to his lips. She looked up into his eyes and realized that his thoughts must be occupied in the same manner as her own. He was noticing the changes, the sameness.

Mostly changes, she thought, dropping her gaze again. She had been twenty-two years old when he had left her—no, when she had driven him away. A mere girl.

"Papa," Sophia said, clapping her hands, "does Mama not look beautiful?"

"Yes," he said. "Very. Come inside, Olivia. My butler and housekeeper are eager to be presented to you. Then Sophia will take you to your room and you may rest and refresh yourself."

"Thank you," she said and laid her hand on the arm he extended to her.

She heard Sophia laugh in delight behind them.

2

He had not known how he was to treat her when she arrived. He had agonized over the possibilities for days. And he was not at all sure that he had made the right decision.

Perhaps he should have treated her as a guest rather than as the mistress of Clifton Court. Perhaps he should have had her put in a guest chamber rather than in the countess's room next to his own. Perhaps he should have had the connecting door between their dressing rooms locked. Perhaps he should have stayed inside the hall to greet her instead of going outside. Or, perhaps he should have insisted on going out ahead of Sophia. Perhaps he should not have given her the function of hostess at dinner, seating her at the foot of the table, facing him across its length, Weymouth beside her. Perhaps he should have been all business and taken her aside soon after her arrival to discuss the matter of Sophia's imminent betrothal.

Perhaps he should not have summoned her at all. Perhaps he should merely have invited her opinion and advice by letter. He had done so several times over the years. Her letters were invariably lucid and sensible.

He felt like a gauche schoolboy again, the Earl of Clifton thought later in the evening as he completed the third hand of cards opposite the duchess. He should be more like his wife. She had been a calm and unruffled hostess all evening and was at present conversing quietly at the other end of the long drawing room with Weymouth and Sutton and Sophia and a few of the other guests.

His wife! It seemed impossible, he thought, glancing across the room at her. His wife of almost nineteen years. Livy. A stranger.

"They make a charming couple, do they not, Marcus?" the duchess said as he took her elbow and steered her in the direction of the tea tray. She was smiling fondly across the room. "Such a lovely and prettily behaved girl. Better than Francis deserves, I must confess, though he is a dear boy and will appear so to all the world once he has sown his wild oats, as William puts it. And I do believe that perhaps they are already sown. Sophia is having a steadying effect on him."

"It seems a long time since they used to play and quarrel interminably," the earl said, avoiding the basic issue. Sutton had offered for Sophia already, but had been given no final answer. He had been told that the matter must be discussed with Lady Sophia's mother. He had been told that there was the serious matter of Sophia's very young age to be considered. And yet the earl's friends, the Weymouths, were behaving as if the delay in consent was a mere formality.

"And he is closer in age to her than Claude would have been," the duchess said, "or Richard or Bertie."

"The christening of Claude's son went well?" the earl asked, trying to turn the subject.

It was a fortunate question. The duchess, accepting a cup of tea from his hands, seated herself, summoned about her a court of younger ladies with a gracious smile, and proceeded to entertain them with an account of the christening of her son's heir. Lord Clifton stood watching her politely.

Sophia, he saw, had moved with several of the young people and seated herself at the pianoforte. Sutton was behind her, leaning past her to set a piece of music on the stand before her. His arms were on either side of her so that when she turned her head to smile warmly at him they almost kissed. The earl felt his jaw tightening. If that young puppy ever laid so much as a single finger on Sophia without his personal say-so, he would . . .

He looked toward his wife. Olivia must help. She would doubtless know what to do to put an end to such an undesirable connection. Just as she had known how to persuade a much younger Sophia to spend Christmas with him that one year when the girl had wished to return home to her mother, with whom she had always lived for most of the year. And when the time came, she had known how to talk their daughter into going to school, although Sophia had been angry and rebellious. She loudly exclaimed that Mama would take her part and not insist that she be packed off to an institution just as if she were not wanted.

It was not easy having a daughter, he had found, with no wife close by to advise him on how best to bring her up. He had never asked Mary's advice, though she was a woman of sense and doubtless would have been willing to give it. Mary and Sophia belonged to quite different aspects of his life.

His wife was talking with Weymouth and smiling. She looked quite at her ease until she glanced his way, catching his eye. She turned sharply away, and seemed discomposed for a moment.

He had wondered if he would recognize her. And perhaps he would not have, if she had not been alone and in Sophia's arms. Perhaps he would have passed her on a crowded street. Though he would undoubtedly have turned his head for a second look. She had been very pretty as a young woman— unusually lovely, in fact. She had had a slender, pleasing figure and a bright, expressive, smiling face surrounded by masses of almost blonde curls.

She was beautiful now, quite extraordinarily beautiful. Her figure was fuller, more alluring, her long hair combed smoothly back from her face and coiled at the back of her head—there was no sign of gray in it. But her face was the part of her that had changed most. Although she smiled now, and had smiled through dinner and most of the evening, it appeared to be an expression she had deliberately assumed. The animation, the brightness had gone, leaving behind only beauty and serenity.

Livy! She had been only seventeen when he had first seen her. Her parents had had no intention of marrying her off so young. She was making her come-out only because an older cousin of hers was also to be presented and the two families had decided to make it a joint occasion.

They had spent most of the evening on opposite sides of the ballroom. He had been very young himself, just down from Oxford, just about to embark upon the life of a man about town. He had been eager to acquire some town bronze, some town swagger—until he had seen her and known all through the evening that she had also seen him, though their eyes never quite met.

But their eyes had met and held, after he had arranged an introduction to her and danced with her after supper. And her cheeks had flushed and her lips had parted, and he had been smitten by a whole arsenal of Cupid's darts. Poor foolish young man, believing that young love could last for a lifetime.

The earl returned his attention to the Duchess of Weymouth in time to make an appropriate comment on something she had said. Sophia must be prevented from making the same mistake, he thought. She must be protected from coming to the same fate as her mother. And yet he himself had not even been a rake—not as Sutton was with his large array of ladybirds and just as large a following of respectable young ladies sighing for his favors. He himself had been an innocent. A dangerous innocent, who had made one mistake and had not had the sense to keep quiet about it.

Livy!

He bowed and turned away from the ladies as the conversation turned to other topics. He strolled across the room in the direction of his wife and Weymouth. And he remembered how she had been as a young bride and how he had been. A pair of young innocents deeply in love and eager to consummate that love, the one as virginal and unknowledgeable as the other.

He had been fumbling and awkward. He had hurt her dreadfully and had been forced to finish the consummation to the sound of her smothered sobs. And yet she had turned in his arms afterward and looked at him with that eager young face and consoled him, one hand smoothing his hair. *She* had consoled *him*! It did not matter, she had assured him. She was his wife now and that was all that mattered.

"And it will be better next time," she had told him. "It will be, I promise you. Marc?" Even in the near darkness he had seen the radiance of her smile. "I am your wife. Not just because of the church and the vicar and the ceremony and the guests. But because of this. You are my husband."

"Forever and ever, Livy," he had promised her, kissing her warmly and lingeringly. "Forever and ever my wife, and forever and ever my love."

Poor fool. Forever had lasted not quite five years.

She looked up as he approached. The smile that she had imposed upon her face stayed in place.

"I have just been telling Olivia how good it is to see her again," the duke said. "She is in good looks. We had some good times together, all of us, did we not, when the boys were small and Sophia a mere toddler?"

"Yes," the earl said. "Bertie and Richard and Claude were always her champions against the various atrocities Francis devised to be rid of her."

The duke laughed. "I think I had a permanently stinging hand that one time you all stayed with us for a month," he said. "I doubtless gave myself far more pain than I meted out to Francis's backside. Do you remember the orchestra pavilion, Olivia?"

The earl chuckled and looked at his wife to find that her smile had changed to one of genuine amusement.

"If it is possible for one's heart to perform a complete somersault," she said, "I think mine did when I saw Sophia sitting on the very peak of the dome, as cool as a cucumber, refusing to admit either that she was frightened or that she did not know how to get down."

"And she was barely four years old," his grace said.

"I did not know," the earl said, "that I was capable of shinning up smooth pillars and up an even smoother dome in less time than it would have taken me to run around the pavilion once."

"And Olivia standing below admonishing you to be careful," the duke said with a chuckle. "And holding out her arms as if she thought she could catch you if you fell."

Lord Clifton met his wife's amused eyes and felt his smile fade with hers.

"And Francis nowhere in sight," his grace continued, "after luring her up there. He had gone fishing, if I remember correctly. And it was Olivia weeping in your arms, Marcus, after it was all over, not Sophia. She was on her way to join the fishing party, I believe."

"Yes," the earl said. "I believe I was so shaken that I even forgot to spank her."

"They were good days," the duke said with a sigh, "when the children were all young and about us. But who would have thought that Francis and Sophia would ever develop an attachment? He would never let her play with him even when they got older. Is that not right, Marcus?"

"Fortunately," Lord Clifton said, "they did not see much of each other once they were both off at school and Sophia was spending most of her holidays at Rushton. They have not met for four years before this spring."

"And now it seems, Olivia," the duke said, "that they want to make us related by marriage. How will you like it, eh? Do you fancy having my scamp of a youngest son for a son-in-law? I would not blame you at all if you were to say no." He laughed heartily.

The earl looked at his wife.

"Marcus and I have had no chance to discuss Lord Francis's offer," she said quietly. "It would be unfair to give my opinion until we have done so, William."

A good answer, the earl thought, looking at her admiringly. Marcus? She had called him that earlier outside. Prior to that, she had not called him by his full name since before their marriage. It had always been Marc. But then he had been calling her Olivia since her arrival.

Which was as it should be. They were after all strangers. Strangers who happened to share some memories and a daughter.

"This is neither the time nor the place to discuss terms anyway," the duke said. "Ah, the young people are leaving the pianoforte."

Sutton was taking Sophia by the hand, the earl saw, and threading his fingers with hers. They were smiling at each other as if they saw the whole world mirrored in each other's eyes. And they were approaching.

"Your permission, sir," Lord Francis said, bowing, "to

take your daughter walking on the terrace outside. Miss Maxwell and Lady Jennifer, Mr. Hathaway, and Sir Ridley will be coming too, if the ladies' parents permit.''

"It is a heavenly night," Sophia said. "We looked out through the windows a short time ago—did we not, Francis—and all the stars are shining and the moon is bright. Do say yes, Papa. It is too warm in here."

She was looking very pretty, her father thought, her dark eyes bright, her cheeks flushed, the radiance of young love giving her a certain glow. She reminded him of her mother, although he had never before thought them alike. There was something in the expression. Olivia had used to glow like that.

"Mama," Sophia was saying, "the fountain looks quite breathtaking in the moonlight. Do you remember that from when Grandpapa used to live here? You should come outside with us. You should come with Papa." She laughed and turned toward him. "What better chaperons could there be, after all, than my parents?"

"I think your mother is probably tired from her journey, Sophia," he said.

"And yet," Lord Francis said with a bow, "there is nothing better calculated to lull one to sleep than a short walk outdoors before retiring. Is there, Lady Clifton? Won't you come?"

There was a brief silence.

"Olivia?" the earl said and found himself almost holding his breath. "Would you care for some fresh air?"

"Thank you," she said after another brief pause. "I think that would be pleasant."

"I shall send up for your cloak, then," he said.

"Look back when you have the opportunity," Sophia said. "Not now. Casually, just as if you are looking at the stars. I cannot look without seeming very obvious. Are they walking together, Francis? Are they talking? Don't do it now or they will think I have asked you to do so. *Not now!*"

Lord Francis had turned his head over his shoulder without any attempt at casualness or subterfuge.

"She has her arm through his," he reported. "They are not talking. At least they were not when I looked. But perhaps one of them had just stopped speaking and was pausing to draw breath while the other had nothing to say."

"I said not now," she hissed at him. "They will think we are spying on them."

"If I had only thought," he said, "I would have brought my telescope out with me. Except that I did not bring it with me to Clifton, of course. And now that I come to think of it, I do not possess one at all. I shall slink across into some bushes if you wish, Soph, to observe the proceedings. Do you think they will miss me? I don't know how they could when Lady Jennifer is shrieking with such mirth. Whatever can Hathaway be saying to her, do you suppose?"

"This is all a joke to you, is it not?" she asked. "My mama and papa are together for the first time in fourteen years and all you can do is talk about stupid things like slinking off into bushes. Do you ever take anything seriously?"

"I do, Soph," he said. "I would worry about getting my knee breeches snagged by thorns."

"Oh!" she said, tossing her head.

"I think it is time for a melting glance," he said. "We cannot have them thinking that our ardor has cooled. I think we have done remarkably well so far, don't you? I don't know about you, Soph, but I am giving serious consideration to going on the stage."

"You might as well," she said tartly. "You would be close to all your actresses."

"Smile, darling," he said seductively, turning his face sideways in order to give an image of his profile to those walking behind them and smiling dazzlingly down at her. "Come on, Soph. It is worth a mint to see you do it."

She turned her head to look up into his eyes and smile slowly and meltingly. He bowed his head a fraction closer and looked down at her lips.

"Don't you dare," she said, her expression not changing at all. "If you want your cheek smacked and your nose flattened and your eye blackened, just come half an inch closer, Francis."

His face moved perhaps a quarter of an inch closer. "That is quite far enough," he said. "Not that your threats would deter me if I really were tempted in even the smallest way to steal a kiss, Soph. But I have a distinct feeling that your father's fist might cause my nostrils to part company with each other if I did."

They both turned their heads to face the front again, the radiant smiles fading as they did so.

"What next?" he asked. "My parents are already planning wedding journeys and drawing up guest lists and wondering which church the wedding is to be in. And my mother is already dreaming of new grandchildren and wondering if there will be time to wash and iron the family christening robes after Claude's baby and before ours. All while I stand by looking complacent and rather as if a falling star had hit me in the eye."

"I don't like to disappoint them," Sophia said, "but I would not marry you, Francis, if you were the last man on earth."

"In some ways we are remarkably well suited, Soph," he said pleasantly. "We think alike. I do not believe I would marry you even under similar but reversed conditions to the ones you mentioned."

"You are no gentleman," she said. "You never have been."

"There is no point in being cross just because I refuse to marry you, Soph," he said. "I was gentleman enough to allow you to refuse to marry me first. But enough of this quarreling. What happens next? We suddenly find that our love has cooled so that my parents and I can take ourselves off tomorrow and I can get back to the congenial life of raking?"

"You would like that too, would you not?" she said. "You would like to abandon me just as if I were a hot potato to be dropped at all cost?"

"In short, yes," he said. "But I gather from your tone that you have further use for me."

"Of course I have further use for you," she said indignantly. "If you leave tomorrow or the next day, Francis,

Mama will have no further need to stay here and she will go home and never see Papa again. And that will be that. And if that happens, I shall never marry anyone for I will not allow myself to be lured into such a life of misery. What are they doing? And *don't look now*!''

Lord Francis looked. ''Strolling and talking,'' he said.

''Talking?'' She looked up at him eagerly. ''That is promising. Don't you think so, Francis?''

''We have been talking too,'' he said. ''Quarreling.''

She sighed. ''Do you think they are quarreling too?'' she asked.

''No idea,'' he said. ''But you can depend upon it that they are too well-bred to come to fisticuffs, Soph. So I am to stay in order to keep them together, am I? Do you think they are going to allow us to become betrothed?''

''Not if Papa can help it,'' she said. ''He says that I am far too young even though I have had my eighteenth birthday already and am older than Mama was when she married. But that would be his meaning, would it not? We are going to have to be distraught, Francis. We are going to have to threaten elopement or suicide.''

''By Jove,'' he said. ''Quite a choice, is it not? The devil and the deep blue sea, would you say?''

''No,'' she said. ''But I would fully expect you to do so. I would choose suicide without the slightest hesitation. It will be best if they do consent, though.'' She frowned in thought. ''We will want to marry without delay, of course. A summer wedding. Mama will have to stay to plan it. There will be a great deal for her and Papa to discuss. And perhaps our wedding will remind them of their own.''

''Ah,'' he said, ''I hate to interrupt this pleasant train of thought, Soph, but did you say our *wedding*? What do we do afterward? Neglect to consummate it and go begging for an annulment?''

''Oh,'' she said. ''You are right. There cannot actually be a wedding, can there? But just the planning of it will remind them. Don't you think? And how could you say what you just said? It would be just like you to humiliate me by annulling our marriage and having the whole world say that

I could not even attract you sufficiently to tempt you on our wedding night.''

"Soph," he said, "I am glad the moon is not quite full. I might hear some words of real madness from you.''

"But really," she said, "you could not have said anything more insulting, Francis. I should die of mortification.''

"Good Lord," he said. "And to think that I gave up a week or two or five of a life of genial civilization in Brighton for this.''

"A life of gambling and carousing and womanizing, you mean," she said tartly.

"That is what I said, is it not?" he said. "Time to bill and coo again, Soph. A kiss on the hand, I believe?" He raised her hand to his lips and held it there while she smiled radiantly up at him.

3

There was a certain familiarity even after fourteen years. A familiar height, her cheek just above the level of his shoulder. A familiar and distinctive way of holding his arm, with her own linked through it. He held it tight to his body so that the back of her hand was against his side.

She had never minded before, of course. She had always walked close beside him. When they had walked unobserved, he had often set an arm about her shoulders while she had set hers about his waist.

"Your curls make a comfortable pillow for my cheek, Liv," he had often said. And sometimes he would rest it there and snore loudly while she had giggled and told him how foolish he was.

She minded now. She had hoped to avoid memories and comparisons. She had hoped to avoid all but purely business encounters with him. A foolish hope, of course, when the duration of her stay was indefinite and there were guests at the house looking for amusement. And when it was summertime at Clifton. Summertime at Clifton. She felt a welling of memories and nostalgia.

Marc. Oh, Marc.

"So what do you think?" he asked now, breaking the silence between them.

"About Sophia and Lord Francis?" she asked. "She is too young, Marcus. Only just eighteen. She is still a child."

"Yes," he said, and they both remembered an even younger child who nineteen years before had insisted on marrying. Two young children.

"She knows nothing of life," she said, "and nothing of people. She finished school only a year ago and was with me in the country until after Christmas. How can she possibly be ready for marriage?"

"She cannot," he said.

"I know how it must have been," she said. "She got caught up in the whirl and glamor of the Season and met Lord Francis again for the first time since they have both grown up, and fell in love with him. It was inevitable. He is a very handsome and charming boy. But she does not know what a sheltered world she has been living in. She does not know that their love cannot possibly last."

"No," he said.

"I know what it is like," she said. "I know just how she is feeling."

"Yes," he said.

Because it happened just like that with me. She did not speak the words aloud, but she did not need to. They hung heavy on the air before them.

"You are agreed with me, then," he said, "that we must prevent the betrothal from happening?"

"Yes," she said. "Oh, yes."

"It will not be easy," he said. "They are quite besotted with each other and you know how stubborn Sophia can be. I have always avoided confrontations with her whenever possible. I am afraid I have sometimes found her unmanageable. You have always done better than I on that score, Olivia."

"Yes," she said. "You have always indulged her, Marcus. Perhaps you were afraid of losing her love. I have always shut my mind to the possibility and refused to allow her her way on every matter."

"I have seen so little of her," he said. "I never kept her long because I felt she needed her mother more than her father. And I always thought you would miss her."

"Yes," she said. "I always did. Oh, Marcus, look at them. They are totally wrapped up in each other."

Sophia and Lord Francis were still walking, but their faces were turned to each other, the moonlight catching his expression of tenderness and utter absorption in her. For one shocked moment Olivia thought that he was going to kiss her daughter, but he drew his head back and they strolled on.

"By God," the earl muttered quite viciously, "he would

have been sorry if he had moved just one inch closer.''

"Oh, Marcus," the countess said, "is he quite as wild
as you suggested? He seems such a pleasant young man.''

"There is nothing vicious about him, as far as I know,"
Lord Clifton said. "He has been known to gamble a little
too much and he involves himself in too many of the more
outrageous and daring exploits in the betting books—things
like racing curricles to Brighton and drinking a pint of ale
at as many inns in London as possible during one night before
becoming insensible. And he spends too much time in the
greenrooms of the theaters. Nothing he will not outgrow in
time in all probability. He is only twenty-two.''

But you did not outgrow them. She wondered with
unwilling curiosity if Lady Mornington was still his mistress
or if it was someone else now. She so rarely heard news of
his doings. Lady Mornington might be four or five years in
his past by now, for all she knew. And probably was. After
all, he had remained faithful to his wife for less than five
years.

"But why would he suddenly wish to marry Sophia?" she
asked. "He is very young and his behavior has suggested
that he is not yet ready to settle down. Why the sudden
change? She is just an infant.''

"But a very pretty and vivacious infant," he said. "We
are looking at her through parents' eyes, Olivia. To us she
is just a child and probably always will be. You were
increasing when you were her age.''

She closed her eyes briefly and remembered. The wonder
of it. The sheer joy of it. Life growing in her. Her child and
Marc's, the product of their love. The only cloud—the *only*
one on what had remained of their married life together after
Sophia had been born was the fact that it had never happened
again, that she had never again been able to conceive despite
the fact that they had made love very frequently.

"Yes," she said. "Marcus, she must be persuaded to give
up this foolishness. I shall have to talk with her tomorrow.
I have had no chance today. I shall explain to her all the
dangers and disadvantages of marrying so young. She will
listen to me. She almost always has. And if she will not,

then you must exert your authority. You must reject Lord Francis's suit.''

"Yes." He sighed. "It will not be easy, Olivia. William and Rose seem to think the betrothal is an accomplished fact already. They are more than delighted. And they have always been such good and such close friends.''

"Then you must speak with them," she said. "We can do so together if you wish. We must explain that Sophia is too young, that her happiness is very precious to us because she is our only child.''

The only link between us in all these years.

"And everyone else expects it too," he said. "That is why they think they have been invited here. And everyone in the neighborhood, doubtless. It is why they think you have come. Sophia has persuaded me to organize a ball for the end of the week, you know. Everyone will be expecting the announcement to be made there.''

"Then they will have to find that they are wrong," she said. "Marcus, don't make a scene. There are two other couples out here. And it is just her hand.''

She had felt the tightening of his arm muscles and had looked up to see the hardening of his jaw as he glared ahead at a besotted Lord Francis holding Sophia's hand to his lips and keeping it there for altogether too long a time.

"Impudent puppy," the earl muttered. "I shall take a horse whip to his hide and do what Weymouth should have done years ago.''

"His behavior is not so very improper," she said soothingly. "Now that I am here we can handle this together, Marcus. It will be all over within a few weeks, I daresay, and then we can return to normal living.''

"I hope you are right," he said.

The Countess of Clifton sat in the window seat of her private sitting room the following day waiting for her daughter to come. It was more than an hour past luncheon already and they had still not had their talk. It was very difficult, it seemed, to accomplish anything of a serious or personal nature while a house party was in full swing. There was always too much else to do.

That morning a riding party had been arranged for the young people, to be chaperoned by Lord and Lady Wheatley, Lady Jennifer's parents. The earl had joined them. And at luncheon Miss Biddeford had talked of nothing else except the bonnet in the village that she should have bought the day before. Finally Mrs. Biddeford had agreed to take her daughter back into the village.

"Though it will be straight in and out again," she had said. "I want to play bowls with the others."

Several of the guests were with the earl on the bowling green at the back of the house. Sophia had been invited to accompany her friend Rachel and Mrs. Biddeford and had looked inquiringly at her mother. The countess had nodded.

But there was no sign yet of the returning carriage. It was really too beautiful a day to be indoors, Olivia thought, looking out beyond the fountain and the formal gardens before the house over the rolling miles of the park in the distance. She had fallen in love with Clifton Court during her very first visit there, though on that occasion her room had been the small Chinese one at the back of the house, overlooking the kitchen gardens, greenhouses, and orchards, and the lawns, bowling green, and woods to the west.

The woods. And the hidden garden. She wondered if it was still there: a small and exquisite flower garden in the middle of the woods, entirely enclosed by an ivy-covered wall and accessible only through an oak door that could be locked from the outside or bolted from within.

It had been designed for and by the crippled sister of Marcus's grandfather, long deceased by the time Olivia first came to the house. Marcus had taken her there the day after their betrothal became official and one month before their wedding—a time when it was deemed proper for them to be alone for short spells without a chaperon.

It was there that he had kissed her for the first time. . . .

The countess got abruptly to her feet and walked restlessly about the room, straightening a picture, shaking a cushion before moving through the open door into her bedchamber and beyond it to her dressing room. She checked her appearance in the mirror, applied more perfume to her wrists. And looked at the closed door opposite the open one leading back into her bedchamber.

She had been curious about it since her arrival the previous afternoon. She was really not sure. Her apartments had been the former countess's. But perhaps his rooms were elsewhere. She set a light hand on the doorknob and listened. Silence. It was probably locked, anyway.

She turned the handle slowly and felt the slight give of the door. It was not. She pushed it inward, her heart pounding uncomfortably, feeling like a thief. It was probably an unoccupied room.

A shaving cup and brush were on the washstand, brushes and combs and bottles of cologne on the dressing table. A blue brocade dressing gown had been thrown over the back of a chair, a pair of leather slippers pushed carelessly beneath. There was a book on the seat of the chair.

She looked unwillingly beyond the room, through the open door leading to a bedchamber equal in size to her own, though its high bed, richly canopied and curtained, was more elaborate than hers. There was another book on the bed, visible through the side curtains, which were looped back.

The only other part of the room she could see was a side table that held a single, framed picture. It was turned away from her. It was doubtful that she could have seen it clearly, anyway, from the connecting doorway between their dressing rooms.

Would it be *her?* she wondered. She had been told that Lady Mornington was a lovely woman. But perhaps it was someone different by now. Someone younger. Someone no older than Sophia, perhaps. Either way, she did not want to see. It was one thing to know of his debaucheries, to think of them occasionally when she could not force her thoughts to remain free of him, to imagine the woman with whom he was currently involved. It was another to see. To see the face of the woman—of one of the women—with whom he committed adultery.

She did not want to see. And yet she was already in the doorway to the bedchamber, looking nervously at the hall door, half expecting it to crash open at any moment. She listened again. Again silence.

The picture was turned so that he would be able to see it from his bed. Was he so little able to live without her, then? Was he longing to have this business with Sophia settled so that he could go back to her? Olivia hoped she would not be very young or very pretty, as she reached out an unwilling hand and turned the picture.

She was indeed very young. And smiling and happy. And pregnant, though the painter had omitted that detail. But she was not in her best looks, she had protested to Marc. She had begged him to wait until after she had given birth. But Marc could be as stubborn as his daughter was now. He wanted her likeness, he had told her, so that he could always have her with him, even when she was busy visiting and gossiping with her friends. She could remember realizing with some shock that he was afraid to wait in case she died in childbed. And so she had consented.

And the painting was now on the table beside his bed, turned so that he could see it from his pillow. Was it always there—from force of habit, perhaps—noticed no more than the rest of the furniture in the room? Or had he placed it there for the occasion, in case she should have reason to look into his room, as she did now?

That smile had been for him. He had never once left her during the tedious hours of the sitting. He had talked and talked and told endless funny stories until the painter had looked reproachfully at him because she had laughed so much.

The smile had been for him.

Marc!

She closed her eyes and drew in a slow breath.

Her eyes flew open at the distant sound of a door opening. She turned the picture back to its original position with hasty fingers and dashed back through both rooms, pausing only for a moment to set his slippers side by side beneath the chair. His valet must have missed them. Marc had never been renowned for tidiness. She closed the door between the two dressing rooms and leaned back against it, breathing with relief.

What in heaven's name would she have said if he had caught her?

"Mama?" Sophia's voice came from the bedchamber.

"In here," the countess called, hurrying through from the dressing room. Her daughter was peering around the door from the sitting room. "I thought you had decided to stay in the village until nightfall."

"Mrs. Biddeford remembered all sorts of things she wanted once we were there," Sophia said. "And Rachel decided that she did not like the bonnet after all. But once we had left the shop and made all the other purchases and were back in the carriage, she changed her mind once more and nothing would do but we must descend again and go back for it. All the way home she entertained us with assurances that she should have waited until she returned to town." She laughed.

"Sophia," her mother said, "we have to talk."

"Oh, dear," the girl said. "I always know you are serious when you smile at me in just that way, Mama."

"Sit down," the countess said, ushering her daughter back into the sitting room.

"It is about Francis, is it not?" Sophia said, looking at her mother anxiously and standing in the middle of the room. "You do not like him, Mama? You are remembering him as he was as a young boy, are you, when he was forever playing nasty tricks on me because I was always following him about? But that was just boyhood, Mama. All boys are like that, horrid creatures. Or you have heard bad things of him recently. He has been sowing his wild oats, Mama. It is what young men do. But that is all behind him now. And it is said, you know, that reformed rakes make the best of husbands."

"Oh, Sophia." The countess laughed despite herself. "Do you have any more platitudes to mouth? Come and sit down, do, and tell me how this all began. You have not seen Lord Francis for several years, have you? I cannot remember your having a single good word to say about him before now.''

Sophia sighed and sank down onto a sofa. "But all our aversion to each other has been converted into love," she said. "He is so very wonderful, Mama. I did not imagine it possible to feel this way. Is this how you felt about Papa?"

"I daresay," the countess said. "Sophia, I find this very difficult. Until the last year or so, it has been easy to deal with you. If we disagreed on any issue of importance, I would merely decide for you whether you liked it or not. Now it is not so easy to force you to do what I wish, even if my greater experience of life helps me to see reality more clearly than you."

Sophia got to her feet again and crossed the room to one of the long windows. "You are not going to forbid me to marry Francis then?" she asked. "But Papa is preparing to do so, is he not? And you wish to do so, do you not? But why, when he is the son of a duke, Papa's close friend, and when he and I are so deeply in love?"

"Sophia," her mother said earnestly, "you are so very young. So very sure that nothing will ever change, that there is such a thing as happily ever after. How am I to explain to you that life is just not so, that your future should be planned with your head and not your heart? I know that such an idea will be quite beyond your comprehension and utterly abhorrent to you. It would have been so to me at your age."

Sophia turned to look at her. "Must I fall out of love with Francis merely because you fell out of love with Papa?" she asked. "Must history always repeat itself?"

"Sophia." The countess looked distressed. "I did not . . . that is not what happened between Papa and me. It is not because of that that I am advising you to think more carefully."

"Yes, it is," Sophia said. "Every girl I know has made or is planning to make her come-out at the age of seventeen or eighteen. And all their mamas and papas are eager for them to make suitable marriages. It is the thing to do. Else, why is London during the spring known as the Marriage Mart? And who could be more eligible than Francis? It is true that he is a younger son, but he is the younger son of a duke and has a large portion, even without the inheritance he expects from his great-aunt. It is true that he has something of a reputation for wildness, but what gentleman does not? Most girls I know, and their mamas too, would kill for an offer from Francis. Cynthia still blushes when she so much as looks at him. Why is it you and Papa alone who say I am too young? Is it because you were too young, Mama?''

''Yes,'' Olivia said, sadly. ''I do not want you to make the same mistake as I made, Sophia.''

''But other marriages work,'' the girl said. ''The duke and duchess are still together and Mr. and Mrs. Maxwell and Lord and Lady Wheatley and—oh, everyone but you and Papa. You are the only married couple I know who live apart. Why did you stop loving Papa?''

The countess felt horribly as if she had lost control of the encounter. It was not proceeding at all according to plan.

''That is not what happened,'' she said, looking down at her hands.

''What, then?''

She looked up. ''Oh, Sophia, he is my husband and your father. I did not stop loving him.''

''And yet you have not seen him since I was four years old until yesterday,'' Sophia said. ''Was it his fault, then? Did he stop loving you?''

''No,'' the countess said. ''I don't know. I don't know, Sophia. Something happened. It was nothing to do with you. I did not stop loving him.''

''You love him still, then?'' There was a gleam of triumph in Sophia's eyes. ''You have not spent any time with him today, have you? But you are bound to feel strange together at first. You will be more at ease as time goes on.''

''Sophia,'' the countess said.

''You are ten times lovelier than she is, anyway,'' the girl said.

''She?'' Olivia raised her eyebrows.

''Lady Mornington,'' Sophia blurted. ''You know about her, don't you? She is Papa's mistress. But not nearly so lovely as you and he must see it too, now that you have come home.''

Olivia swallowed. Still Lady Mornington, then? After six years? His liaison had lasted longer than his marriage? He must love the woman, then. A more lasting love than his first had been.

"Sophia," she said gently, "I am not here to stay. I am here only so that Papa and I can discuss your future with you and each other without the awkwardness of exchanging letters. As soon as everything is settled one way or the other, I shall be going home again. Rushton is my home. This is Papa's home. But we have strayed a long way from the subject I wished to discuss with you."

Sophia smiled radiantly at her. "No, we have not," she said. "When Francis and I are betrothed, you and Papa and I can discuss the wedding. It will be much easier than trying to do it by letter. And since we wish to have the banns read as soon as the betrothal is announced, you might as well stay for the wedding. It is too far to travel back here from Lincolnshire less than a month after you leave."

"Sophia," the countess said, "have you been hurt dreadfully by the fact that Papa and I have lived apart for most of your life? It has not been in any way your fault, you know. Papa and I both love you more than we love anyone else in the world. And I cannot call my marriage a mistake, you see, for without it there would not have been you. And I am as sure as I can be that Papa feels the same way. But what are we to do about you and Lord Francis? Do come and sit down again and let us talk about it sensibly."

"We want to get married in the village church," Sophia said eagerly, coming to sit beside her mother, "even though it will mean having only family and close friends as guests. I want to get married where you and Papa were married, and Francis says that he wants to get married wherever I happen to be the bride walking down the aisle." She laughed. "He says the most absurd things. Tell me about getting married there, Mama. Did Papa kiss you at the altar? Did you cry? I was born less than a year later, was I not? I think you must have been very much in love."

Olivia sighed. "Oh, Sophia," she said. "Yes, we were. You were a child born of love. You must never doubt that."

4

Lord Francis Sutton, standing beside the bowling green, having completed his own game, drew Sophia's arm through his. He smiled warmly at her, and strolled a little farther along with her, quite out of hearing of either the bowlers or the small cluster of spectators.

"It must be age that is coming upon me unexpectedly early," he said, "or some strange malady that has struck me within the past couple of months and is proceeding apace. It must be the country air, perhaps, or the country foods. A strange deafness. *What* did you say?"

"She can be won over," Sophia said eagerly, her cheeks flushed becomingly. Her look could easily be mistaken for one of complete adoration. "She is uneasy about the match, Francis, but it is merely anxiety for my happiness. She said—or she implied very strongly—that she will not forbid our marrying even if she does advise strongly against it."

"That part I understood very well," he said. "You must have been speaking more loudly and distinctly when you said that. It was the next part I misunderstood—or I think I surely must have, anyway."

"The part about the wedding?" she said. "I told her we were eager to marry in the village church, or that I was eager, anyway, and that you wished only to do what pleased me. I told her that as soon as our betrothal was announced, she could stay and help plan the wedding."

"You are getting close," he said. "I believe it was the next sentence."

"We want the banns read immediately after the betrothal announcement," she said.

"That was the one," he said. "And I might have saved you the trouble of repeating yourself, Soph. I heard correctly the first time. May I ask you something? Are you trying to

trap me into marriage? Are you playing a more clever game
than all the other females who fancy me? It is a good thing
you don't wear stays, Soph—you don't, do you? You would
be popping them all over the place at this moment.''

''Well!'' The word finally found its way past Sophia's lips.
''The conceit. The unmitigated conceit. All the other females.
All? How many dozen, Francis? How many hundred? Or
should I go higher? I would marry a toad sooner than marry
you. I would marry a snake sooner than marry . . .''

''I follow your meaning,'' he said, smiling even more
warmly and lifting her hand briefly to his lips. ''It is just
that you are chuckleheaded then, Soph? Smile, darling.''

She smiled. ''Don't you 'darling' me,'' she said from
between her teeth.

''When on the stage,'' he said, ''you have to throw
yourself heart and soul into the part. Once the banns are read,
my darling, we are going to be dead ducks, you and I. It
will be bad enough to have to face down a broken engage-
ment, Soph. But that? It is out of the question.''

Tears sprang to her eyes. ''But she will go back home,''
she said. ''As soon as this is settled one way or the other,
she said she will return to Rushton. Whether we become
betrothed or not, she will go. And what is the point of being
engaged, Francis, if she does not stay?''

''What indeed?'' he said.

''She will stay if there is a wedding to prepare for,'' she
said.

Lord Francis scratched his head and apparently watched
the bowlers for a few moments. ''Maybe so, Soph,'' he said.
''But will she go home anyway after we are married? That
is the question. And what am I talking about, saying *after*
we are married? Insanity is infectious. It must be.''

''She still loves Papa,'' Sophia said. ''She as much as
admitted so to me. And he must love her, Francis. She is
so much lovelier than his mistress.''

''Good Lord, Soph,'' he said. ''You are not supposed to
know anything about mistresses, and even if you do, the word
should never be allowed to pass your lips.''

''His ladybird then,'' she said, exasperated. ''His bit of
muslin. His . . .''

"Yes," he said, tossing a look up to a fluffy white cloud that was floating by. "Lady Clifton is certainly a better looker than Lady Mornington. But it does not follow that he therefore wants her more, Soph. If you want my opinion, trying to bring them back together again after fourteen years is rather like trying to flog the proverbial dead horse. Oh, Lord, waterworks?"

"No," she said crossly, turning with hurried steps back toward the house. "Just a little insect in my eye, that is all. And the sun is too bright. I forgot to bring my parasol with me."

He caught up to her, drew her hand through his arm, and patted it. "Perhaps I am wrong," he said. "Perhaps I am, Soph."

"No, you are not," she said, fumbling about her person for a handkerchief, then taking the one he offered her. "She has been here for a whole day and they have scarce said a word to each other except last night out on the terrace when we forced them together. It is quite hopeless. She will go back home whether it be tomorrow or next week or next month."

He curled his fingers beneath hers on his arm. "Perhaps all they need is time," he said. "It must be awkward meeting again after so long and with so many other people around to provide an interested audience. Perhaps in time they will sort out their differences."

"Oh, do you think so?" she asked, looking up at him hopefully.

"Yes, I do," he said. "No, you keep the handkerchief, Soph. It looks rather soggy. You certainly are not one of those females who can keep their eyes from turning red after a few tears, are you?"

"Oh," she said. "The word 'compliment' is not in your vocabulary, is it, Francis? I am sorry in my heart that you have to escort me about in all my ugliness. Perhaps you should resurrect one of your old tricks. You always used to be able to get rid of me, usually by stranding me somewhere."

"The island I always thought was the best one," he said. "How many hours were you there, Soph? And you would have been there longer if I had not eventually whispered your whereabouts to Claude.''

"It was most cruel of you to row back to shore before I could get down from the tree,'' she said, "knowing that I could not swim and that the water was just too deep to be waded.''

"I never confided another secret to Claude after that,'' he said. "He almost broke a leg in his haste to take the glad tidings to our father. I believe I was too sore to sit down for the rest of that day.''

"There was not a great deal of it left,'' she said tartly. He grinned.

"Do you really think there is still hope?'' she asked.

He shrugged. "Your father has taken himself off from the bowling green already,'' he said. "Perhaps they are talking even now.''

"Do you think so?'' she asked. She looked back to the bowling green to verify the fact that her father had indeed disappeared. "You will do it then, Francis?''

"Do what?'' he asked suspiciously.

"Allow the banns to be read if they will consent to our betrothal,'' she said. "Will you?''

"And allow the ceremony to take place too?'' he asked. "And the wedding trip in the hope that she will remain here to greet our homecoming? And our first child to begin his nine-month wait for birth in the belief that she will stay for the happy event and for the christening to follow? Perhaps we can have ten children in a row, Soph. Or an even dozen. Perhaps at the end of that time your mother will think it not worth returning to Rushton. Our eldest will be coming up to marriageable age.''

"You are making a joke of my feelings,'' she said, "as usual. It will not get as far as that, Francis. Of course it will not. I shall break off the betrothal before the wedding, whatever happens. You have my word on it.''

"Good Lord, Soph,'' he said. "Do you have any idea of the scandal there will be?''

"I do not care about scandal,'' she said.

"You will,'' he said. "No one will want to touch you with

a thirty-foot pole after you have jilted a duke's son almost at the altar.''

"That will suit me," she said. "I have already told you that I have no intention of marrying anyone. I don't want to be touched with a pole or anything else.''

"I am not talking only of suitors,'' he said. "No one will want to invite you anywhere, Soph. You will be an outcast, a pariah.''

"Nonsense,'' she said.

"Well,'' he said, "never say that I did not warn you. But go ahead and do it if you must. As long as I have your word on it that you will do the jilting, that is. I will certainly not be able to do it.''

"Oh, Francis," she said, looking up at him with bright eyes, "how kind you are. I did not think I would be able to persuade you to agree. You are wonderful.''

"Soph," he said, frowning, "a little less enthusiastic with the *kinds* and the *wonderfuls*, if you please. They make me distinctly nervous coming from you. I think we had better hope that your papa says no and sends me on my way. We had better hope quite fervently, in fact.''

"A wedding in the village church," she said, her eyes dreamy. "With the bells ringing and the choir singing and the rector decked out in his grandest vestments. And the organ playing. Oh, Francis, it cannot fail to remind them and affect them, can it? *Can* it?''

"Ah, Bedlam, Bedlam," he said. "Your doors are wide open to me and beckoning, it seems.''

The Earl of Clifton was almost finished with a game of bowls when he saw his daughter walking up from the house. Olivia must have had her talk with her, then. Mrs. Biddeford had come out almost an hour before.

He relaxed somewhat. Olivia would have talked sense into Sophia. She seemed to have a gift for doing so. It had been a great relief to read her letter announcing that she was coming. A great relief—but something else too. He had not been at all sure that he really wanted to see her again, even though her portrait followed him about wherever he went.

It always stood beside his bed, where it was the last thing he saw at night before blowing out the candles and the first thing he saw in the morning before getting out of bed.

But there was something quite different between a portrait and reality.

He excused himself at the end of the game and laughed when Lord Wheatley remarked that it would be a pleasure to let such an expert at the game go.

"I'll wager you spend every waking moment of your summers out here practicing, Clifton," he said, "just so that you may make the rest of us ordinary mortals look like clumsy oafs."

"I have an especially large umbrella that I use to keep myself dry during the rainy weather," the earl said, "so that I don't have to waste a single one of those moments."

Sophia and Sutton had strolled a little apart from everyone else, he noticed, and were deep in conversation. Was she telling him? But she did not look particularly tragic. He had no misgivings about letting them out of his sight. They were surrounded by his houseguests, including Sutton's own parents. He made his way back to the house.

His wife was not in her private apartments. Neither was she in the drawing room or the morning room or any of the salons. Her ladyship had stepped outside, a footman told him when he finally thought to ask. To the bowling green? But he would have passed her on the way. He went out onto the terrace and looked along all the walks through the formal gardens. They were deserted. The seat surrounding the fountain was empty, he discovered when he walked all about it to see the stretch that was not visible from the terrace.

Where could she be? The village? But she would have gone with the Biddefords and Sophia earlier if there had been anything she needed, surely. The hidden garden? Would she have gone there? Would she remember it?

It had been allowed to deteriorate during his father's last years. The lock had been rusty and the garden hopelessly overgrown when he had gone there after his father's funeral. He had stood on the spot where he had kissed Livy for the first time and felt even more bereft than he had felt in the churchyard looking down at the box that had held all that remained of a much-loved father. He had felt that the state of the garden somehow mirrored the state of his life. Tidying it up, putting it to rights seemed a monumental task and somehow futile.

Why tidy up a garden that almost no one knew about, that almost no one now living cared anything about? After all, there were the large gardens surrounding the house and the well-kept miles of the park beyond. Who needed a small garden hidden in the middle of a wood?

He needed it, that was who, he had decided. Like the portrait, it was one small memory he had left of her. She had loved the garden. He had always known during that month before their marriage where he might find her and he had frequently gone to her there. She had never bolted the door against him, though together they had bolted it more than once against the world so that they might enjoy a private embrace.

Would she remember it? Would she go there? Would it not be the very last place she would go?

And yet he had hoped from the start. He had left the door unlocked since he knew she was coming, hoping that perhaps she would find it again, hoping that no one else would do so. He did not want his guests, or even Sophia in the hidden garden.

He strode through the woods, veering off the main path until he came to the ivy-colored wall. The arched door was almost hidden by ivy. It was shut. He set his hand on the latch. She would not be in there. It was the most foolish place of all to look. And even if she were, it would be wrong to go in. If she had come there, it would be because she wanted quiet and privacy. If she were there, she would have bolted the door from the inside.

But it was not bolted. It swung inward on well oiled hinges when he lifted the latch.

The contrast between the scene inside the garden and that outside would have caught at the breath of a stranger not expecting it. Outside all was tall old trees and muted colors and semidarkness. Inside all was exquisite blooms and riotous cultivated beauty and color. A stone sundial in the center was surrounded by delicate fruit trees between the seasons of blooming and bearing fruit. Smooth green lawns were on either side of the cobbled path inside the door and sloping rock gardens, carpeted with a profusion of flowers, at the opposite corners. Roses climbed the walls.

The earl's gardeners spent a disproportionate amount of their time keeping the hidden garden immaculate.

She was sitting on a flat stone in one of the rock gardens, her arms clasping her knees. The green of her muslin dress was as fresh as the grass. He closed the door quietly behind him. He did not bolt it. She was looking steadily at him, her eyebrows raised.

"You have kept it, then, Marcus?" she said.

"Yes." He strolled toward her.

"Why?"

He did not reply for a while. How could he tell her the real reason? "Family sentiment, I suppose," he said at last. "And because when something is so exquisitely beautiful one feels the need to cling to it."

She nodded. She seemed satisfied with his answer.

She was exquisitely beautiful, he thought. The portrait beside his bed no longer did her justice. And yet the bloom of youth was no longer there. She was a woman, more lovely than a mere girl.

"Well?" he said.

"I do not know if it can be prevented, Marcus," she said. "She has her heart set on the match and I did not notice that anything I said made her feel even the slightest doubt about the wisdom of her course."

"You failed?" he said.

"I told her at the start," she said, "that I would no longer treat her as a child and make her decisions for her. I told her I would not forbid the betrothal, though you well might. But I also told her that I would do all in my power to persuade her that she would be making a big mistake in persisting."

"You did not forbid the match?" he said, frowning.

"She is eighteen years old, Marcus," she said. "I was a married lady at her age."

''But can she not see how foolish it is to lose her head over almost the first man she has seen?'' he asked. ''She is eighteen, for God's sake, Olivia. A child.''

''But she reminded me,'' she said, ''that all about her in London were the young girls of the *ton*, come to be presented and to find husbands. It is the way of the world. And she is right, Marcus.''

''You approve of the match, then?'' He set one foot on a stone a little below the level of that on which she sat and rested one arm across his knee. ''You think we should approve the betrothal?''

She looked troubled. ''I don't know,'' she said. ''All my instincts are against it. I cannot believe that she will be happy with Lord Francis. And I cannot believe that she can possibly know her own mind or realize that being in love is not always a sound basis for a marriage. But she turned the tables on me when I gave her those arguments.''

He looked at her while she plucked a carnation and held it to her nose.

''She says it is because of you and me,'' she said, raising her head to look at him. ''She says we are opposed because our own marriage failed and we find it impossible to believe that hers will not. She listed other marriages that have not failed. In fact, ours is the only one that has, as far as she knows.''

He swallowed.

''Marcus,'' she said, ''could she be right? Are we being unduly pessismistic and overprotective? Would we feel the same way if nothing had happened and we had stayed together? Or would we feel rather pleased at the prospect of her marrying Rose and William's youngest son? Despite his reputation, would we be pleased? He seems excessively fond of her. I don't know the answer. I cannot put myself into the position of a normal, contentedly married woman to know how I would feel. I came here to try to think of the answer.''

He could not think of the answer either. He looked down at her bowed head, at the smooth, almost blonde hair parted neatly down the middle and combed back from her face. And he watched her twirl the carnation and bury her nose in it.

If nothing had happened. If Lowry had not decided to get married in London and invited him and Livy to the wedding. If he had not appeared quite so eager to go because Lowry had been a particularly close friend of his at Oxford. If Sophia had not come down with the measles just the day before they were due to leave and Livy had not persuaded him, much against his will, to go alone because his heart had been so set upon it. If there had not been that stupid party for Lowry two nights before the wedding and all the interminable drinking.

If the rest of their university cronies had not laughed at him for being such a staid married man when he was still so young and had not dared him to come with them to a certain tavern of low repute. If he had not been so drunk and so foolish, foolish, foolish. He had never afterward been able to remember either the girl's name or what she had looked like. Only the fact that he had bedded her and hated it while he was doing it and hated himself after he had paid her and staggered out into the street and vomited into the gutter to the hearty amusement of those cronies who were still with him.

Foolish idiot of a young puppy. Having behaved so, he should have found some salve for his conscience and pushed the experience out of his mind. The girl had meant nothing to him and he knew that none of his friends would ever tell what he had done. He had known that he would never be tempted to do such a thing ever again.

But he had gone home and shut himself away from Livy for four days, puzzling her with his insistence that he needed to be with his books and catch up with what had happened on his property since he went away. And at night he had been unwell and too tired to make love to her. On the fourth night he had been too unwell to sleep in her bed. He had gone into his own little-used bedchamber.

"What is wrong, Marc?" she had asked him, coming quietly into his darkened room half an hour later as he stood staring out of the window.

"Nothing is wrong," he had said. "Just this stomach ache, Livy."

"What happened in London?" she had asked.

"Nothing," he had said. "A wedding. Parties. Too much eating and drinking, Livy. I'll feel better soon."

"Is there someone else?" She had whispered the question.

"No!"

He had almost yelled the word, turning to face her. It had been the time to cross the room and take her into his arms, kiss her, take her through to her own room again, and make love to her. He could have forgotten once he had been inside her familiar and beloved body. And even if he could not have forgotten, he should never have told her. Never.

"There was a girl," he had blurted. "A whore. Nobody, Livy. I cannot even remember her name or her looks. I was foxed and dared to it. It meant nothing. Nothing, Livy. It is you I love. Only you. You know that. She was no one. It will never happen again. I promise."

Even in the darkness he had seen the horror and revulsion on her face. She had said nothing as they stood and stared at each other, his hand stretched out to her.

And then she had turned and fled. Both her bedchamber and dressing room doors were locked by the time he had gone staggering after her.

She had refused to forgive him. And she had kept on refusing until he had been forced to believe that she never would.

She set the carnation down on the stone beside her.

"You think I should have a talk with Sutton, then," he said, "and find out what his intentions and prospects and plans are? You think I should give our consent if his answers are satisfactory, if it appears that he is in earnest and intends to be good to Sophia? Is that what you think I should do, Olivia?"

"I don't know," she said, looking up again. "We have to make the most important decision concerning her that we have made in her life, Marcus, and reason and good sense no longer seem good enough guidelines. What is the reasonable or sensible thing to do? Mama and Papa and your parents did not stop us from marrying when they saw that our hearts were set upon doing so."

"No," he said.

She spread her hands palm up on her lap and looked down at them. "Perhaps they should have," she said.

"Yes."

"But does that mean that we should stop Sophia?" she said. "Perhaps it will turn out to be a happy marriage."

"Yes."

"Oh, Marcus," she said, lifting her face to him, "what do you think? I would so like you to make this decision because you are her father. But I know that is not fair."

"It strikes me," he said, "that in six months' time or a year or two years we will be going through this all over again, Olivia, if we say no this time. And I believe Sophia will always be too young and there will always be something wrong with the young man."

"Yes." She smiled ruefully.

"I think I had better hear what Sutton has to say for himself," he said.

"Yes."

"I will not make it easy for him," he said.

She smiled. "I remember your saying that Papa was a veritable ogre," she said. "Though he was normally the mildest of men."

"You were seventeen," he said, "and his only daughter."

"Yes."

"You will be prepared to live with this betrothal, then?" he asked.

"I suppose so," she said. "Sophia said that they will want the banns read immediately, Marcus. They wish for a summer wedding at the village church."

"Do they?" he asked. And he had the sudden memory of Olivia, her face raised to his, its expression tender and wondering and utterly vulnerable as the rector pronounced them man and wife. It was a memory all mixed up with organ music and the smell of flowers and the pealing of bells. "You would stay until after the wedding, then?"

The color deepened in her cheeks. "If there is a wedding," she said. "Yes, if I may."

"This is your home," he said.

She shook her head. "No," she said. "Rushton is my home."

"Are you happy, Olivia?" he asked and wished he had not turned the conversation to such a personal matter.

She did not answer for a moment. "Contented," she said. "I have my home and my garden and my books and music. And the church and my charitable works and my friends."

"Clarence?" he said. "Is he still your friend? I rarely see him in town."

"He does not often go," she said. "He prefers to remain in the country. Yes, he is still my friend, Marcus. So are a dozen other people and more."

"I am glad," he said. "You have never been willing to use the house in London, even when I have assured you that I would not be there."

"No," she said. "I am happier at home."

"I always loved the place," he said. "I am glad you are contented there."

"Yes," she said.

He straightened up and lowered his foot to the grass. "Are you coming back to the house with me?" he asked. "Or would you rather stay here a little longer?"

"I shall stay here," she said.

He nodded and turned away. But her voice stopped him when he had his hand on the latch of the door.

"Marcus," she said. He looked back over his shoulder. "I am glad that you have kept the garden."

He smiled and let himself back out into the wood.

I kept it for you, he wanted to tell her. But it would not have been strictly true. It was for himself that he had kept it. Because it reminded him of Livy and the perfection of the life they had had for almost five years before he had destroyed it on one stroke by trying to prove to a crowd of drunken men who meant nothing whatsoever to him that he was a real man.

He closed the door quietly behind him.

5

She had not played charades for years, the Countess of Clifton thought, laughing after a particularly energetic round and seating herself to catch her breath. She always attended every assembly and social gathering in the neighborhood of Rushton, but for years she had been considered a member of the older generation and had sat with them, merely observing the more energetic sports of the young.

But Sophia had insisted that she join in the game this evening and Mr. Hathaway had echoed her urgings. Marcus had left the drawing room soon after the gentlemen joined the ladies following dinner, taking Lord Francis with him. Sophia had been flushed and frenzied ever since.

A footman had come into the room and was speaking with the duke and duchess and then turned in Olivia's direction. "His lordship requests the pleasure of your company in the library, ma'am," he said quietly for her ears only and then looked about him for Sophia.

The countess smiled at the duke and duchess as all three of them made their way to the door.

"So we are to be put out of our misery, Olivia," his grace said. "Is it to be yes or no, eh?" He chuckled.

"The interview has certainly lasted long enough," the duchess said. "All of an hour. Have they been talking business all of that time, do you suppose?"

"And so, Olivia," the duke said, as they all paused outside the library for another footman to open the doors for them, "we are to be rid of our last boy and you of your only girl all at the same time. We will have nothing to trouble our old age except the arrival of grandchildren."

The earl was the only occupant of the library. He was standing with his back to the fireplace, his hands behind his back. He smiled at them.

"Well, Marcus," the duke said, "did that scamp of a son of mine impress you sufficiently, or did you send him packing?"

"I have consented to his making his offer to Sophia," the earl said. "I believe he is doing so at this very moment."

"Splendid, splendid," the duke said, rubbing his hands together while the duchess fumbled in a pocket for a handkerchief and the countess watched her husband. "And when are the nuptials to be? Before Christmas, I hope. There is no point in waiting around once the intention has been expressed, I always say."

"In one month's time," the earl said. "Your son wishes to have the betrothal announced tonight, William, if Sophia will give her consent—and I don't believe there can be much doubt that she will do so. He wants the first banns read on Sunday."

The duchess shrieked and buried her face in her handkerchief.

"Here?" his grace said. "Not in St. George's like our other boys? Well, a quiet country wedding has its charm, I must admit. You and Olivia were married here, were you not, Marcus? A charming wedding, as I remember. So Francis is proving to be as impulsive as ever, is he, and insisting on no delay? Now don't take on so, Rose. No one has died. And, indeed, little Sophia may yet refuse him."

"But how can we be ready in one month?" her grace wailed. "Olivia?"

"I am sure it can be done," the countess said soothingly. "The invitations can be sent off tomorrow. They are the most urgent. Then we can sit down and plan everything else."

"I think for this evening we might as well relax," the earl said, "and await developments. Do have a seat, Rose. Olivia? And you too, William. What can I offer you to drink?"

"This is quite like old times," the duke said, beaming about him a few minutes later when they were all seated cozily, drinks in hand.

It was and it was not, Olivia thought. They were together, the four of them, talking and apparently relaxed, as they had often been in the past. But she was no longer seated beside her husband, their hands almost touching—they had never embarrassed their family or friends by showing open affection in public. He was sitting in a chair by the fireplace, she on the sofa beside the duchess. And she no longer felt quite part of the group. The three of them had continued the friendship over the fourteen years when she had been at Rushton.

She had agreed with Marcus that afternoon that the betrothal should be consented to if his interview with Lord Francis was satisfactory. She still did not know if they had made the right decision. Probably they would not know until several years had passed and they could see how the marriage developed. But she wished after all that they could have done something to prevent it.

If there were to be no marriage, she would be able to go back home without further delay. Home to the safety and familiarity of Rushton and to her friends—Clarence and Emma Burnett in particular.

But now she was to be at Clifton for at least another month, amid all the fevered excitement of an approaching wedding. And it was to be at the church in the village. It was going to be very difficult.

And difficult to be in company with him daily, both of them mingling with his guests. And there would be innumerable occasions when they would have to be alone together, working on the arrangements. It was going to be difficult to bear. Every bit as difficult as she had expected. More so.

He was so very attractive. She had never particularly thought of that word in connection with him before. He had been excessively handsome and vital and very, very dear to her. But she could not recall ever feeling this aching pull toward his masculinity. It was not a pleasant feeling. She had no wish to feel it. She was not a schoolgirl to be sighing over a handsome man. She was a mature woman.

Besides, he was Marc—Marcus—and she did not want to be reminded of a marriage that had failed a long time ago and from the misery of whose ending she had fought her way back to life through a year and more of hell. She wanted only to be away from him, to be at peace again. And she knew very well what had made him so very much more attractive than he had been when they were together. It was experience—experience gained with countless other women.

She wanted nothing to do with his experience. She had preferred her innocent Marc.

They were interrupted less than half an hour after sitting down by the sudden and unheralded opening of the doors and the arrival of Sophia and Lord Francis, hand in hand, their faces brightly smiling.

"Ah," Lord Francis said, "you are all together here. Very opportune. Sophia has just agreed to marry me."

"I have," she said, flushing and laughing.

They were all on their feet suddenly, talking and laughing. And the duchess raised her handkerchief to her eyes again.

"Oh, my boy," she said. "My baby. And it seems no longer than a year ago that you were in leading strings." She hugged him and wept over him.

"Sophia, my girl," his grace said, opening his arms to her, "we have wanted you for a daughter-in-law from the time when you could climb stairs after our boys but not descend them again. And now our wish is to be granted. Come and have a father-in-law's hug."

Everyone had to hug everyone else, it seemed. Olivia submitted to a bear hug from the duke, who assured her that he could not be better pleased at the closer link there was to be between their families, and to a teary one from her grace. Sophia threw her arms about her and danced her in a circle, declaring that now they would have a whole month together, all of them. Lord Francis smiled sheepishly at her until she cupped his face in her hands and kissed his cheek and told him that she would be proud to have him for a son-in-law.

And then her husband was there as she turned, smiling, from Lord Francis and he was releasing their daughter. The duchess was sobbing loudly in her husband's arms and lamenting the fact that their baby was leaving them and there would be no more weddings to look forward to until Bertie's girls grew up.

"Well, Olivia," the earl said, smiling at her. "We are to be the parents of a bride, it seems."

"Yes." She bit her lip and felt the unexpected emotion of the moment work at her facial muscles.

And then his arms came beneath her own and about her and he hugged her hard against him. Her own arms, for lack of anywhere else to go, went about his neck.

All she could feel was shock. Shock that he was quite unmistakably Marc, this older, broader man with the silvering dark hair. Quite unmistakably. It was something about the way he held her, perhaps. Something about the way he caused her body to arch itself against his. Something about the familiar cologne he wore. And something else, quite undefinable.

Marc!

His cheek rested briefly against hers. "We must be happy for them, Olivia," he murmured into her ear. "We must believe that they will be happy."

"Yes." She closed her eyes and then was standing alone again, aware of the duke's booming laugh and the duchess's sniffles and Sophia's chatter.

And she watched as Lord Francis set an arm about Sophia's shoulders, drew her close against his side, and bent his head to kiss her briefly but thoroughly on the lips. The girl looked stunned, almost angry, for a moment, her mother thought, before flushing scarlet while everyone laughed.

"We want to be married just as soon as the banns have been read," Lord Francis said. "Don't we, Soph? It will not be worth anyone's going home. There is going to be a wedding to celebrate."

"Go home!" the duchess exclaimed. "Did you hear that, Olivia? We will be fortunate indeed, Francis, if there is even time to go to bed within the next month. Do you have any idea whatsoever of all that is involved in planning a wedding? No, of course you do not. You are a mere man. Olivia, my dear, I have the headache merely thinking about the coming month."

The duke chuckled. "What Rose actually means, Olivia," he said, "is that she is now in her element and woe betide anyone who tries to distract her from the sheer delight of wearing herself into a decline over the coming nuptials."

"Shall we adjourn to the drawing room?" the earl suggested. "Our guests will be wondering why they have been abandoned for so long, though I daresay they will have guessed. I believe my wife and I have a betrothal to announce. Olivia?" He held out an arm for hers.

"And what did you think you were about in the library?" Sophia demanded as soon as they were clear of the others.

She and Lord Francis had been permitted to step outside alone for a breath of air in light of the fact that they were now officially betrothed. Everyone else had appeared too tired from a day of outdoor activities and an evening of charades to accompany them. Or too tactful, perhaps. They were strolling along one of the diagonal paths of the parterre gardens.

"What was I about?" he asked, frowning. "I was about announcing our betrothal and trying to look suitably besotted."

"Looking suitably besotted does not include kissing my lips," she said. "You will stay far away from them in future, Francis, if you know what is good for you. You were fortunate indeed not to find yourself with a fat lip."

"If you cannot control your passion sufficiently, Soph," he said, "it would be better to bite me on the neck rather than on the lips. I can cover up the evidence with my cravat."

"Oh," she said, "you are disgusting. Who in her right mind would wish to bite your neck? Ugh!"

"You turned an interesting shade of scarlet when I did kiss you," he said. "I thought perhaps you were about to swoon in my arms, Soph."

"Yes, well," she said, "you said yourself that when you are acting you have to throw yourself wholeheartedly into the part. I had to convince Mama and Papa that it was my first kiss."

"It probably was too," he said. "Was it?"

"Wouldn't you like to know!" she said, tossing her head.

He chuckled. "The worldly wise look does not suit you, Soph," he said. "We are going to have to steal several kisses, you know, over the next days. People will expect it."

"Oh, nonsense," she said.

"There are probably a dozen people lined up behind the darkened windows of the house right now," he said, "just hoping to see our silhouettes merge."

"What a ridiculous idea," she said, glancing across to the house. "I do not see a single watcher."

"Naturally," he said. "You would not exactly expect them to be lined up there, a candle in each hand, would you, Soph? They are standing back out of sight or hiding behind the curtains."

"Sometimes, Francis," she said, "I think you must have windmills in your head."

"It sounds painful," he said. "Shall we thrill them?"

"What?"

"Your mama and papa might be among them."

"Mama and Papa would not spy on me," she said indignantly.

"They would not think of it as spying," he said. "They will want to see for themselves that they made the right decision concerning us, Soph. They will want to see that we are not out here quarreling or walking ten feet apart."

"Well, we are not," she said. "Walking ten feet apart, I mean. We are always quarreling."

"I think we had better do this right," he said. "Stand still, Soph, while I kiss you."

"Lay one hand on me," she said indignantly, "and I will . . ."

"It will have to be two hands," he said, "and my mouth. You aren't afraid, are you?"

"Afraid?" she said scornfully. "Of you, Francis?"

"It is as I thought," he said, stopping and setting one hand on her arm. "You are afraid."

"Well," she said. "Of all the . . ."

"Half a minute should be a decent enough time for a newly betrothed pair, I believe," he said. "Count to thirty slowly, Soph. It will take your mind off your jitters."

And while she still looked up at him in mingled indignation and embarrassment and fright, he set his mouth to hers, took her free arm in his other hand and merged their silhouettes.

"What are you doing?" She drew her head back when she had counted no higher than twenty-one and glared at him. "What do you think you are doing?"

"Trying to open your lips with my tongue, actually, Soph," he said. "It becomes a little tedious merely to rest still lips against still lips, don't you think?"

"No, I do not think," she said. "That was a quite unnecessary part of the act. It could not be seen from the house. And if it had, Papa would doubtless be out here by now brandishing a whip about his head. Don't you ever do that again. *Ever,* do you hear me? It made me feel all funny."

"Did it, Soph?" He grinned. "You had better not go falling in love with me, you know. I don't want to be responsible for broken hearts or anything like that."

"Do you know, Francis," she said, "I do not believe I have known anyone—*anyone*, male or female—who comes even close to you in conceit. Fall in love with you, indeed! I would be as likely to fall in love with a toad. I would be as likely to . . ."

" . . . fall in love with a snake," he said. "Sometimes you are not very original, Soph. Let us change the subject, shall we? Are you happy, at least? Are you satisfied?"

"Oh, Francis." She looked up at him with a radiant smile as they resumed their walk. "Was it not wonderful? Even more wonderful than could possibly have been imagined? They hugged each other. Did you see? Actually hugged. And I do believe he kissed her cheek too. And in the drawing room afterward he kept her on his arm while everyone came about to congratulate us and kept his hand over hers too and talked about 'my wife and I,' just as if they had the most normal of marriages. Did you notice, Francis? Everything is going to be all right, is it not? After a month everything cannot fail to be all right."

"It was definitely promising," he agreed. "But I cannot help feeling that we have got in a little deeper than we expected, Soph. Good Lord, my mother must have soaked three handkerchiefs. And they were all so very pleased."

"Your mother and mine are going to love planning the wedding," she said, smiling up at him. "We must not forget that the guest list is to be drawn up directly after breakfast tomorrow. You must think of any special friends you want to invite, Francis, apart from Mr. Hathaway and Sir Ridley, who are here already, and I will think too. I don't believe I will be able to sleep tonight.''

''Soph,'' he said.

''What?''

Lord Francis sighed. ''Nothing,'' he said. ''Just a little thought from that alien world of sanity that I used to belong to.''

''Oh, that,'' she said, sobering. ''Yes, of course.''

The Earl of Clifton could have gone through the connecting door between his dressing room and hers. She was, after all, his wife, and there had been a time when the door between their rooms was permanently open. But times had changed, of course. Or he could have knocked on the door and waited for her maid to answer. He could hear the two of them talking behind it. But there was something demeaning about knocking on the door of his wife's dressing room.

He strode around to the door of her sitting room and knocked.

She was dressed when she came through from the bedchamber a few minutes after her maid had let him in. But he must have taken her by surprise. He should have left his call until a little later in the morning, perhaps. Her hair had not been done. It hung smooth and shining halfway down her back. She had pushed it behind her ears. He tried to keep his eyes from it. It used to be short.

''I came to see if you had had second thoughts,'' he said, smiling. God, but she was beautiful.

''Second and third and thirty-third.'' She returned his smile. ''I suppose we have to realize that we cannot live her life for her, Marcus, any more than our parents could live ours.''

''They seem happy enough,'' he said.

''He is a pleasant young man,'' she said. ''I think his charm is more than just of the surface. I like him.''

''It seemed strange,'' he said, ''to see him kiss my little

girl in the library and no longer have the right to plant him a facer.''

"Oh, Marcus," she said, "she was such a sunny natured little girl, was she not?"

"Do you remember how she used to try to run across the grass almost before she could walk?" he said. "She used to be angry rather than upset when she continually fell down." He laughed.

"And then you would take her riding on your shoulders," she said. "And she would clutch on to fistfulls of your hair so that you used to swear that you would be bald by the time you were thirty."

He turned away suddenly and crossed the room to look out of a window. "Did you notice what she kept saying last night, Olivia?" he asked.

"About our all being together for the next month?" she said. "Yes. She said it more than once."

"She has never said much," he said. "I always thought she accepted the situation for what it was. Perhaps she did. Perhaps it is only being here with us like this that has made her realize that she grew up without a family."

"Yes," she said. "I did not realize either, Marcus."

"This month is going to be very important to her," he said. "*We* are going to be important to her. We together. Her mother and father."

"Yes."

He turned from the window to look at her broodingly.

"Can there be some peace between us for one month?" he asked. "I know you have not liked me for many years, Olivia, and have made a new life for yourself in which there is no room for an old marriage. And I know there has been a dreadful awkwardness between us since you arrived— married but not married, separate parents to the same child. Can we at least outwardly be more together—for Sophia's sake? Is it possible?"

She stared back at him, her face pale. She looked rather as she had looked the morning he left home never to return, he thought unwillingly, although at the time he had not dreamed that he would not see her again for fourteen years.

He had gone away to give her a few weeks to come to terms with his infidelity. To give her a few weeks to forgive him.

She never had.

She licked her lips. "I would do anything in the world for Sophia," she said. "You know that."

"Yes," he said. "And so would I. It will mean a little more than being under the same roof for a month."

"It will be like last evening?" she said. "My hand on your arm? 'My wife and I'? 'Our daughter'?"

"Smiling at each other," he said. "Doing things together."

"Planning the wedding together," she said.

"Can you do it, Olivia?" he asked. "For one month can you hide your aversion to me—at least in public?"

She raised her eyes to his. "Yes," she said. "For one month, Marcus. For Sophia's sake."

"A family for one month," he said. "I think it will be important to her, Olivia."

"Yes," she said.

"Let's go down to breakfast then," he said, extending his arm to her.

"My hair," she said.

He smiled in some amusement. "It is lovely," he said. "I like it long, though I always liked the curls too. Go and have it dressed. I shall wait for you here, shall I?"

"Yes," she said.

He watched her leave the room and turned back to the window. A family for a month. It was a sweet seductive thought. One he must not allow to take a hold on his feelings. After Sophia's wedding she would be going home again. Back to Rushton. He must not let down the guard on his emotions during that month. It had taken him too many years to build it up.

6

It would be impossible to invite all the *ton*, as the duchess seemed to wish to do. Large as Clifton Court was, there was a limit to the number of guests who could be housed in its rooms. And the village church was not large. Members of the *beau monde* would not enjoy sitting outside in their carriages or standing in the churchyard while the marriage ceremony was in progress, the earl pointed out, because there was no room for them inside.

The guest list would have to be drawn up with care. All of the guests then staying at the house were willing and eager to stay or at least to come back again. Family had to come next and then close friends—those of Sophia, Lord Francis, the duke and duchess, the countess, and the earl.

The meeting of the interested parties lasted for all of two hours until, at last, the list was just the length it needed to be. Then her grace, Olivia, and Sophia spent the rest of the morning writing the invitations while the men went into the village to visit the rector.

After luncheon, the earl insisted that everyone take a rest from the wedding preparations in order to ride for a few hours and take a picnic tea on the hill north of the house.

"After all," he assured the alarmed duchess, who insisted that there were not enough hours left in which to arrange everything satisfactorily, "we cannot have you and Olivia looking quite hagged on the wedding day, now can we? Rose? And I do assure you that I have a perfectly competent housekeeper and cook, who are even now making arrangements to ensure that we will not all starve. I have also sent for most of my staff from the London house to come."

"And it is a beautiful day, my love," the duke told her. "Far too lovely to be wasted on the hysterics indoors."

"We are not having the hysterics, are we, Olivia?" her grace said. "We are merely busy."

"Besides," Lord Clifton said, "the other guests have been neglected quite shamelessly for half of the day. Olivia, can the time be spared?"

"We do need half an hour to finish the invitations," she said. "And they really should be sent today, Marcus."

"Half an hour it is, then," he said. "Not one moment longer."

And so while the afternoon was still early, they all rode out, hats shading their eyes from the brightness of the sun. They rode along the smooth miles of the park to the south of the house and back along the wooded banks of the river that formed the border of the park to the east. Cultivated acres stretched beyond it to the horizon. The river circled back around the house until, finally, the riders branched away from it toward the heather-covered hill a few miles north of the house. There carriages of food and footmen awaited them.

The ride had been a long one, even though the trees along the course of the river had shaded them from the worst of the sun's heat. They all dismounted at the foot of the hill and set the horses free to graze on the grass there. Most of the guests were grateful for the blankets set down on a piece of level ground halfway up the hill and sank down onto them before accepting glasses of wine from the footmen.

"That is my riding done for this year," Lady Wheatley said. "And it is more than I did last year at that."

Several people laughed.

"I never feel quite right if I do not begin each morning with a three-mile ride," Mrs. Biddeford said. "Though I do not have quite the energy of these children, I must confess." She grimaced as she watched several of the young people and the earl and countess climb the remainder of the slope to stand on top of the hill.

"Dear Olivia," the duchess said. "She is looking well, is she not? She seems not to have aged like some of us."

"I am glad you said *some,* my love," his grace said with a chuckle, "or you would have mortally offended several ladies here, I do not doubt. Though you too look quite as youthful as you did on the day I married you."

"William!" the duchess said scornfully and fanned her face with a napkin. "But how delightful it is to see them together again, is it not?"

"I never could quite understand what the problem was," Lord Wheatley said. "I was always under the impression that it was a love match."

"That is precisely what the problem was," his grace said.

Sophia, who had ridden with her friend Cynthia for much of the way, the two of them with their heads together wondering over the success of the original plan and discussing how best the mock betrothal was to be put an end to when the time came, found her hand being taken by Lord Francis when they dismounted.

"What are you doing?" she asked.

"Lacing my fingers with yours," he said. "It looks far more intimate, Soph, than linking arms or merely holding hands. And while good manners would demand that we be with and converse with our friends during the ride, sentiment now dictates that we steal a few minutes together." He smiled into her eyes and she smiled back.

"Mama and Papa have not been together all afternoon," she said. "This is not going to work, Francis."

"Nonsense," he said. "After being away from their guests all morning, of course they would have felt obliged to mingle this afternoon as we did. They did well enough this morning."

She brightened. "Cynthia said they came down to breakfast arm in arm," she said. "Do you suppose that means . . .?" But she stopped and blushed scarlet.

"Probably not," he said. "But they sat side by side in the library when they need not have done so, and they were both very insistent that the other's friends be invited to the wedding."

"Yes, they were, were they not?" she said. "Where are we going?"

"To the top of the hill," he said. "Young lovers have boundless energy, you know."

"No, I did not know," she said. "But there is a rather splendid view from the top."

"I know," he said, grinning. "I remember."

She looked at him blankly for a moment and then her look became indignant. "You were quite horrid," she said. "I do not know why I even talked to you in town this spring."

"Don't you?" he said. "It is because I am a duke's son and have fairly or unfairly acquired a reputation as something of a rake, Soph. An irresistible combination to the ladies, I have found. And yes, that does make me conceited, I must admit. I have saved you from having to say it yourself, you see."

"You went fishing," she said accusingly.

"I did," he said. "With my brothers. Blissfully free of female companionship."

"While I kept watch at the top of the hill for hours and hours," she said.

"Oh, come now, Soph," he said, "it could not have been for longer than two at the most. And we needed someone to keep watch, you know, while the rest of us went hunting poachers and highwaymen and brigands. You did a splendid job. You kept them all at bay so that we were able to enjoy a peaceful hour or two of fishing."

"You were fortunate," she said, "that I did not tell your father on that occasion. Or your brothers, either. They did not know what story you had told me to keep me away. Claude would have punched you in the nose."

"A manly punishment at least," he said. "Bertie would have spanked me, and my father would have walloped me. A subtle difference, you know—something to do with the weight of the hand. My father's was invariably heavy."

"You would have deserved it," she said.

"Doubtless." He grinned. "But you should be hoping fervently that I have not changed, Soph. I always managed to get rid of you, did I not? I must say, I felt uncomfortably hot under the collar when we called on the rector this morning and started to discuss banns and weddings and such."

"Did you?" Her eyes widened. "Papa has already sent for half the staff from the London house. Have you heard?"

He grimaced.

"Here we are at the top," she said. "Oh, how lovely. There is a breeze. Look, Francis, half the others are coming up, too. I thought everyone was tired from the heat and the ride."

"Ah, an audience," he said, catching her about the waist with one arm, drawing her against him, and kissing her soundly before releasing her and taking her hand again.

"I told you not to do that again," she said indignantly.

"Kiss you?" he said. "But we have probably restored the spirits of a dozen or so weary riders and climbers, Soph. And there is a play to be acted out, you know."

"I meant that business with your tongue," she said. "The breeze was just cooling me nicely. Now I feel hot again."

"Soph!" he said. "Only a total innocent would say such a thing aloud and expect it to discourage me from trying again. If we are going to have to steal kisses, we might as well make them enjoyable, after all."

"Enjoyable!" she exclaimed. "You may speak for yourself, Francis. For my part, I would as soon kiss . . ."

"I know," he said. "Look who is coming up there to your left, Soph. And with arms linked. And talking with each other and seemingly oblivious to everyone else."

She looked, saw her father and mother approaching, grabbed Francis's arm, and squeezed it tightly.

"Oh," she said, "it is working, I knew it would. I never doubted it for a moment. It will work, Francis, will it not?" She looked up anxiously into his face.

"I don't see how it can fail, Soph," he said, "with the weather cooperating so gloriously and you and me so deeply in love, and all the joy of a wedding beginning to catch everyone up in its excitement."

"Oh, you are wonderful to say so," she said, squeezing his arm again. "I could kiss you, Francis."

"Once is enough for the time being," he said. "And not too free with the *wonderfuls* if you please, Soph. I might start to think that you mean them and really start to feel choked by my cravat."

Sophia turned with a bright smile to greet the group of

friends who were reaching the summit of the hill and beginning to exclaim on the splendor of the view.

He had given her the details of the visit to the rector. She had told him of some of the plans she had discussed with the duchess as they wrote the invitations.

"Was it a good idea to agree to let the wedding take place here?" she asked. "Rose seems a little disappointed that it is not to be at St. George's."

"It is what they both want," he said. "And these large *ton* affairs can be cold, you know."

"Yes," she said. "I never regretted that we married here, Marcus. It was a wonderful wedding, was it not?"

"Yes," he said. "But then I think a clay hut would have seemed wonderful to us on that particular day, Olivia."

She could think of nothing more to say and indeed was embarrassed that she had spoken so freely and thoughtlessly. They did not need to speak of their own wedding. Doing so would only cast a blight on their daughter's and make them anxious for her happiness again.

"You are content to invite only two friends from Rushton, Olivia?" he asked. "It seems not quite fair when I chose five of my close friends."

"Emma and Clarence will be enough," she said. "But I would be sorry if they could not come for Sophia's wedding. Clarence said, after I had received your letter, that it was quite what was to be expected at her age. I suppose a mere friend can see more clearly than a parent that a child is growing up."

"Yes," he said. "I have not seen Clarence for many years. Or Miss Burnett either."

"Emma has never been far from home," she said. "And Clarence has not for quite some time."

She was breathless from climbing the hill and talking at the same time. He paused and drew her arm more closely against his side. It would be so easy, she thought, to relax into this new state of amity, to believe that their natural and mutual concern for their daughter was a totally binding force, to imagine that the truce they had agreed to was a permanent peace. It was a feeling she must hold firm against. She did not want to have to go home in a month's time to fight all the old battles again.

But it was easy to remember just why she had been so happy with him, why she had loved him so much.

"I think perhaps we have done the right thing, don't you?" he said. "None of our guests threw up their hands in amazement that we would allow the betrothal of so young a daughter. And the rector seemed to feel that it was the most natural thing in the world for Sophia to be getting married. They look good together. They look as if they belong together."

"Yes." Olivia looked to the top of the hill, where their daughter and Lord Francis stood close together in animated conversation, their fingers laced. "They have known each other all their lives. That must help. It is not as if they have just recently met and have had romance blind them to each other's faults. They talk to each other a great deal. They seem to be friends, Marcus."

"Do you remember this hill?" he asked.

They had walked there the day before their wedding, when they had been able to escape from the frenzied activities going on at the house. They had climbed right to the top, as they were doing now, and let the wind blow in their faces and wished that the following day were over already so that they could be married and alone together.

"I don't care about the houseful of guests and the feasting and all the rest of it," he had said. "I just want you, Livy."

"And I you," she had said, turning into his arms. "Tomorrow, Marc. It seems an eternity away."

"Tomorrow," he had whispered against her lips. "And then no more separations. Night or day. Never or ever, Livy, until death do us part."

"I love you," she had told him, and he had kissed her long and deeply while they were buffeted by the wind.

"I wonder if they feel as we did then," he said, and she knew that he was thinking of the same memory. "I wonder if they feel their wedding to be a mere nuisance standing between them and eternal bliss."

"But it was a wonderful day after all, was it not?" she said.

"Yes," he said. "They will discover that too."

Before they could remember that they should not reminisce together, they were at the top of the hill, and the breeze greeted them—and their daughter. She had released Lord Francis's hand and pushed her way between them, taking the arm of each.

"Is this not wonderful?" she said, her cheeks glowing from the wind and happiness. "Miles and miles of countryside to see, the lovely sunshine, the cool breeze, and the three of us together again. Is it not wonderful beyond belief?"

"Yes, wonderful, Sophia," Olivia said nad found herself fighting tears for some reason.

"You are truly happy, Sophia?" her father asked. "You have not rushed into anything merely because you are eighteen and it seems the thing to do to marry?"

"I am truly happy, Papa," she said, squeezing his arm. "I am betrothed to the most wonderful man in the world and the most wonderful parents in the world are here to help me celebrate. This is going to be the happiest month of my life so far. And then all the years ahead with Francis. We want you to spend Christmas with us—you andd Francis's parents too, of course. And the New Year. Don't we, Francis?"

Lord Francis had been laughing and joking with some of the other young people. He turned at the sound of his name. "Don't we what?" he asked with a smile.

"Want Mama and Papa and your mother and father to spend Christmas with us," she said. "And New Year. It is what we were talking about a few minutes ago when we were coming up the hill, is it not?"

"The very topic," he said, smiling deep into her eyes. "And we were both agreed that by Christmas we will probably be able to take our eyes off each other for long enough to entertain relatives. We will be disappointed if all four of our parents cannot be there."

"Mama?" Sophia asked eagerly.

"We will have to see," she said. "That is a long time in the future."

"Papa?"

"I shall be there, Sophia," he said quietly.

"Doubtless there will be numerous other occasions too," Lord Francis said. "Won't there, Soph?" Somehow he had possessed himself of the hand that had been linked through her mother's. "Perhaps for the christening of our first child in a year's time or less."

Olivia heard her daughter suck in her breath as Lord Francis smiled at her again and raised her hand to his lips. Good heavens, had they talked about such a thing already?

"It looks as if the food has been taken from the baskets," Mr. Hathaway said loudly enough for all to hear. "And I feel as if I could devour it all myself."

"You would not be so unsporting," Rachel Biddeford said.

"Oh, yes, he would," Sir Ridley said. "I think those of us who hope to eat a bite had better race for it."

"Well, Soph," Lord Francis said, "you must lift your skirt above the ankles and grasp my hand. I don't intend to be the last to the chicken slices."

And they were gone, all of the young people, laughing and shrieking and rushing down the hill.

The earl looked at his wife and smiled. "What was that we have been saying about their having grown up?" he said. "Were we like that at their age, Olivia?"

"Christmas," she said soberly. "It is not really that far in the future, Marcus. Will Sophia be very disappointed, do you think, to have to entertain us separately? Surely she cannot expect everything to change just because she is marrying Lord Francis."

"We will have to wait and see," he said. "All we have agreed to is this month, Olivia. And we have done the right thing. She is very happy to have the three of us together again. Let us just live this month through, shall we, and worry about the rest when it is over?"

"Yes." She sighed. "I have not looked forward to Sophia's growing up. If I had known that it would lead to this sort of complication, I think I would have looked forward to it even less."

"Shall we go down?" he said. "Are you hungry?"

"I suppose so," she said, shrugging.

"I have had some of the trees cut back from the river-bank down there," he said, pointing down the north side of the hill. "Those very old ones. Unfortunately, they kept shedding ancient branches and sometimes whole trunks into the water and caused flooding. It seemed sad at the time, but actually the cutting back has made for a pleasant walk or ride. Would you like to see?"

"Yes," she said. "Have you made many changes, Marcus? I remember that you used to accuse your father of being quite unprogressive."

"The ravings of a younger man who had not yet learned to appreciate tradition," he said. "It is a good thing, perhaps, that most men are older when they eventually inherit. I have far more sympathy with my father than I used to have. Take my arm, Olivia. This section is steeper than it looks. Yes, I have made changes, of course, but nothing to destroy the character of the place."

"What others have you made?" she asked.

A whole hour passed and several of the guests, having finished their picnic tea, had already ridden back to the house before the earl and his wife came strolling around the bottom of the hill and began the climb to the remains of the feast.

"Oh, dear," the countess said as if suddenly recalled to the present, "we have been neglecting our guests dreadfully, Marcus."

"They do not look neglected," he said. "In fact, I would say they look remarkably well fed. Is that Hathaway stretched out fast asleep? And several people are actually beaming down upon us—most notably Sophia. And Rose. Are you hungry yet, Olivia? I could eat a bear."

"And I forgot to have bear patties packed in the hamper," she said without stopping to think. His comment and her reply had been common ones during the years when they were living together.

"Cucumber and cheese and chicken will have to do instead, then," he said. The old reply again.

Olivia felt a heavy ball of panic lodged deep in her stomach. Their plan must not be allowed to work too well.

The plan was for public appearances for Sophia's sake, not for private exchanges.

Sophia and Lord Francis rode off together, Cynthia and Sir Ridley Bowden a little behind them.

"What did you mean," Sophia said accusingly when they were on horseback and on their way, "talking about our first child like that in front of Mama and Papa. I could have died of mortification."

"Or of burst blood vessels in your head," he said. "To say you turned scarlet, Soph, would be to understate the case. I was merely following your lead, that's all. You are the one who started talking about Christmas and New Year and all that sort of sentimentality."

"Inviting them for Christmas and a christening are two entirely different matters," she said. "I scarce knew where to look. In one year's time or less indeed. What a disgusting idea. I would rather . . ."

He held up a staying hand. "We are not going to have to go through all this toad and frog and snake business, are we?" he said. "Have done, Soph. The thought of infants and nurseries actually is enough to make me run all the way to Brazil without stopping or even noticing the ocean, so you need have no fear. Especially if you were to be the mother."

"And that is just like you too," she said indignantly, "to give me such a very ungentlemanly setdown. I would rather be childless to my dying day than have you father my children. So there."

"They were an hour alone," he said, "out of sight of the whole company. And looking quite pleased with themselves and the world at the end of it too. Very promising I would have to say, Soph. Another few days like this and we will be able to put an end to this charade before the wedding guests start to arrive."

"Do you think so?" she said. "They did look almost like an ordinary married couple, did they not, Francis? But how are we to know that they will stay together after we have put an end to all this?"

He shrugged. "I don't know," he said. "You will have

to ask them, I suppose, Soph. You are their daughter, after all.''

"Oh," she said, "how can I go up to them and ask if they are going to remain together?''

"Ask them one at a time," he said.

"I suppose so." She frowned. And then she smiled radiantly at him. "The Christmas idea might work, though, Francis, even if this does not," she said. "There is no time quite like Christmas for love and families and peace and warmth and everything else that is wonderful. If we can get them to come to us for Christmas, they surely will remain together afterward. Don't you think?''

"Christenings sometimes have the same effect, too," he said dryly. "Soph, I am coming more and more to the belief that you are either the wickedest schemer it has ever been my privilege to know or that you are a case for Bedlam. I rather lean toward the latter.''

"Oh, yes, of course," she said, mortified. "It will just have to happen this month, then, won't it?''

"And sooner rather than later would be good for my peace of mind too," he said. "Promise me one thing.''

"What?" she asked, looking at him.

"That after this you will consider yourself fully revenged for all those nasty things I did to you as a boy," he said. "That we will shake hands and go happily on our separate ways.''

"But you agreed quite freely to this," she said. "I never agreed to all those horrid tricks. Don't tell me that you are having second thoughts, Francis, and wish we had never started all this. You are, aren't you?''

"Who? Me?" he said. "Having second thoughts? Why ever would I do that, Soph, when I am having so much fun? And when I am in imminent danger of being dragged off to the altar just so that we can have your parents for Christmas? It has never once occurred to me to have second thoughts or to give in to an attack of acute anxiety.''

Sophia looked doubtful. "Well, then," she said, "why are you talking about shaking hands and going our separate ways? If we do that, Mama will go home before she and Papa have realized that they cannot live without each other and I shall never marry because I will be finally convinced that no good can come of marriage. Do you want to be responsible for those two disasters?''

Lord Francis sighed. ''When you get back to Bedlam, Soph,'' he said, ''ask them to reserve a room for me, will you? There's a good girl. I am going to be needing it soon.''

Sophia clucked her tongue and spurred her horse to a canter. Lord Francis shook his head and went after her.

7

They really did not need the distraction of the ball less than a week after the announcement of the betrothal, the duchess said. There was so much to do without all the preparations for that. She seemed oblivious to the fact that the earl had organized the ball several weeks before and that his servants were quietly and efficiently carrying out all the work that was to be done. She seemed equally oblivious to the fact that various competent persons had taken over the preparations for the wedding and that everything was progressing smoothly.

As his grace commented to the earl and countess one afternoon when her grace had finally been persuaded to rest in her room for an hour on the understanding that the world would not collapse about her if she did so, her mind must not be disabused. She was entirely happy being in a panic about nothing.

Besides, the duchess had assured everyone, herself included, the ball was entirely necessary as an official celebration of the betrothal.

The countess and Sophia, accompanied by Lord Francis, were to go to London for a few days the following week in order to be fitted for wedding clothes and bride clothes. Olivia had mixed feelings about the approaching journey. So many years had passed since she had been to town. And yet, she had always loved it there. Her come-out Season had been magical.

The duchess kept her busy most days about real and imagined preparations for the wedding. And there were guests to entertain. She grew accustomed to being the hostess at Clifton, to spending hours in company with her husband, behaving for Sophia's sake as if theirs was a real marriage. And it was a worthwhile effort. Sophia glowed and was utterly happy.

And yet, there was the need to spend time alone. For fourteen years she had been a very private person, bringing up a daughter, having a circle of good friends, participating in the social life of her neighborhood, and yet being essentially alone. She had grown accustomed to the life.

She needed time to think. Time to regain her equilibrium, her sanity. Sometimes she found herself almost forgetting that things were not as they seemed. Sometimes she found herself seating herself next to her husband or speaking to him or even seeking him out when there was no real need to do so. She had strolled beside him throughout one afternoon walk, for example, and had realized, only after they had returned home, that she need not have done so since Sophia and Francis had gone with a few other young people to the village.

And there were the mornings, two of them, when he had mentioned at the breakfast table that he must ride out about estate business for a few hours and she had asked him privately afterward if she might accompany him. She had always done so when they had been together. She did not want to be merely the lady of the house, she had always said. She wanted to be part of his world. She wanted to understand the workings of his land. She wanted to be able to talk meaningfully with her husband about the things that really mattered.

It was training that had stood her in good stead during the intervening years. Although Marcus remained in close communication with his steward, he never came home and had learned to trust her with the day-to-day decisions concerning Rushton.

And so she rode with him about Clifton and enjoyed those mornings more than she had enjoyed anything else for a long time. She watched and listened and asked him questions and made comments. They scarcely stopped talking during all the hours they were gone. During those hours, she had not once felt any awkwardness with him, or any strain from their long separation and the knowledge that it would resume once Sophia was safely married. It had seemed quite like old times. They had felt like friends. Friends and comrades.

Dangerously like.

She needed some time to herself. And she found it not in her rooms, where she could in all probability have gone undisturbed, but in the hidden garden. It became almost a regular part of her day to steal away there for an hour in the afternoons. Only one rainy day had kept her away.

She would sit in the rock garden, merely thinking or dreaming, her eyes feasting on the beauty and color of the flowers, her nose drawing in the heady scent of the roses. Or sometimes she would take her book and read. Sometimes she stretched out on the grass beneath the shade of one of the trees and watched the clouds float across a blue sky and let the peace of nature seep into her very bones. Once, she fell asleep.

It was like a place apart, a dream world, a little heaven on earth. Not Clifton, not Rushton, not the past, not the present. Not of this world at all.

She never bolted the door behind her, but she always hoped that no one else would discover the hidden garden. It would not be the same once someone else had been there to exclaim on its beauty. Except one person, of course. She went there each day to escape from him—not so much from his physical person as from the influence he was beginning to have over her emotions. And yet, of course, she took him there with her, for it was there he had first kissed her. It had been their garden—Marc's and Livy's. Two different persons.

She fought against the knowledge that in reality they were still the same people.

She was sitting there on the afternoon of the ball, rather than resting in her room before getting ready, as the other ladies were doing. The sun was hot again and the sky cloudless, as it had been so often recently. She was beneath the shade of a weeping willow tree, beside a bed of hyacinths. She was wishing that the remaining three weeks until the wedding would pass by quickly. And she was wishing that time would stand still.

She did not know what she wished, she thought, smiling ruefully at the contradiction in her mind and reaching out to touch a purple bloom.

And then the arched door opened and she looked up to

see him come inside. She was not surprised. She had been expecting him.

Had she? Cetainly she had not consciously done so. If she had, then surely she would have sought out privacy else-where. Had she wanted him to come? Onto magical ground like this, no part of the real world. Did she want him there?

He leaned against the door as he shut it behind him and she knew, although she could neither see nor hear it happen-ing, that he had bolted it. She had expected it. Wanted it?

"You are not resting?" he asked her, strolling toward her along the path and around the sundial.

"Yes," she said. "Here."

He smiled and stopped below her. She was sitting on a rock on a level with his shoulders. "You come here every day, don't you?" he asked.

"Yes."

It was a dream world indeed. He stood there looking up at her, his eyes roaming over her face, her hair, her body. And she looked at him, at the man he had become while she had not been there to observe the gradual changes. Neither seemed to feel the embarrassment of silence or the need to say anything.

Surely he was more handsome now than he had been. Or perhaps it was just that she was looking at him through older eyes that demanded more than a slender, good-looking boy. There were lines in his face—not wrinkles exactly—but lines of maturity and character. Lines that revealed that he had some experience of life. And his silvering hair was unexpect-edly attractive. It was as thick as it had ever been.

His shoulders were broader, and his chest too. And yet his stomach was flat and his waist and hips still slim. He was not showing his age in increased flabbiness as Clarence was doing. Clearly he looked after himself, as he had always done. The muscles of his calves showed that he walked and rode a great deal. She wondered if he still liked to spar at Jackson's boxing saloon when he was in town.

When he reached out his arms to her, she did not hesitate to set her hands on his shoulders and lean forward so that his hands could grasp her by the waist and lift her to the ground in front of him. He held her above him for a few moments and she looked down into his upturned face.

It was inevitable. It was what she had known for days was going to happen. Had she? The conscious thought had not crossed her mind. But she had known it. She had been coming to the hidden garden and she had known that he would eventually come there, too. It was their garden after all, and it was still as lovely and remote as it had been when they shared their first kiss. It was the one thing in their world that had not changed.

He lowered her slowly, sliding her along his body until her feet touched the ground. And then he lowered his head and kissed her.

She could only feel shock at the sameness and the difference. He was Marc as he had always been, bending her body to his, his height arching her head back. And so familiar that the years instantly rolled back. There were no years. Only Marc and her and the rightness of their being together. He was the only man who had ever kissed her or touched her in any way intimately.

And yet so different. He had used to kiss her with parted lips. They had always enjoyed the warmth and intimacy of kisses. She had liked to curl against him on a sofa or on his lap, indulging only in kisses, without any particular thought to going to bed. It had been a warm and wonderful form of communication.

But he had never kissed her openmouthed as he was kissing her now, his mouth wide over hers, his tongue pushing up behind her lip and creating strange vibrations against the soft flesh there.

And then his face was above hers and they were looking at each other again, exploring each other's eyes this time. And he was lowering his head and pecking light kisses on her temples and cheeks. She ran the back of her fingers softly over his jaw, her elbows up over his shoulders. His jaw was smooth. He must have shaved very recently.

They had always been able to look into each other's eyes without embarrassment and had laughed together once after two friends had told them that they hated to sit opposite each

other at table when alone because doing so forced them to
look into each other's eyes as they talked. She had laughed
about it with Marc, and the two of them had tried it, sitting
opposite each other at a small card table, their elbows
touching on its top, their chins cupped in their hands, trying
to stare each other down. They had laughed and occasionally
leaned forward to exchange brief kisses, but succeeded in
staying where they were for half an hour before they had
been called away to some unremembered task.

They looked at each other now until he wrapped one arm
about her shoulders and the other about her waist, drew her
close against him, and kissed her again.

And this time the unfamiliarity was total. He slid his tongue
all the way into her mouth until she felt filled with its firmness
and heat, and withdrew it as slowly before pushing inward
again. And she realized, as her knees almost buckled under
her, what act he was simulating and then had no more time
for thought. Only for reaction.

She had never felt desire before, a strange truth in light
of the fact that their five years together had been ones of
almost daily intimacy, and that she had always—with the
possible exception of their wedding night—enjoyed their
couplings. She had enjoyed them because they always gave
him such pleasure and because there was joy in being so
intimately possessed by the man she loved more than anyone
else in the whole world. If asked, she would have said that
she felt both desire for and fulfillment with her husband.

But she knew now, beyond the realm of rational thought,
that she had never felt desire before. Never this raw throbbing from her mouth to her throat to her breasts to her womb
and lower. A throbbing and an insistent longing to be possessed. Never this uncontrolled need to have his body fill
her and give her peace.

She arched herself into him as one hand twined tightly in
his hair and the other went up under his coat and waistcoat
to the warm silk of his shirt at the back. And she held her
mouth wide to the rhythm of the simulated loving of his
tongue.

He was looking down at her again, his dark eyes gazing

knowingly and heavy-lidded into her own. And he was turning her until their feet discovered soft grass, and lowering her down onto it, raising her muslin dress to her waist as he did so. His hands stripped her of her lower garments, removed his coat to set beneath her head, and undid the buttons of his breeches.

Was this going to happen? Was she going to allow it? It was one thing to share kisses with him in the hidden garden, however intimate, and quite another to couple with him there. Should she not put an end to the madness? She looked about her at the trees and the grass and the banked flowers spilling over the rocks. She could see the sundial behind her and the clear blue sky above. And she knew clearly what was happening and what was about to happen. She would never be able to accuse him of ravishment, she thought quite deliberately.

And yet she was like two persons. The one was detached and rational. The other ached for him and wanted him and needed him and knew that it had all been inevitable from the moment when she had read his letter asking her to come. For how could she see him again and not love him? How could she see him again and keep dormant within herself the knowledge that she had always loved him, had continued to love him even when she had hated him the most?

There was no stopping what was about to happen. And she would not stop it now, even if she could. She would think later of the shame of it, of the complications she was adding to her life, of the hell she would be facing after she had returned home, alone again.

He was beside her on the grass, pulling free the sash beneath her breasts with one hand as the other slid up her naked body beneath her clothes and covered one of her breasts. She closed her eyes and opened her mouth in a silent cry.

What he did to her breasts, to first one and then the other, was achingly familiar to her. She bit down on her lower lip and smiled with the wonder of it after all these years. Marc. She wanted to open her eyes and speak his name, but that was one thing she could not do.

And his hand moved down between her legs as he kissed her again, and began to do unfamiliar things, things that brought her desire to a boil and had her arching up against his hand, crying out into his mouth, begging for a release she had never suspected a need of before.

And then his weight was on her and his hands beneath her and his knees pushing between her own and widening them and he came up into her with one sharp thrust and something shattered inside her and inside her world so that she clung to him with her arms and legs, her body shaking out of control as he moved quickly and deeply in her to his own climax.

She was hardly aware that he moved off her almost immediately because of the hardness of the ground, taking her with him so that she lay on her side against him, her head on his arm while he lifted his coat and spread it over her. She slept almost immediately.

He had guessed that she came to the hidden garden daily, though he had not spied upon her. And he had tried to stay away from there himself, sensing her need to have somewhere to go where she could be alone. It must be difficult for her, coming into his world at a moment's notice and forced to remain in it for a whole month. He realized that. And difficult, too, to be forced by her love for Sophia into spending more time with him than inclination would lead her to do otherwise.

He had tried to leave her alone and had failed on this particular afternoon. The ladies were all in their rooms resting in preparation for the evening's ball. The gentlemen were all variously employed and did not need his company. There was no work that particularly demanded his attention. And the weather was glorious—perfectly sunny and hot. It was an afternoon made for love.

And he loved her. He had never doubted it, had never even tried in all the years of their separation to stop loving her. Olivia was his wife, the woman he had chosen to spend his life with. Nothing had happened to change those facts.

He had known that he still loved her even before she

arrived. What he had not expected was the force of his need for her. Not just physical need, though there was that too, but also emotional need. He needed her companionship again, her support and respect. Her affection. He had never found a substitute for those qualities, even with Mary.

He needed her, but knew what a strain he had put on her emotions by pressuring her into playing out a charade for Sophia's benefit. He tried very hard to keep conversation easy and light between them, to do or say nothing that would embarrass or distress her, and in some ways it had been easier than he had expected. She still had her interest in estate business and the well-being of his tenants. They were able to talk impersonally, but with genuine interest on those matters.

He tried very hard to keep anything personal out of their relationship. She had made herself very clear on that score years before and had always been quite adamant in her refusal to forgive him. He had written almost daily when he first left home. Six months had passed before he finally wrote to her to inform her that it would be the last time he would beg her forgiveness. If she refused it that time, then he would be forced to consider their marriage at an end in all but name. He would leave her alone to live her life in peace, writing to her only about business matters and matters concerning Sophia. He had informed her that he would never take Sophia from her, but would need to see their daughter with fair frequency.

He had informed her yet again that he had been unfaithful to her only that once, that there had been no repetition of the infidelity during the six months, and never would be if she would but forgive him and take him back. She had written to tell him that after deep and careful reflection she had concluded that she could never again be his friend or his wife or lover after what had happened. It would always be there to come between them. She would be grateful if he kept the promises made in his last letter. She would never deny him Sophia for visits.

He had done as she asked. And a month after her letter arrived he had set up Patty, a young dancer, as his mistress.

He had found a measure of forgetfulness with her for the year after that—a very small measure. The girl had been a very experienced young courtesan. But it had not been experience he had been in search of. It had been a substitute for Livy. After a year he had paid her off and never repeated the experiment, though he had occasionally—rarely—hired a woman for a single night.

He rested his cheek against the smooth hair on top of his wife's head and looked at the roses climbing the wall opposite. He would not sleep, explosive as their coupling had been. He wanted to smell the sweet fragrance of her hair and to feel the warmth and softness of her lower body, still unclothed, against his own. He wanted to feel the weight of her head on his arm and to listen to her even breathing.

Except that he felt rather sick. He had come to her at last, half hoping as he walked through the woods that she would not be there, but would be safely resting in her own apartments. He had come to talk with her, he had convinced himself as he entered the garden and slid home the bolt on the door behind his back. He had come to smell the flowers with her and enjoy the sunshine. He had come . . . because he had had to come.

He would just hold her, he had decided a few minutes after that. He would just kiss her as he had kissed her during those days of their betrothal. He would indulge in a little nostalgia. And in a little self-indulgence too, he had decided very soon after that, using his tongue on her in the sensual, suggestive manner taught him by Patty many years before.

And then it had been too late. He closed his eyes and turned his face into her hair.

He was feeling sick and despairing. What further proof would she need that he was uncontrolled and selfish in his passions? Locking the door of the garden and taking her on the grass as if she had been any whore. As if he had come there for no other purpose.

And he was feeling sick for another reason too. She had changed. Her body was more mature and voluptuous. That was understandable. She had been twenty-two years old the last time he had slept with her. She was thirty-six now. But that was not the difference. It was a difference in experience.

She had been an innocent when he had left her, just as he had been. She had never initiated anything in their love-making and had never given any signs of great physical passion. She had always enjoyed their beddings. He had known her well enough to realize that. And they had always made love in the literal meaning of the term. But he had never known her aroused beyond a hardening of her nipples and an increased warmth. Even after five years of a very intimate marriage, she had been an innocent.

The woman with whom he had just coupled was no innocent. He had been startled by her early and total arousal, by the way she had arched herself to him, explored his body with pressing palms, sucked on his tongue, moaned out her desire, and half dragged him down to the grass. She had touched him with knowing hands after he had unclothed himself and while he had touched her. And she had twined herself about him and abandoned herself to physical release at his first inward thrust into her body.

It was not the Livy he had known with whom he had coupled. It was Olivia as she had become in fourteen years. He lay on the grass, her body nestled warmly against him, and stared at the roses. He wondered who had taken her from innocence to the glorious flowering of passion and sensuality he had just been witness to.

Clarence, he supposed. Clarence almost certainly. He had been a handsome enough man and had always been her friend as much as his own. Not that he suspected even for one moment that there had been anything between the two of them before the separation. But there clearly was a great deal between them now.

There was a dull ache of despair in the pit of his stomach and a growing anger too. An unfocused anger. Not entirely against her. He knew from experience that it was nearly impossible to remain celibate for fourteen years. And not entirely against Clarence, though at least partly so—oh yes, at least partly. And not even entirely against himself for causing it all.

Just an anger against fate, perhaps, for bringing about this present pass. For allowing Sophia to break out with the measles just when she had, and not a day or two later. For making Livy the type of woman who would want him to go to that wedding alone because he had had his heart set on it. For making him go even though he would twenty times have preferred to remain at home with his wife and daughter. For that stupid party and his criminal weakness. For all the rest of the chain of events leading to the end of their marriage and to this bitter-sweet moment.

Perhaps they had loved too dearly. Had he loved her less, perhaps he could have kept quiet about his infidelity and punished only himself with it. Had she loved him less, perhaps she could eventually have forgiven him. Had he loved her less, perhaps he would have forced her to take him back and they might have eventually worked out some sort of peace. Had she loved him less . . .

It was all pointless thinking. Matters were as they were. And he found himself physically satisfied and mortally depressed. And disturbed by the beginnings of anger.

She was awake. He could tell by the change in her breathing and by the slight tensing of her body. He closed his eyes. If she smiled at him, he thought, then he would talk to her from the heart. He would ask her once more, after all these years, to forgive him even though there was now much more to forgive. He drew a slow breath, opened his eyes, and eased his head back to look down into her face.

She looked back at him, her eyes blank. Not the blankness of a consciousness not fully returned, but a deliberate blankness. A mask. A brick wall. There was not even the suggestion of a smile on her face.

He felt his jaw hardening as he clamped his teeth together. He eased his arm from beneath her head, sat up, and adjusted his clothing. He lowered her dress beneath the cover of his coat and then lifted the coat away and pulled it on. He got to his feet and brushed the grass from his clothing. And he turned to look down at her.

She had not moved or changed her expression or uttered a word.

"After all, Olivia," he said, and he hardly recognized the coldness of his own voice, "you are my wife."

Then he strode across the grass to the door, unbolted it, and let himself out, closing it firmly behind him.

8

All of her father's neighbors were delighted at the news of her betrothal, Sophia discovered at the ball that evening. They were equally delighted by the fact that she and her prospective husband had decided that the nuptials were to be held at their own village church.

"It must be nigh on twenty years since there was such a grand wedding in these parts," Mr. Ormsby said. "Your mama and papa's, my dear Lady Sophia. And a lovely one it was too."

"The sun was shining," Mrs. Ormsby added, smiling and nodding toward the earl and countess, who stood next to their daughter and future son-in-law in the receiving line. "And such a beautiful bride."

"But no lovelier than you will be, my dear," Mr. Ormsby said before extending his hand to Lord Francis. "So you are the fortunate young man, are you?"

"The very one, sir," Lord Francis said, bowing.

The neighbors were also pleased to see her parents together again, Sophia saw, and she glowed with hope and happiness. They looked so splendidly good together this evening, her papa in black with sparkling white linen, her mama in turquoise silk. They looked not old enough to be her parents, she thought fondly, despite Papa's silvering hair. It only made him look more distinguished.

Sophia smiled and curtsied and turned her cheek for yet another series of kisses from beaming well-wishers.

Color glowed in her mother's cheeks, Sophia had noticed earlier when she had called at her room so that they might come downstairs together for dinner. It was such a deep color and so perfect that at first Sophia had thought that her mama had taken to wearing cosmetics. But no, the color was natural, and had not faded at all in the course of the evening.

Her father was rather stiff and formal this evening. He had scarcely smiled, though he was treating his guests with courtesy and friendliness. But it was understandable, Sophia thought fondly, that his manner would be a little unnatural this evening. It was not every day that a gentleman held a ball in celebration of his only daughter's betrothal.

Sophia felt a stab of guilt and darted a look up at Francis. He smiled warmly back at her and one of the Misses Girten sighed and simpered as she approached along the receiving line.

"Such a very fine-looking couple," she commented to the earl and countess. "And clearly a love match."

Sophia felt even more guilty. But she quelled the feeling instantly. It was all worthwhile if it would finally bring Mama and Papa together again. They so obviously belonged together.

It was a pity that Bertie and Richard and Claude were not present, the duchess said with a sigh when it appeared that all the guests had arrived and the dancing could begin. She still could not quite believe that her baby was to be married within the month. But then, she said, cheering up visibly, the boys and their wives and families would be coming to Clifton more than a week before the wedding. Soon she would have all her family about her again.

"And soon you will have another daughter-in-law to add to the flock, Rose," the duke said, patting her hand and looking about the ballroom, which they had all just entered. "And doubtless another occupant for the nursery too, within the year. Our boys are nothing if not prompt about such matters. They take after their father."

"William, love!" the duchess said, embarrassed.

Lord Francis, in view of all the guests in the ballroom, smiled meltingly into Sophia's eyes and raised her hand to his lips.

"The moment can be likened only to standing on a trap-door, a noose about one's neck, waiting for the door to be sprung," he murmured fondly into her ear. "And knowing that one did not commit the crime but has cheerfully admitted to it all along on the foolish assumption that the real culprit would come to take one's place at the last moment."

"How can you liken a ball to a hanging, Francis?" she said, looking about at the floral decorations that she had helped with earlier in the day. "And it is all in our honor. Was there ever a more wonderful feeling? Look." Her hold on his arm tightened. "Papa is going across to the orchestra to instruct them to begin playing. And I believe he is going to make an announcement."

"The trapdoor hinges are creaking," Lord Francis said.

The Earl of Clifton raised a hand for silence. He got it easily since almost all eyes were on him and the gathered guests were eager for the ball to begin.

"Welcome to Clifton Court," he said, looking about him at all his friends and neighbors and houseguests. "The reason for this evening's celebration is well-known, so I do not intend to give a long speech."

"Bravo!" a voice said from a far corner, and there was a flurry of laughter.

"This is just an official announcement of the betrothal and coming nuptials of my daughter, Sophia, and Lord Francis Sutton, youngest son of the Duke and Duchess of Weymouth," the earl said. "They will lead the first dance, a waltz. Please feel free to lead your partners onto the floor after a few minutes, gentlemen. And enjoy the evening, ladies."

Sophia flushed at the applause and looked anxiously up at Lord Francis as he led her to the middle of the dancing area. "Everyone is going to be watching," she said. "I shall have two left feet, Francis."

"You are fortunate," he said. "I will be dancing with a noose about my neck."

"How foolish," she said.

"Smile," he commanded, and she tipped her head back to show that she was already doing so, and they began to waltz.

"Oh, Francis," she said. "This is very wonderful, is it not? I had no idea quite how it would be. I think that after all, provided Mama and Papa remain together, and perhaps even if they do not, I will marry." Her eyes grew dreamy. "At the village church. And make very, very sure that nothing stupid ever happens to keep me away from my husband for the better part of my life. I think I will live happily ever after.''

''Er, those plans don't include me by any chance, do they, Soph?'' he asked. ''I mean, you aren't expecting me to play the part of radiant bridegroom and happy husband as well as besotted fiancé, are you?''

''Of course not,'' she said. ''You do not have to worry that I will break my word, Francis.''

''What?'' he said. ''Nothing to add about snakes and toads and such? You aren't coming to like me by any chance are you, Soph? I don't particularly want any softening of feelings here for a while yet, you know.''

''Oh,'' she said indignantly, ''how could I possibly like you, Francis? You always go out of your way to be obnoxious.''

''Now that I know the secret of my success with you,'' he said, ''I shall be sure to continue with it, Soph. A little twirl about the corner here, I think. We have guests to entertain. Ah, our respective mamas and papas have joined us on the floor, I see.''

''Papa does not look at all relaxed,'' Sophia said with a frown. ''He looks almost as if he is not enjoying himself. But they waltz beautifully together, do they not? And how could he fail to fall in love with Mama all over again, Francis? I think it is happening, don't you? They have been together far more than they needed to be in the past week. She has even been out with him about estate business.''

''Lord,'' her partner said, looking harassed before putting his smile firmly in place again, ''my mother is going to weep floods of tears when you jilt me, you know, Soph. She probably will not talk to you for the next ten years or so.''

''I am not going to jilt you,'' she said indignantly. ''What a horrid word.''

''Oh yes you are,'' he said firmly, ''even if the word were ten times more horrid.''

''I am going to end the betrothal,'' she said. ''That is all.''

''And that is not jilting?'' he asked.

''No,'' she said. ''Is that what people are going to say, Francis? That you have been jilted? It is going to be dreadful for you, is it not? People will wonder what is wrong with you. I am most awfully sorry.''

''I will live with the ignominy, Soph,'' he said hastily. ''Believe me, I will live with it.''

Perhaps the hardest thing she had ever had to do, Olivia thought, was come downstairs to dinner. Harder even than alighting from her carriage outside the doors on her arrival at Clifton. Yes, harder even that that. She was more grateful than she could say when Sophia came to accompany her down.

Her mind had refused to stop teeming with a whole host of conflicting thoughts and emotions since earlier that afternoon. She had lain on the grass in the hidden garden for a long time after he had left, reluctant to move, afraid to set her thoughts in motion, to face what she had done, to wonder at his final look and his final words.

She had lain there trying to cling to mere feeling and reaction. She was sore and her breasts felt tender. And it had been wonderful, quite wonderful. It had been such a very long time. She had dreamed of it, ached for it so often over the years, and yet when it had happened it had been so much more wonderful and so much more—physical than she remembered. She knew that she would want it again.

With him. Only with him. Emma had once suggested to her, during one of her dreadfully restless periods, which had mercifully become less frequent over the years, that she go to one of the spas or even to London and take a lover for a month or two. Emma had always prided herself on being enlightened and had quite deliberately chosen the spinster life for herself. Olivia had been horrified. She was a married lady, she had protested. She could not dream of doing that with anyone but her husband.

She would not want to do it with anyone but Marc even if he were not her husband. She had always known that.

Taking a lover had never been an option in her life. And yet her aloneness, her loneliness, her celibacy were her own fault. She had recognized that almost from the start. Refusing to forgive him after one infidelity, which he very clearly had

regretted bitterly, was harsh and foolish. She should have
forgiven him. She had wanted to forgive him. She *had*
forgiven him in the privacy of her own heart. But she could
not live out that forgiveness, she had realized during those
first months alone, when his letters were coming almost
daily. She could not live with him as before, be intimate with
him, be his friend. There would always be that between them.

Olivia had finally left the garden, returned to the house,
and sent down for hot water for a bath, recognizing the fact
that her thoughts could not after all be kept at bay. The real
world intruded, even into the hidden garden.

She had been too deeply in love. She knew that. Their
marriage had been too perfect. She had not known it at the
time, but had only realized it since, looking about her at the
marriages of her friends and acquaintances. Her marriage
had been unreal. Quite perfect for an unbelievable five years.
There had never been a cloud on their horizon.

The storm, when it came, had killed everything. She had
not afterward believed she could live with an imperfect
marriage. She had believed that she could not be fair to him
any longer. She would surely always look on him with
suspicion and disappointment. He could never again be her
Marc as she had known him. And she was afraid even to
try to get to know a new Marc. Perhaps she could not love
the new Marc.

The thought of not loving him had filled her with panic.
Better never to see him again. Better to live on alone as if
he were dead.

And so she had written to him at the end of six months
to tell him—untruthfully—that she could not forgive him. She
had tried to explain her reasons, but she had been unable
to explain.

She had been very young. Very immature. Very ignorant
of life.

Making love with him that afternoon had surely been the
most wonderful experience of her life. But of course she had
given in to the unreality of the hidden garden. She had
believed that that one experience could erase all the bitterness of fourteen years. She had believed as she woke up and

remembered where she was, and with whom, that it would all be at an end, that he would smile at her, kiss her, and say something that would erase the past just as if it had never been.

Foolish woman. Even in fourteen years she had not fully matured. She had looked up at him with anxious eyes to find his own unsmiling and hooded. And then he had got up and dressed himself without a word or a look just as if it had all meant nothing to him. And finally his voice. His cold voice telling her that after all she was his wife.

She had just been one of his women. One of his countless women. But on this occasion, he had been able to excuse his promiscuity with the irrefutable truth that she was his wife.

She had been no more to him than any of his women! And she had been forgetting during the past week—deliberately forgetting, perhaps—that things had changed, that there was now a great deal more wrong with their marriage than just that first regretted infidelity. There had been other women in his life, probably untold numbers of them. There was Lady Mornington.

She had felt sick as she dressed reluctantly for dinner and the ball. Physically sick. And dreaded meeting him again more than she had dreaded anything in her life. Going downstairs, seeing him again, behaving as if nothing had happened between them, was the hardest thing she had ever had to do.

He was dressed in the newest fashion, one she had heard of but never seen before. His evening coat and knee breeches were black, his waistcoat silver, his shirt and stockings white. White lace frothed over his hands. He looked far more handsome than any other man present. And she had to allow Sophia to take her across the drawing room to where he stood, talking with Mrs. Biddeford and Lord Wheatley. She had to smile at them all and accept a glass from his hand.

"Thank you," she said as he complimented her on her appearance, her eyes on the contents of her glass.

Sophia took a hand of each of them in hers and joined them, her two hands holding them together.

"This is going to be the most wonderful night of my life," she said. "And you are both here to celebrate it with me. Mama and Papa, how wonderful this all is."

He was looking broodingly at their hands, Olivia saw when she glanced up at him and then smiled at their daughter. His face was quite unsmiling.

They sat facing each other at dinner, but such a length of table lay between them that there was no necessity of even looking at each other and no possibility of talking. It was relatively easy. And then there was the receiving line, where they stood shoulder to shoulder for almost an hour, greeting guests, making small talk, and smiling and smiling. And not once glancing at each other or exchanging a single word.

"We must dance, Olivia," he said to her finally, after Sophia and Lord Francis had been waltzing alone for a few minutes. "It is what is expected."

It was the hardest moment of all, the necessity of standing face to face with him and setting one hand in his and the other on his shoulder, the whole roomful of guests watching. And she had no doubt that they had drawn eyes from Sophia and Lord Francis. All these people, after all, knew that she and her husband had been estranged for many years.

"We must smile," she said, smiling.

He did not respond. "I suppose I must say I am sorry," he said after a few moments of silence.

"Why?" she asked. "You are not sorry, are you?" And she looked up into his cold eyes.

"And you are never in the business of forgiving, are you?" he said. "I would be wasting my breath."

"Do you apologize to all your women?" she said. "It must become tedious."

His jaw tightened. "All my women," he said. "No, Olivia, there is never any need. They always enjoy what they get. As you did this afternoon."

"Yes," she said. "It would be hard to resist such expertise."

"Well," he said, "no great harm has been done, then, has it? We are, when all is said and done, man and wife. And you have looked after yourself over the years, Olivia. You are still beautiful."

"A crumb thrown to the dogs?" she said. "Thank you, Marcus. I am to feel the thrill of being complimented by my own husband, I gather?"

"You may feel what you wish," he said. "The caustic tongue is new, Olivia."

"There is a great deal that is new," she said. "I am no longer a person you know, Marcus. It is fourteen years since I was your wife. I am *not* your wife, though in the eyes of church and state we are still married."

"Ah," he said. "So fornication comes lightly to you?"

"Not as lightly, perhaps, as adultery came to you once upon a time," she said.

"Touché." He watched her from cold, hooded eyes. And then his eyes strayed beyond her. "Sophia is watching us," he said, "and looking puzzled. This is the most wonderful night of her life, Olivia. That is what she said before dinner, is it not? I think we must defer our quarrel until a more private moment." He smiled suddenly and looked down into her eyes. "Did you have a glimmering of an understanding of all that it would mean to be a parent, Olivia? Did you know how smitten we both would be with love for our only daughter?"

"Enough that we would do this for her?" she asked, smiling back into his eyes. "No, I did not. Marcus, I would die for her. I know you will say that is pure melodrama, but it is true. I would."

"And smile at me for her," he said. "In some ways that is worse than dying, is it not, Olivia?"

"Don't invite me to quarrel again," she said.

"It is an art we never learned, is it not?" he said. "Five years and not one harsh word. We were the fairy-tale lovers, Olivia. The happily-ever-after lovers. Two children living in bliss together and together bringing a third into the world."

"Yes," she said. "Two children. But there is nothing wrong with childhood, Marcus. It is less painful than adulthood."

"Yes," he said. "But in real childhood, there is always someone who will kiss the hurt better and make all well. There was no one to do that for us, was there?"

"No."

His hand at her waist increased its pressure a little. "Let us separate that absurdly happy pair of children," he said. "Dance with your future son-in-law, Olivia. I want to dance with my daughter."

"Yes," she said, relieved and sorry. Relieved because they would no longer have to touch and look into each other's eyes and make conversation. Sorry for the same reasons.

"This ballroom is deuced hot," Lord Francis said to Sophia when they came together again later in the evening. "Hathaway was just saying how warm it still is outside. Warm, Soph, not stifling hot as it is in here. Shall we take a turn about the garden? I daresay we are expected to go slinking off together some time during the evening, anyway."

"Like thieves in the night?" she said. "How foolish."

"Like lovers in the night," he said. "Those older ladies in a row over there—the ones who have not stopped nodding and simpering since they arrived—will be thrilled beyond words."

"The Misses Girten and Mrs. and Miss Macdonald?" she said. "They will more likely have a collective fit of the vapors, Francis."

"Fit of imagined ecstasy," he said. "Shall we go?"

"It *is* hot in here," she said. "I wish Mama and Papa would dance together again."

"It would not be right," he said. "They are the host and hostess, you know. And there is a prodigious number of unattached ladies that your papa must feel obliged to lead out."

"Do you think that is all?" she said, allowing him to take her out through the French windows onto the terrace at the west side of the house. "I could have sworn that they were quarreling just before they came to separate us during the first dance."

"I would say that is a promising sign, Soph," he said. "If they are quarreling, they are probably airing out their differences."

"Do you think so?" She looked doubtful. She followed his lead out onto the lawn, which led to the distant stable block. "But we always quarrel, Francis, yet we are not ironing out differences. We are merely quarreling."

"True enough," he said. "The terrace is black with people, Soph. I wonder they don't all run into one another at every turn. They have probably all poured out to catch a glimpse of me stealing a kiss from you."

"How absurd," she said. "As if people have nothing better to do with their time."

"There is nothing more romantic than a newly betrothed pair, though," he said. "Shall we satisfy them?"

"But Mama and Papa are not out here," she said. "And they are the only ones we are really trying to convince, Francis."

"True enough," he said. "But rumor will soon get back to them if we appear cool, and then they may never settle their own differences."

"Do you think so?" she said doubtfully. "Very well, then. We had better kiss. But don't do that with your tongue."

He sighed. "Your next beau or your next fiancé is going to think you a dreadful innocent if you don't know how to kiss, Soph," he said.

"I know how to kiss," she said indignantly.

"You know how to pucker your lips," he said. "That is child's stuff, Soph."

"Well!" she said, offended. "If you do not like my kisses, Francis, you do not have to kiss me, you know. It is all the same to me."

"Perhaps you had better learn while you have the chance," he said.

"From you?" she said. "From a rake?"

"Who better to learn from?" he asked.

Sophia could think of no suitable answer.

"You have to relax your mouth," he said, "and let me do the leading."

"Just as in dancing," she said.

"Just as in dancing," he agreed. "And never mind the puckers. They are not part of good kissing."

"Oh," she said.

He set a hand beneath her chin and raised it. "I have the

feeling that it is a good thing it is dark out here," he said. "What color are you, Soph?"

"Is there a color brighter than scarlet?" she asked.

"Yes," he said. "The color of your face right now. Relax your mouth. And your teeth."

"But they are chattering," she said.

"Let me worry about that," he said and set his mouth to hers.

Sophia gripped his shoulders as if trying to inflict bruises as his lips teased hers apart and his tongue began to explore with exquisite lightness the soft flesh behind her lips and the warm cavity of her mouth beyond her teeth. He touched the tip of her tongue with his and circled her tongue slowly. Then he lifted his head away.

"You are a reasonably apt pupil," he said as her eyes fluttered open. "You can release your grip, Soph. I shall catch you if you fall."

"You flatter yourself," she said, her voice shaking. "You think I will fall merely because I have allowed myself to be kissed as a rake would kiss his . . . ? Well, as a rake would kiss?"

"I think there is a distinct possibility, Soph," he said. "Your knees are shaking."

"That is because it is cool out here," she said scornfully. "And I don't think that was proper kissing after all, Francis. I think it was improper. Oh, it is so hot out here."

"Somewhere in that last speech," he said, "there was a minor contradiction. But no matter. You will have some experience now to take to your next beau, Soph."

"I would never allow anyone to do that to me ever again," she said. "It was disgusting."

"Good enough to make the temperature soar, though, was it not?" he said. "We had better go back inside, Soph, before you decide you want more, and before you decide that perhaps you want a lifetime of it."

"Ohhh!" Sophia's bosom expanded with her indignation. "The very idea. Do you think yourself quite irresistible to women, Francis, just because you know how to kiss? Yes, obviously you do. I have never in my life known anyone so conceited. Why I would rather . . ."

"The old familiar litany," he said. "The music has stopped, Soph, and it is supper time. I would hate to get back and find all the food gone. Let us walk."

"By all means," she said. "Let me not keep you from your supper, Francis. I would hate to be responsible for that cruelty."

"Thank you, Soph," he said. "You have a kind heart. But it is not quite elegant to snort, you know."

"I shall snort if I want to snort," Sophia said.

"Quite so," he said. "Go ahead then. Don't let me stop you."

"I happen not to feel like snorting again," she said, on her dignity.

9

Most of the earl's houseguests announced their intention of leaving Clifton Court within a few days after the ball in order to give their host more freedom to prepare for the wedding. Everyone, though, promised to return a few days prior to the event.

It was just as well, the duchess declared, since there was so much still to do, and Olivia was going to town for a few days with Sophia and Francis. She would like nothing better than to go with them, she said, but how could she leave Clifton Court at such a time? She sent for her personal dressmaker to come to her there.

"You may avail yourself of her services too, Olivia, if you wish," she offered. "I am sure you would be pleased with the results. And dear Sophia too. There is nothing Madame Blanchard loves more than the chance to dress a bride."

But Olivia had her heart set on going away for a few days. She must get away, she felt. She needed to think. And so they were to leave three days after the ball.

Sophia was despondent. The idea she had had to bring her parents together again seemed to have developed a life of its own and taken itself somewhat beyond her control. The preparations for her wedding seemed unstoppable, and now she was being taken to town to buy bride clothes—all at her papa's expense.

She had been hopeful at first. After the first awkward meeting, her parents had seemed comfortable, almost happy in each other's company. And yet in the past few days, and especially since the ball, she had looked at them and wondered. Were they merely strangers being polite to each other? Would the approach of her wedding bring them closer? But how soon would that happen? How much longer could she wait before finding an excuse to end the betrothal?

And *had* they been quarreling during the ball? They had spent no time together at all after the opening waltz.

She was outdoors with Cynthia the afternoon before she was to leave for town with her mother and Francis. Cynthia, who lived only ten miles away, was also to return home the following day. Cynthia wanted to know when the charade was to end.

"It *is* to end, is it not, Sophia?" she asked. "You have not decided to marry Lord Francis after all?"

Sophia's answer included references to toads and snakes.

"But he is so very handsome and charming, Sophia," her friend said with a sigh. "Mr. Hathaway has been wondering too. We both agreed that things have gone so far that they are well nigh impossible to stop."

Sophia grimaced. But the earl, who had been out riding with some of the gentlemen but had stayed in the stables longer than they after their return, was striding back to the house at that moment.

"There he is now, Cynth," Sophia said. "I am going to ask him if he and Mama have reconciled."

"Just right out like that?" Cynthia said. "Is it wise, Sophia?"

"But I must ask some time," Sophia said. "They are unlikely to tell me what they decide or do not decide. Perhaps I will not know until after the wedding, Cynth. And yet when I say things like that to Francis, he almost has an apoplexy on the spot and either bellows 'What wedding?' in that obnoxious way of his or tells me I should be in Bedlam, which is not at all a complimentary thing to say to his betrothed, is it?"

"Except that you are not his betrothed," Cynthia reminded her.

"As he tells me ten times a day," Sophia said. "As if I could ever forget the fact. Who would want to be Francis's betrothed?"

"Just about every woman between the ages of eighteen and twenty-five who has laid eyes on him," Cynthia said.

"Don't let him hear you say that," Sophia said hastily.

''He is too conceited for his own good as it is. I am going to talk with Papa. Do you mind?''

And she waved her arm to her father and tripped across the grass toward him as he slowed his stride and smiled at her.

''What?'' he said. ''No Francis in sight, love? Is this normal?'' He lowered his cheek for her kiss.

''He is playing billiards,'' she said. ''I came outside with Cynthia.'' She linked her arm through his.

''So tomorrow you are off to town for bride clothes,'' he said. ''I suppose you intend to beggar me, Sophia.''

''Oh, yes,'' she said, laughing, ''but I daresay Mama will not allow me to, Papa. I wish things were not moving quite so fast.''

He looked sharply down at her. ''With the wedding?'' he said. ''You are not having second thoughts, are you?''

''Oh, no,'' she said. ''I love Francis dreadfully, Papa, and three weeks still seems a frightfully long time to wait. But I just wish . . . Oh, I just wish we had longer to be with you and Mama. Always I was with one or the other of you but never with both. I can scarcely remember the time when we were all together. There must have been such times, weren't there, and many of them?''

''Yes,'' he said. ''We spent a great deal of time together, Sophia, the three of us.''

''And now only three more weeks,'' she said, ''and I will be married and going away with Francis, and when we come back from our wedding journey, I will be living with him and not with you and Mama any longer. But when I do visit, Papa, will it be the two of you together, or will I have to make separate visits?''

''Sophia.'' He covered her hand with his. ''You have been dreadfully hurt over the years, have you not? You have never said anything until now. I did not realize it, and neither did your mama. I am sorry, love. I am sorry more than anything that you have been the innocent sufferer.''

''What happened?'' she asked. Her father, she noticed, had changed his course so that they were no longer walking toward the house but toward the parterre gardens before it.

"Why did you never come back? Why did you not send for Mama? Why did I always come alone when I visited you? What happened?"

"We just discovered that we could no longer live together," he said slowly.

"Papa," she said, "I am no longer a child. Something must have happened. Was it Lady Mornington?"

He looked at her sharply. "What do you know of Lady Mornington?" he asked.

"That she is your mistress," she said. "Though she is not one tenth as lovely as Mama. Is *she* what happened?"

"No," he said. "I did not even meet the lady until six years ago, Sophia. And good Lord, she is my friend, not my mistress. Whatever gave you that idea?"

"It was someone else, then," she said. "Another woman. It was your fault, wasn't it, Papa? But how could you have wanted another woman when there was Mama? That is what men do, though, is it not? They marry and then they become bored with their wives and take mistresses. If Francis ever tries to do that, I will kill him. I will take the very largest book from our library and break his skull with it. I swear I will. But how could you have done it, Papa? I always looked up to you. You were my hero."

"I was your mother's hero too," he said harshly. "I am human, Sophia. You say you are no longer a child. Well, learn that, then, that I am human. But it was not quite as you think. I did not take a mistress. Not until we were irrevocably apart, anyway. And I did not become bored with your mother. Never that. I loved her. I want you to know that. You were a child of our love and the two of you were my world."

"Then what *happened*?" she said rather petulantly considering her claim to be an adult. "If you loved her, you should have lived happily ever after. Why have you been estranged for most of my life?"

"Sophia," he said, and he gripped her hand very tightly as she fought to control her tears.

"Don't you love her any longer?" she asked. "Don't you, Papa? Are you merely being civil to each other because of the duke and duchess and the other guests? Is it all for show? Don't you love her?''

"I love her," he said. "I have never stopped, Sophia. Never for a single moment.''

"Well then," she said, brightening instantly and stopping in order to throw her arms up about his neck to half throttle him. "I will have the two of you to come back to after my wedding. My mama and papa together again. Oh, just wait until I tell Francis. Just wait until I do.''

"But it is not as simple as that, Sophia," he said, taking her gently by the waist. "Life never is, love. What happened, happened. Fourteen years ago. It is a long time. We have both built and lived new lives since then. We are different from the people we used to be. There is no going back. There never is in life. Only forward. And love cannot bind two people who have lived apart for that long.''

"Why not?" The tears were back in her eyes.

He shook his head. "It is hard to explain," he said. "Your mother was twenty-two, Sophia. Now she is thirty-six. I was twenty-six. Now I am forty. We cannot resume our relationship just as if those years had not passed.''

"You could if you loved each other," she said. "I don't believe you, Papa. I don't believe you really love her after all. You just say you do because you are talking to me and it would seem wrong to tell your own daughter that you do not love your wife. Nothing is going to change, is it? This past week and a half had been for nothing, and nothing more will be accomplished in the remaining three. There will be Francis with his parents and his brothers and their wives. And then there will be me with you. And with Mama. And the two of you will be wonderfully civil to each other.''

"Sophia," he said.

"No," she said, "don't say it. There is nothing more to say. You must be longing for this nuisance of a wedding to be over so that you can rush back to Lady Mornington. Your *friend.*''

"Sophia," he said, and he took and held her hands very tightly. "I am sorry in my heart that you have conceived the wrong idea about Lady Mornington. But forget about her anyway. I shall not be returning to her even as a friend. I promise you. And I will tell you the reason why too. Having seen your mama again, I know that I cannot return to a relationship that has been generally miscontrued—not just by you. Having seen your mama again, I know that she is the only woman I have ever loved or ever will." He squeezed her hands even more tightly. "But that does not necessarily mean that we will ever live together as man and wife again, love."

She dropped her head forward to look at their clasped hands.

"But there is one bond between us," he said. "A firm one that has never ever wavered. We both love you to distraction, Sophia. We both want your happiness more than anything else in life. For the next three weeks and for your wedding day we will not merely be practicing civility. We will be rejoicing together in your happiness. Together, love. And if it is important to you in the future to see us together, then I daresay we will come together occasionally. We love you that much. Both of us. Together, Sophia."

She raised her hand suddenly and set it against his cheek. "Papa," she said, and her voice was thin with suppressed tears, "I would do anything in the world to see you and Mama together again. Not just because of me, but because of each other. I would give up Francis if that could happen."

He laughed softly. "What?" he said. "Give up the love of your life, Sophia? For us?"

"Yes, I would," she said.

"Well," he said, releasing his other hand and stroking her hair, "that is quite an offer. You love him very much, don't you?"

"But I would give him up." She closed her eyes very tightly.

"You must marry him," he said, "and be very happy with him, Sophia. That is the very best thing you can do for Mama and me. And I will promise you that I will see what I can do about the rest of it. Do we have a deal?"

She jerked back her head and looked up at him with shining eyes. "You are going to keep Mama here?" she asked. "You are going to be reconciled? You are? You promise?"

He frowned and shook his head. "Only that I will see what

I can do, Sophia,'' he said. ''I cannot make any promises about the outcome.''

''Oh,'' she said, ''but you always meant yes, Papa, when you used to say you would see what you could do. I always knew you meant yes, though. I would pretend still to look anxious. Oh, I knew it would work. I knew all would be well. I am going to tell Francis. He will be so excited for me. I am going to find him now.''

And the Earl of Clifton found himself with arms outstretched to the disappearing figure of his daughter, who was dashing down one diagonal path and across a flowerbed toward the house with quite unladylike haste.

He bowed his head and set one hand over his eyes.

Sophia burst into the billiard room just as Lord Francis was bent over his cue, fully concentrating on a difficult shot.

''Francis,'' she said, totally forgetful of the fact that ladies did not normally enter that particular room. ''You must come. You are going to be so very pleased.''

Lord Francis, unable to prevent the forward movement of his cue, hit by far the worst shot of anyone all afternoon. He straightened up, shaking his head ruefully.

The Duke of Weymouth chuckled. ''Just in time, Sophia, my dear,'' he said. ''Francis had not missed in ten minutes. The rest of us are feeling a trifle bored.''

''Oh,'' she said as Lord Francis turned toward her, a resigned look on his face, ''I am so sorry, Francis. I would have crept in had I known and waited until you had finished.''

''Don't mention it, Soph,'' he said, smiling. ''What better way is there of losing a game?'' He took her hand on his arm and patted it. ''You will excuse us, Papa? Gentlemen?''

''More than that,'' the duke said. ''We will rejoice, lad, at your quitting the table.'' He laughed heartily.

''Well, Soph,'' Lord Francis said when they were outside the room, the door closed behind them, ''this had better be worth losing a game over. You have told your father? And he now has all the embarrassment of breaking the news to mine? I had better go upstairs and make sure that all my things have been packed. I had better take myself off before my mother finds out and drowns me with her tears. If I were you, Soph, I would hide.''

''Whatever are you talking about?'' she said, frowning and leading him in the direction of the front doors.

''You have not ended our betrothal?'' he asked.

''No, of course not,'' she said. ''How absurd.''

''But you said I would be so very pleased,'' he said.

She looked at him indignantly. ''Oh,'' she said, ''it is just like you, Francis, to remind me just how delighted you will be to be free of me. It will happen, never fear.''

''But when, Soph?'' he asked. ''There are nineteen days to our wedding. Can a fellow be blamed for getting a trifle nervous?''

''I have heard that men always get nervous before their weddings,'' Sophia said kindly. ''Women get excited and men nervous. It is quite natural that you should be feeling so.''

''Soph,'' he said, ''can I save words and just mention the word *Bedlam*? Would you understand my meaning? And don't bother to answer. What will I be so very pleased about?''

''I am to marry you and live happily ever after,'' she said, drawing him down the steps outside the house onto the cobbled terrace. ''And in the meantime, Papa will see what he can do about getting Mama to agree to stay with him. He just said so. We agreed on it.'' She beamed up at him. ''You see? It is working after all and I need not have been burdening you with all my doubts in the past few days.''

Lord Francis scratched his head with his free hand. ''The one is not totally dependent on the other, by any chance, is it, Soph?'' he said. ''Am I to sacrifice my freedom just because you have an agreement with your papa?''

''Of course not, silly,'' she said. ''But he told me that he loves her, you see, and he has agreed to see what he can do. That always means an undoubted yes when Papa says it. And he will work on it immediately, Francis, because there is not much time left. Within a week all their differences will be settled and they will be together again. You mark my words. And then we can announce that we have irreconcilable differences.''

"Just to help them celebrate," he said.

"It will be quite a blow to them, of course," she said. "To all four of them. We will have to break the news gently."

"Is there a gentle way to break such news?" he said. "The trouble with us, Soph, is that we have no imagination. Neither of us. We did not picture it being quite like this, did we?"

"No," she said. She reached across and touched his hand with her free one. "And it will be worse for you, Francis, for you will be the jilted one. Would you prefer it to be the other way around? Shall we pretend that I still love you dreadfully and that you are the one with no heart?"

"Good Lord," he said. "There is not a stronger word in the English language than Bedlam, is there, Soph? If there is, you had better tell me what it is, because I am in dire need of it."

"I am merely trying to save you from some humiliation," she said. "I would take it on myself if I could, Francis. After all, I am the one to blame for all this."

"No you are not," he said. "No one exactly stuck a dueling pistol to my head to make me to it. I thought it would be amusing. Amusing—ha!"

"I am sorry," she said. "Perhaps we can make it a mutual thing, Francis. We can go to Mama and Papa and your parents together, and tell them that we have discussed the situation quite rationally and in a perfectly amicable manner and have decided that after all, we would not suit. Then neither one will bear the blame or be humiliated. Shall we?"

He sighed. "We had better see how things develop after we return from London, Soph," he said. "But good Lord, you are going to be returning with five trunkfuls or so of bride clothes, aren't you?"

"Yes," she said. "Or perhaps not quite so much. You had better tell me where we are going for our wedding journey, Francis. There is a difference between the type of clothes I will want if we are going to Italy, and the type I will need if we are going to Scotland."

Lord Francis merely looked at her.

"But I have to know," she said. "You must tell me, Francis. Where would you take me if we really were about to be married, and if we really were going on a wedding trip?"

"To bed probably," he said. "And you may well blush and look outraged, Soph. You could not expect any self-respecting male to resist that invitation, could you?"

"To bed," she said, both her cheeks and her eyes flaming. "With you, Francis? I would rather . . ."

"Austria and Italy," he said. "For the rest of the summer and probably the winter, too, Soph. We would dance in Vienna, and ride in a gondola in Venice, and lean with the Tower of Pisa, and get stiff necks in the Sistine Chapel, and shelter your complexion from the sun in Naples."

"And Rome?" she said eagerly. "Would we go to Rome, Francis?"

"Where do you think the Sistine Chapel is?" he asked. "The Outer Hebrides?"

"I forgot," she said. "You do not need to be quite so scornful, Francis. I am not a featherbrain, you know."

"Well," he said, "that is where I would take you, Soph—during the daytime. I suppose my first answer would still hold true for the nights. And don't get all puffed up again. We are talking only of where I would take you *if* we were getting married, the key emphasis being on the *if.* You will need light and pretty clothes."

"All right," she said. "But it is going to be dreadful to spend Papa's money on such a deception, is it not? And all the other expenses of the wedding. Oh, dear, I lay awake a whole hour last night just worrying about it all."

"Perhaps it will be worth the expense if we succeed in mending a broken marriage," he said, patting her hand again.

She looked up at him, suddenly happy again. "Even if by some chance it does not happen before the wedding," she said, "there is still hope. I have just remembered something Papa said. He said that if in future it is really important to us that we see both of them together, then they will come together. We will have other chances, you see, Francis—

perhaps at Christmas or Easter or at a christening if one happens fairly soon.''

Lord Francis continued to pat her hand and look down at her, an expression almost of amusement on his face.

''Oh,'' she said, her smile fading. ''I forgot. No, that will not work, will it?''

''Perhaps they will come together the next time you are betrothed,'' he said. ''Perhaps you could make a regular thing of this, Soph.''

''Don't make fun,'' she said. ''This is serious, Francis. And you don't think I would deliberately humiliate other gentlemen in this way, do you?''

''Only me?'' he said.

''But you are different,'' she said, looking earnestly up into his face. ''You are . . . Oh, I don't know. You are— Francis, that is all. I could not do this with anyone else. No one else would understand. I would not be able to talk like this with anyone else. And you do not have to say what you are about to say. Anyone else would have taken me straight off to Bedlam, I know.''

''That is not what I was about to say,'' he said. ''I was about to warn you again, Soph. You are not falling in love with me by any chance, are you? I don't altogether like this business of feeling comfortable with me and all that.''

''In love with you?'' she said, her eyes blazing to life again. ''How stupid. What I meant was that I did not have to worry with you because you are just Francis and I really do not care if I hurt your feelings or not. Partly because you have no feelings, and partly because I have a whole lifetime of getting even with you to accomplish. Falling in love with you!'' There was a world of scorn in her voice and on her face.

''Ah,'' he said, ''that is all right, then. I was getting a little uncomfortable for a moment, Soph. Nineteen days. That means eighteen at the outside for being betrothed to each other. I suppose we can survive that long, can't we? And who knows? Perhaps it will be less than that. Perhaps your mama and papa will fall into each other's arms when we return from London. Perhaps they will have missed each other.''

"Do you think so?" she said hopefully. "Oh, do you really think so, Francis?"

"I have to consider it at least a possibility," he said, "if I am to cling to my sanity."

10

Lord Francis might as well be sitting inside the carriage instead of riding his horse, Olivia thought. For much of the journey Sophia had had the window down, her betrothed riding alongside talking with her. It was a good thing that the day was glorious and the open window necessary for their very survival. Twice, Olivia had noted, Lord Francis reached across to touch Sophia's hand as it rested on the window. That was before she closed her eyes.

It made her heart turn over to see the love of those two for each other. She yearned to urge them to hold on to their love, not to let even the strongest tempest shake it. She wanted to warn them not to set each other on pedestals, not to expect perfection just because they were in love. She wanted to tell them to allow for human frailty. She was desperately afraid that they were too much in love.

"She is sleeping," Sophia said softly. "You do not need to keep on doing that, Francis, thank you very much."

"It is no trouble at all, Soph," he said cheerfully. "How do you keep your skin so soft?" And he chuckled for no apparent reason.

"Did you see?" Sophia's voice, still almost a whisper, sounded very eager. "Did you see them kiss?"

"Very promising," he said. "The footman holding the carriage door open almost swallowed his tongue. I'll wager it will be the *on dit* belowstairs today, Soph, and probably for the whole week."

"I could have swooned with happiness," she said.

"I'm glad you did not," he said. "I never know quite what to do with vaporish females. Does one douse them with water, slap their cheeks, rush all about the house yelling for vinaigrettes, or kiss them back to consciousness? I suppose that last would be strictly dependent upon the female involved, of course. I might have tried it on you, Soph.''

There was a small silence. "I might wake her if I respond as I would like," Sophia said, and Lord Francis chuckled.

So it had worked, Olivia thought. Sophia had been delighted by it, and she would not be able to conclude that it had been done for the benefit of the guests. There had been no one else out on the terrace except a few servants and Sophia and Lord Francis. There had been no other witnesses.

She was reacting like a girl, she thought with some disgust at herself, retiring behind closed eyes so that she might relive a brief kiss.

"Remember to buy yourself some pretty clothes, Olivia," he had said, setting an arm about her shoulders after kissing their daughter farewell. "And don't let Sophia drive you to distraction." He had winked and grinned at their daughter. "I shall be watching for you in about a week's time."

And he had bent his head and kissed her—a firm kiss with closed mouth, neither too long nor too brief. A prearranged kiss, to reassure Sophia. The sort of kiss one might expect from a father or brother. Not one to dream about and live through over and over again in the mind just like a love-starved woman.

Which she supposed she was.

She had lain awake during the nights reliving every moment of their lovemaking in the hidden garden. Though lovemaking was hardly an appropriate term to describe what had happened. They had satisfied a voracious hunger and slaked a parching thirst. That was all. He had been away from the diversions of town and the arms of Lady Mornington for some weeks; she had been without a man for fourteen years. It had not been a lovemaking.

Yet she hugged to herself each night the memory of an uncontrollable passion that at the time she had mistaken for love. And had felt her body aroused anew by the remembered skill of his caresses. And had felt sick at the remembered evidence of his experience.

He had come to her dressing room the evening before, after she had finished dressing. He had opened the door from his own room after knocking, not waiting for an answer. She had flushed at the thought that she might have been undressed or even in her bath. Though doubtless he would have looked coolly at her and remarked that after all she was his wife.

"Have you further need of your maid?" he had asked.

"You may leave, Matilda, thank you," she had said, and the girl had left the room quietly.

They had scarcely spoken to each other since the ball, when they had quite alarmingly begun to quarrel in the middle of the dance floor. They had never quarreled. It was something new in their relationship, something she had no idea how to handle.

"Sophia is upset," he had said abruptly, his feet set slightly apart, his hands clasped behind his back. He had seemed to fill her very dainty dressing room. "She has seen through the facade of our amiability and believes it to have been adopted for the benefit of the other guests. And she has noticed the slipping of that amiability since the day of the ball. She was in tears when I talked with her this afternoon."

Olivia, sitting on the stool before her mirror, had twisted a brush in one hand. "Perhaps she will have to face the truth, Marcus," she had said at last. "Perhaps we can protect her no longer."

"No longer?" he had said. "Have we ever protected her, Olivia? If we had loved our daughter as we have claimed to do all her life, would we not have somehow patched up our differences and remained together for her sake?"

"Our differences," she had said, laying down the brush and looking up at him. "You were the one who decided that a whore's caresses were more exciting than mine, Marcus. You were the one who ruined life for Sophia."

"Oh, no," he said. "I am not going to carry the guilt of that indiscretion to my grave, Olivia. And I am certainly not going to add to the burden of my conscience the belief that I ruined our marriage and our daughter's happiness. There is such a quality as forgiveness, you know. Unfortunately it is something beyond your capabilities."

"I suppose," she had said, "you have been celibate from the time of that whore until a few afternoons ago, Marcus. I suppose I am to believe that of you."

"No," he had said. "I would not like to damage your impression of me as a depraved philanderer, Olivia. I have done too much other damage to your life, it seems. But I did not come here to quarrel with you."

"Did you not?" she had said. "Why did you come, then?"

"We had an agreement," he had said, "to make this month a very special one for Sophia. Can we not keep to it? We have been selfish enough for most of her life, Olivia. Must we also have her in tears as she prepares for what should be the happiest day of her life? It was the happiest of ours, was it not? Can we not at least do our part to see that it is so for Sophia, too?"

"And what about afterward?" she had asked. "Is it fair, Marcus, to allow her to believe that we have an affection for each other when immediately after her wedding she must know the truth?"

"She hopes that she can visit us together afterward," he had said. "Will it be too much to do for her, Olivia? To spend some time together with her once or twice a year? Must we be bitter enemies just because I once spent an hour with a whore and because you would not forgive the transgression? Do you find me so abhorrent?"

She had looked down at her hands.

"You did not find me abhorrent two afternoons ago," he had said.

She had looked up sharply at him. "That was the garden," she had said, "and the sunshine and warmth and . . ."

"And appetite," he had said. "It seems that we still find each other somewhat appetizing, Olivia."

"Yes." She had looked back at her hands.

"Well," he had said, "short of resuming a marriage that seems to have died many years ago, can we at least be mutual parents to the child who survived that marriage? You will be away for a week. By the time you return there will be less than two remaining before the wedding. Perhaps once or twice a year in the future we can force ourselves to spend a week or so in the same house. Can we do it?"

"I suppose so," she had said.

"She said she would give up Francis if only she could bring

us back together again," he had told her. "Foolish child. But she meant it with all the earnestness of youth, Olivia."

She was twisting her hands hard in her lap, she had realized suddenly. *Very well then,* she had wanted to blurt out to him, *let us give her exactly what she wants, Marc. A marriage that is real.* But the words could not be spoken aloud. He had been standing stiffly before her, his manner business-like, his voice abrupt and almost cold. He was trying to persuade her to agree to a workable proposition.

"We must try again, then," she had said. "We did well for the first week."

"This evening," he had said. "We must remain in the drawing room together. Tomorrow morning, when you leave, I must kiss you just as I will kiss Sophia."

"Yes," she had said.

He had stood there for a while not saying anything, as she examined the backs of her hands.

"I wish I could come with you," he had said. "I don't like to think of the two of you on the road with only young Sutton and my servants for protection. You will be all right, Olivia?"

"I came here alone," she had reminded him.

"You will have new clothes made?" he had said. "As many as you wish, Olivia, and have the bills sent to me with Sophia's?"

"You give me a generous enough allowance," she had said.

"My daughter is getting married," he had said. "At least allow me to buy my wife new clothes for the occasion. Will you?"

She had nodded.

"There are enough servants left at the house in town to see to your needs," he had said.

"Yes."

"Well." He had moved abruptly and set his hand on the knob of the door into his dressing room. "You have lived safely for fourteen years without my assistance. I daresay I need not worry about you now."

"No," she had said.

Come with us, she had wanted to beg him quite unreasonably. *Three weeks is all the time we have left.* And the memory caused a tickle in her throat now as she sat with closed eyes in the carriage and did not even hear the occasional chatter of Sophia and Lord Francis. They could not expect to return within a week at the very least. A week—seven whole days!

But there would be countless years without him again after Sophia's wedding, with perhaps the teaser of a week once or twice a year. She felt the desperate need to cry, but her daughter's presence in the carriage forced her to resist the urge.

How foolish—how indescribably foolish—she had been fourteen years before. Imagining that she could no longer love him because he had fallen off his pedestal. She had loved him anyway all those years, but had deprived them both of the chance of a mended marriage. She had deprived all three of them of the chance for a happy family life.

She wished, and felt guilty at the wish, that Sophia had not met Lord Francis again and fallen in love with him. She wished she had not seen Marc again. For now, having seen him, she knew with a new pain all that she had missed in those empty years. And all through her own fault. Not Marc's really. All people make mistakes and have the right to be forgiven—once at least. But she had refused to forgive. She had been afraid to forgive, afraid that their relationship would have changed. She had been too young and inexperienced to know that relationships are always changing, that they must change in order to grow and survive.

His lips had been warm on hers, his arm strong and sheltering. The side of her head was against the soft cushions of the carriage. She imagined that it was against his chest, his arm still about her, his cheek against the top of her head. She imagined herself falling asleep in the shelter of his arms, warm and relaxed and assured of his love.

It felt wonderful to be in London again. She had always loved being there right from the moment of her arrival for her come-out Season. It was there she had first seen Marc and admired him from across the width of a ballroom for several hours before he had suddenly appeared at her side, their hostess with him to perform the introductions. She had fallen in love with him during the set of dances that had followed.

And had not fallen out of love since, though her love had brought her joy for only five years and misery and heartache for all the years since. And Sophia, of course. Her love had brought her Sophia.

She had never been given to extravagance. Even during that first year, when her mother had taken her to a fashionable modiste to have new clothes made that would be more suitable for town living than the ones she had brought with her, she had been horrified at the large number that had been deemed necessary. She had been afraid that she would make a beggar of her papa. In the years since, she had used the modest services of a local seamstress and had even made some of her own clothes.

She felt alternately hot and cold when she discovered just how much Sophia's bride clothes were going to cost. But Marcus had given her specific instructions to make sure that their daughter had all that was needed. Olivia supposed that her husband was a very wealthy man. He had had a comfortable fortune even before the death of his father. After that event, he had inherited a number of prosperous properties. He had also doubled her already generous allowance.

It was with only the greatest reluctance that she picked out patterns and fabrics for clothes for herself. But she would need some fashionable clothes for the week of the wedding, when Clifton would be overflowing with guests. Her own parents were even coming from the north of England.

Everything was to be made with the greatest haste, the dressmaker assured Olivia. She had received a letter from his lordship just a few days ago and had taken on extra seamstresses and deferred working on other orders so that Lady Clifton and Lady Sophia could take all their new clothes with them back to Clifton within a week.

And so they had four days to kill. Lord Francis took them to Kew Gardens and the Tower and St. Paul's and they spent a few evenings quietly at home. But news of their arrival in town was quick to spread and several hasty invitations were sent by hostesses eager to entertain the newly betrothed couple or curious to see again the long-absent Countess of Clifton.

They chose to attend a soirée at the home of Lady Methuen. Young Donald Methuen was a friend of Lord Francis. Olivia felt apprehensive about attending. It was so very long since she had been in town. She fully expected to be confronted with a roomful of strangers. It was a relief on their arrival to find that there were still some people who remembered her, and who made an effort to include her in a group and draw her into conversation. Sophia and Lord Francis had immediately been whisked away by a group of young people.

It was really quite pleasant, Olivia thought, after an hour had passed. It was good to be back. And she still seemed to have the social skills to cope with a large town gathering. Lord Benson, looking considerably more portly and florid of complexion than when she had known him as a rather handsome rake and gentleman about town, even tried to flirt with her. It was not altogether unpleasant to know that she was still young enough and was still in sufficient good looks to invite flirtation.

If she could only have left after the hour, she thought afterward, she would have been thoroughly charmed by the evening. As it happened, she did not leave, and the evening gave her a sleepless night.

A lady joined the group with which Olivia was currently conversing. Another lady, Mrs. Joanna Shackleton, a friend of Olivia's during that long-ago Season when they had both made their come-out, took her arm firmly and would have drawn her away. But Olivia merely smiled at her and resisted the pressure on her arm. She was listening to a story being told by Colonel Jenkins.

"Good evening, Mary," the colonel said when his story was at an end. "You are feeling better?"

"Oh, yes, I thank you," the lady said. "It was just a slight chill, you know. Nothing to keep me at home for more than a couple of days."

"James and I were wondering if your literary evening

would have to be cancelled,'' a lady to Olivia's left said. "I do hope your recovered health will make that unnecessary, Lady Mornington."

"Oh, absolutely." The lady smiled. "I would not cancel those plans for all the chills of a cold winter. It promises to be an interesting evening. Mr. Nicholson is to be there."

Olivia felt the pressure on her arm being renewed, but she ignored it. The lady was quite different from what she had expected. What had she expected? A tall, voluptuous woman with flaming red hair, she supposed, and scarlet lips. A woman whom one would only have to glance at to know her as a harlot.

In fact Lady Mornington was petite with short dark hair and a refined, quiet manner. She was not at all pretty, and it was not just spite that forced her to such a conclusion, Olivia decided. She was not pretty, though she did have fine intelligent gray eyes.

"Have you all received your invitations?" the lady asked, looking about the group. "If not, it is a dreadful oversight for which you must forgive me." Her eyes stopped on Olivia even as the pressure on the latter's arm intensified.

"Olivia," Joanna said, "there is someone . . ."

"But I am sorry," Lady Mornington said, smiling. "I am afraid you are a stranger to me."

"Oh, the devil!" Colonel Jenkins said. "I just realized."

"Olivia Bryant," Olivia said.

"Bryant?" Lady Mornington's eyebrows rose. "Oh. You are the Countess of Clifton."

"Yes."

"Mary," the colonel said, "what are you drinking? Let me take you to find a tray."

"Olivia," Joanna said, "there is someone . . ."

"You are here alone?" Lady Mornington asked.

"With my daughter," Olivia said. "We have come to have her bride clothes made. My husband stayed at Clifton Court."

"Ah, yes," the lady said. "I read the notice of the betrothal in the *Morning Post*. The wedding is to be soon?"

"In a little over two weeks' time," Olivia said, "at Clifton. We will be returning there the day after tomorrow."

Lady Mornington smiled. "This must be an exciting time for you," she said. "Your daughter is a pretty and charming young lady and took well earlier in the Season, I heard. And Lord Francis Sutton is a gentleman with a good sense of humor. I like him."

"Yes," Olivia said. "Marcus and I are pleased with her choice."

Lady Mornington smiled again and turned back to the colonel. "By all means," she said, taking his arm, "let us find this tray, colonel. I am as dry as the Sahara Desert."

"Olivia, I am so sorry, my dear," Joanna said, leading her away in the opposite direction. "I tried to save you from that embarrassment. You do know, I assume?"

"That Lady Mornington is Marcus's mistress?" Olivia said. "Yes."

"But I would not be worried," Joanna said. "You are many times lovelier than she is, Olivia, and certainly no older. But men seem to find it necessary to have a *chère amie* as well as a wife. They are all the same."

That was another thing she had expected, Olivia thought. She had expected Lady Mornington to be a very young woman.

But the facts did not console her, she found when she was alone that night, tossing and turning on her bed, trying to sleep. If Marc's mistress had been more as she had expected, she would have been less concerned. The woman would have been obviously nothing more than an object for physical pleasure. But Marc could not have chosen Lady Mornington merely for his bed. There must be far more to their relationship than the physical.

She did not know why the thought should disturb her. Or rather, she pretended not to know. And she pretended not to be disturbed. It did not matter to her, she told herself, what his mistress looked like. Indeed, there was probably a dozen other women with whom he slept but who were not dignified by the title *mistress*. She did not care.

But the not caring kept her as wide awake as caring would have done. And it was somehow different, she found, imagining what the woman looked like, and actually seeing her and talking with her. That woman, she told herself,

picturing Lady Mornington as she had appeared in the
Methuen drawing room, had been with Marc for about six
years. He had kissed those lips and touched the body countless times. He had slept in her bed probably more times than
he had slept in his wife's.

It did not matter. She did not care.

But at some time before dawn, she got up hastily from bed
and vomited into the close stool, retching until her stomach
was empty and hurting. And then she lay shivering and crying
in bed, telling herself over and over again that she did not
care, that it did not matter.

And that it was all her own fault anyway.

The day after Olivia, Sophia, and Lord Francis had left
for London, Clifton was empty of all guests except the duke
and duchess. Very empty, the earl thought as he rode out
late in the morning to pay a promised call on one of his
tenants.

He was missing her—them. Somehow, though he had not
fully realized it until she left, she had taken charge of most
of the wedding preparations. He had thought that his housekeeper and cook were doing the bulk of the planning, but
it seemed that Olivia had been guiding them, and without
her to run to, they were running to him. And so was Rose,
with a hundred different concerns that he supposed she had
taken to his wife in the previous week and a half.

He was missing seeing her and hearing her voice. And he
was becoming thoroughly annoyed with himself. He had got
over her years before, although he had never stopped loving
her. He had even been happy, or comfortable at least. He
had found the perfect woman in Mary—one who accepted
his need for conversation and companionship but did not
press other claims on him.

There had been a time—one evening—when their relationship might have developed into something more intimate.
But they had both agreed, rather shamefaced, when they were
already in her bedchamber, that it would be impossible. She
still mourned a dearly beloved officer husband killed in

Spain; he still loved a wife from whom he was estranged. After that they had been content with a warm friendship, unusual between a man and a woman. And of course it became the common belief that they were lovers. They had always scorned to try to put an end to the rumors.

Mary was the perfect woman for him. He did not need Olivia any longer.

Except that the missing her was like a gnawing toothache.

And except that he had meant what he had said to Sophia, that he would not go back to Mary, having seen Olivia again, and having loved her again, though he had not, of course, said that to Sophia.

She was gone for ten days, three longer than any of them had expected when they left. But it had been ambitious to have expected all those clothes to be made within a week, he supposed. In the meantime, early wedding guests began to arrive, mostly family. The duke's three older sons arrived with their wives and children. The earl's mother came with her sister from Cornwall and Olivia's parents from the north of England. Clarence Wickham came, escorting Emma Burnett. Each time a carriage appeared, he expected it to be his own returning from London. Each time he hastened out onto the terrace only to find himself greeting other guests.

But finally they came, late one afternoon when it was raining. He knew this time as soon as he got outside that it really was his carriage. And he felt as if butterflies were dancing in his stomach.

"Hello, sir," Lord Francis said cheerfully, vaulting out of the carriage as soon as it came to a stop and the door had been opened. "A pea-soup day, would you not agree? But the roads are good hereabouts. No overturned carriages and shrieking ladies or any drama like that."

The earl shook his hand and turned to hand Sophia out. But young love proved too fast for him. Lord Francis turned and lifted her by the waist.

"Ugh," she said. "It has not stopped raining all day. Papa, how wonderful to see you. We were afraid that we would not get home today after all. Is the rain not dreadful? Wait until you see all the clothes I have bought. You will have ten fits. Francis, put me down, do. I shall have bruises at my waist.''

"I thought you might not like to get your feet wet," he said.

"Better wet feet," she said, "than have you carry me like this into the hall and be the laughingstock among the footmen. Put me down."

"As you wish, Soph," he said, setting her feet on the wet cobbles.

Th earl had turned to the carriage, feeling as eager and as timid as a schoolboy. She was wearing a blue dress and pelisse and a straw bonnet decorated with bright flowers. She looked like a little piece of summertime caught in all the gloom of the rain. He smiled at her.

She smiled back and set a hand in his.

"Welcome home, Olivia," he said. And then he released her hand and imitated his future son-in-law. He took her by the waist and lifted her carefully to the wet ground. "I have missed you."

"And I you," she said. "We were away far longer than we had planned. One of the new seamstresses proved not worth her hire, I am afraid, and all sorts of alterations had to be made."

"No matter," he said. "You are home and safe now." And he kissed her warmly on her parted lips.

He was glad that Sophia and Francis were still outside and watching them. She could not realize how deeply from the heart his words had been spoken or how eager he had been for that kiss.

"Yes." She smiled up at him and took his offered arm. "It feels like heaven to be home again. Does it not, Sophia?"

11

The dismay at having so given herself away as to glow at him as soon as she set eyes on him; to set her hands eagerly on his shoulders to be lifted to the ground instead of extending one cool hand; to assure him that she had missed him too; and to raise her face for his kiss—the dismay soon faded. After all, Sophia had been standing there watching them eagerly and for her sake they had agreed to show each other affection.

Besides, as soon as they had all hurried inside out of the rain, noise and near chaos greeted them. Guests had begun to arrive, it seemed, and soon Olivia was in her mother's arms, and then her father's. And Marc's mother was nodding rather stiffly to her from a little distance away. Emma and Clarence were there in the background—the former waiting to hug her, the latter to squeeze her hand and kiss her cheek.

Sophia and Lord Francis were being besieged by his brothers and their wives and by grandparents and even two children inexplicably escaped from the nursery. There was a great deal of laughter and noisy banter.

"So you finally ran him to earth, Sophia," the duke's eldest son, Albert, Viscount Melville, said, setting an arm about her shoulders. "We all thought he might keep running from you all his life. But the more fool he if he had. And we might have known you would be more persistent than to allow that."

"She finally stuck out a slippered foot and brought him down actually, Bertie," Claude said. "At least that is what I heard. Is it true, Sophia?"

"I heard it a little differently," Richard said. "I heard that Frank waited until your foot was reaching out to take a step, Sophia, and then deliberately tripped over it."

There was loud merriment from everyone gathered in the hall.

"Unfair, unfair," Sophia protested, her cheeks bright with color. "He made me a very pretty offer, did you not, Francis?"

"On one knee," he said. "It was a great shame to waste such an affecting scene on an empty room, wasn't it, Soph?"

Olivia felt a hand at her waist. "Emma and Clarence have been impatiently awaiting your return, Olivia," her husband said, smiling at her friends. "As have I. But we have had a chance to get reacquainted since yesterday afternoon."

"Is that when you arrived?" Olivia asked, looking at them. "We were away three days longer than we expected. It was very frustrating when we longed to be back home. There is so much yet to do," she added hastily.

"You must call on me for assistance," Emma said. "You know that I am never happier than when I am busy, Olivia."

"I want to hear all about London, Olivia," Clarence said. "Most especially if it is still in the same place as it used to be. It is an age since I was there last."

The hand at Olivia's waist tightened slightly. "If you will excuse us," he said to her friends. "Have you said hello to Mama and Aunt Clara, Olivia? They arrived the day before yesterday."

"No," she said. "Not yet." And she turned in dread to speak to the dowager Countess of Clifton. They had used to be on friendly terms.

"Well, Mama," the earl said, "they arrived home safely despite all our worries." His arm drew his wife closer against his side. "Olivia kept the youngsters in line, it seems." He looked down and smiled at her.

Olivia was grateful. "How are you, Mother?" she said uncertainly and reached out rather jerkily to kiss her mother-in-law on the cheek. "Aunt Clara? Did you have a good journey? I am sorry I was not here to greet you." And she was sorry she had spoken the last words. She had not been there to greet them for fourteen years. And indeed fourteen years before, Clifton had not even belonged to Marc.

"I am well, thank you, Olivia," the dowager said.

"You are in good looks, dear," Aunt Clara said, kissing Olivia too. "The years have been kind to you."

"Thank you," Olivia said and was thankful when the arm at her waist turned her again.

"Do you remember Francis's brothers?" the earl asked her. "They have done some growing up since you saw them last."

"Indeed they have," she said. "Bertie still has his smile and Claude his cleft chin. You must be Richard. I would never have known you." She smiled at the tall sandy-haired young man with the small girl in his arms.

"And you look not a day older, ma'am," Claude said gallantly. "I can remember those times when you were constantly pleading with Papa not to be too harsh on Frank. It was understandable that an active young boy would find entertaining your daughter something of a burden, you used to say."

"And yet his hand never felt one mite the lighter than it did on those occasions when you were not there to intercede for me," Lord Francis said. "You caused me a great deal of pain in those days, Soph."

"You have not met our wives, ma'am," the viscount said. "Allow me to make the introductions."

Sophia caught her mother's eye and then looked to her father. She looked entirely happy, Olivia thought.

"I don't know why we are all standing down here," the earl said, raising his voice after the introductions had been made, and the two children, one of the viscount's and one Richard's, had been identified. "I believe tea was about to be served in the drawing room when we were distracted by the sound of the carriage. Shall we go up?"

"A cup of tea will be most welcome," Aunt Clara said.

The earl kept an arm loosely about his wife's waist as they ascended the stairs. "We can release you from your duties at the tea tray this afternoon, Mama," he said, "now that my wife is home."

"Olivia will doubtless wish to freshen up after her journey," the dowager said. "It will be no trouble, Marcus."

"Then we will wait for her," he said. "Olivia is never long about these things. Sophia, you had better go up with your mama too."

Oh goodness, Olivia thought, there was a seductive warmth about the atmosphere of Clifton Court—a family atmosphere. And her husband had thrown himself wholeheartedly into the role they had both agreed to before her departure for London. *My wife is home.* Her feet felt heavy on the second flight of stairs.

"Mama," Sophia said. "I am frightened. I am so frightened."

Olivia looked in surprise at her daughter, whose face was suddenly chalky white.

"What have I done?" Sophia said. "All these people, Mama!"

Olivia took her arm. "Oh, Sophia," she said, "it is overwhelming, is it not? When you first think of marriage, you imagine that it involves only you and your partner. And then you realize that so much more is involved. It seems to get beyond your control, does it not? Almost as if you could not stop it, even if you wished to do so."

"And there are many more people yet to come," Sophia said.

Her mother squeezed her arm. "You don't want to stop it, do you?" she asked.

Sophia turned at the top of the stairs in the direction of her room. She gulped. "I am just terrified," she said. "They are all so very happy, Mama."

"It can be stopped, of course," Olivia said. "You must never be in any doubt about that, Sophia. You will not be irrevocably married until the ceremony has been performed and the register signed. You must not feel as if all your freedom has been taken from you. But neither should you give in to panic for its own sake."

Sophia drew in a ragged breath. "I did not know it would be like this," she said. "And Mama, there are two trunkfuls of clothes."

"Papa would have been disappointed if you had brought home less," Olivia said. "Sit down, Sophia, before you fall down. Now, tell me." She took her daughter's hands in a firm clasp. "Everything else aside—the clothes, the guests, all the preparations that have been made—do you still love

Francis? Do you want to spend your life with him as his wife?"

Her daughter's eyes filled with tears.

"Do you, Sophia? Those are the only two questions that matter. The only ones."

One tear spilled over. "But you did not spend all your life with Papa," she said. "Only a few years."

"Is that what you are afraid of?" Olivia asked. "That your marriage will not last? Your papa and I have been very foolish, Sophia. We threw away something very precious. You must learn from our mistake. You must learn not to love blindly, not to expect perfection from each other. You must not be alarmed if you occasionally quarrel. You must learn that your life together is more important than anything else."

"Will you stay together now?" Sophia asked, withdrawing one hand from her mother's in order to wipe away a tear. "You really are happy to be home, Mama, aren't you? And Papa was happy to see you. You will stay together and love each other again?"

"We have discovered at least," Olivia said, "that there is joy in being together with you again, Sophia. Your betrothal has accomplished that. Now that we are about to lose you to a husband, you see, we realize how important those times together can be." She smiled. "Your marriage will bring us together at least occasionally. Neither of us will be able to resist seeing you whenever possible, and if that means seeing you together, then together we will be. Will that make you happy?"

"At Christmastime?" Sophia said. "And at christenings?"

"And for other occasions too, I daresay," Olivia said.

"If I marry," Sophia said.

"If you marry." Olivia smiled. "Have you recovered from some of your terror? There is some color back in your cheeks. Do you love Francis, Sophia? Do you want to be his wife?"

Her daughter stared back at her and licked her lips. "Of course I love Francis," she said. "I always have, even though he used to be so horrid to me." There were tears in her eyes again. "I have always, *always* loved him, Mama.

I wish I had realized that sooner. I would not have been so foolish.''

Olivia smoothed a lock of hair back from her daughter's face. "Yes," she said. "Love is terrifying sometimes, isn't it? Sometimes it seems safer to run from it rather than face all the joys and heartaches it might bring. Don't run, Sophia, if you truly love. You will always be sorry, believe me. Do you feel better now that you have answered the essential question? We must be going down. I am supposed to be pouring the tea.''

"Yes." Sophia got to her feet. "I will wash my hands.''

For the rest of the afternoon and most of the evening Lord Francis was called upon to give a full accounting of his days in London to his father, to listen to a detailed description by his mother of all the wedding preparations that had been made in his absence, to allow himself to be quizzed by his sisters-in-law about his courtship of Sophia, and to be teased by his brothers about his betrothal to the very girl he had named the Prize Pest as a child.

Sophia was faring no better, with two grandmothers and a grandfather to fuss over her, a great-aunt to kiss her and pat her hand, all her future sisters-in-law to want an exhaustive description of her bride clothes, and her future brothers-in-law to tease her.

"It is still raining," Lord Francis said, staring gloomily from a drawing-room window late in the evening.

"The gardens are not very romantic at night when rain is dripping down your neck, or so I have heard, Frank," Claude said. There was a general chuckle.

"And it is tricky to hold an umbrella and one's betrothed at the same time," Richard added.

"I am just remembering why I have envied Soph's being an only child," Lord Francis said, not turning away from the window.

"When it rains, Frank," the viscount said, "one has to improvise. The gallery is still where it used to be, Lord Clifton?''

"In the very same place," the earl said, "complete with all the family portraits."

"There you are, then," Bertie said. "Problem solved, Frank."

"Just remember that all of Sophia's ancestors will have an eye on you," Claude said.

"Don't do anything to upset them," Richard added. "Or anything I wouldn't do, Frank."

"And if he tries to hide from you, Sophia," Claude said, "come and tell me and I shall tell Papa, and Frank can discover if his hand is as heavy as it used to be."

"London was remarkably peaceful, was it not?" Lord Francis said, turning from the window. "No brothers to set up a predictably idiotic chorus. Did you spend all day yesterday rehearsing while we were still away, the three of you? Come on, Soph. Let's go and stroll in the gallery. There will be no peace for us here if we do not."

"Just make sure you keep him strolling, Sophia," Richard said.

"Supper will be in half an hour's time," the earl said. "You will have her back down by then, Francis?"

"Yes, sir," Lord Francis said, and ushered his betrothed out through the door and up the stairs to the long gallery on the top floor.

They walked side by side up the stairs after Lord Francis had picked up a candlestick with a lighted candle from a hall table. They did not touch or exchange a word.

"We have to keep up appearances," he said when they reached the gallery, using his candle to light two set in wall sconces and setting his own down on a table. "We could hardly have said we did not want to be alone after such brotherly concern, could we, Soph? We have hardly had a chance to exchange a word all evening."

Sophia was examining a portrait next to one of the wall sconces.

"Oh, lord," he said, sinking down onto a cushioned bench against one wall, "what are we going to do next?"

"Mama and Papa like being together with me," Sophia said. "Mama said so. After we are married, they will come together occasionally just to spend time with us. It is better than nothing, I suppose, but I don't think they will ever live together again, Francis. Too much time has passed. Almost my whole lifetime.''

"After we are married," he said.

"Yes." She turned to look at him. "We ought to have thought more carefully, ought we not?"

"That sounds rather like the understatement of the century," he said. "Lordy, Soph, a family gathering and all in their best wedding humor. And not a suspicion among the lot of them or a single expression of uneasiness about our possible incompatibility considering our childhood relationship. I am beginning to know what a trapped animal must feel like.''

"We have to end it now," she said, her voice shaking. "Tonight, Francis. Right now. We have to go down and tell them all that we have had a dreadful quarrel and have put an end to our betrothal. In a few days' time there will be many more people. It will be harder then.''

"Do you want me to slap you around a bit first?" he asked. "Do you want me to stand still while you rake your fingernails down one of my cheeks?''

"Don't make a joke of it," she said. "This is deadly serious, Francis.''

"A joke?" he said. "Have you ever had fingernails down your cheek, Soph, and the blood dripping onto your cravat?''

"We have to do it now," she said.

"I can't see your person very clearly in this light," he said. "But if your body is shaking as badly as your voice, Soph, you had better come and sit down. I have told you of my difficulty with vaporish females before.''

"I am not vaporish," she said, coming to sit beside him. "Just terrified. We had better do it without further delay, Francis. Let us not think about it longer or talk about it either. Let us go and do it.''

"We have not had enough time for such a nasty quarrel," he said.

She looked at him in incomprehension.

"If we go down now, two minutes after coming up here,''

he said, "we can hardly expect them all to believe that we have quarreled so violently as to have called off the whole wedding."

"Then we shall say we quarreled this afternoon," she said. "Or yesterday."

"Soph!" he said. "Why would we have waited until this evening, and smiled and received everyone's congratulations in the meantime, if that had happened? Have some sense."

"Then we must wait awhile," she said. "How long? Five minutes? Ten? My courage will have given out by then."

He took her hand in his. "Perhaps we should wait a few days," he said. "Imagine how it would be, Soph. Carriages emptying themselves of smiling, festive guests every hour for the next several days. And we would have to greet each carriageful with the same story."

She gulped noisily.

"It does not bear thinking of, does it?" he asked.

"Oh, Francis," she said, "what are we going to do?"

"The very question I asked you a few moments ago," he said. "Though I might have saved my breath. You have just thrown it right back in my teeth. And if you gave an answer, it would probably be something corkbrained like suggesting that we stand up at the front of the church, the rector behind us, and make the announcement there."

"Don't be horrid!" she said. "I am the one who wanted to go down immediately and put an end to it."

"Or you will be suggesting that it will be easier for all concerned if we get married anyway," he said.

"Oh," she said, jumping to her feet and standing before him, her hands on her hips, "I don't know why I agreed to this stupid scheme in the first place, Francis. The scheme itself is bad enough. But I must really have had feathers in my brain to have agreed to do it with you of all people. Do you imagine that I am still running after you just because I was always stupid enough to do it when we were children?"

"The thought had crossed my mind, I must confess," he said. "You aren't wearing stays by any chance, are you, Soph? You are about to burst them if you are."

"You toad!" she said. "You eel! You . . ."

"Snake?" he suggested.

"Rat! You conceited rat!"

"Quite so," he said. "We'll wait until everyone has arrived, Soph, and then make one grand announcement. Maybe by that time, your mama and papa will have decided that they cannot live without each other after all."

"It is just not going to happen," she said. "I was foolish to think it would. It was stupid to think I could bring them together when they have lived apart forever. This whole business has been stupid."

"If we are to wait a few days," he said, "we had better look when we go down as if we have been doing what everyone thinks we are doing."

"Making love?" she said scornfully.

"Er, I think your papa might be up here with the proverbial horsewhip if he thought that, Soph," he said. "Kissing is what everyone is imagining us doing."

"Well, there is no one to observe us," she said, "so we do not need to feel obliged."

"But there is definitely a just-kissed look," he said. "Everyone will be looking for it when we return, especially my esteemed older brothers. For the sake of my self-respect, Soph, I can't take you back down looking totally unkissed, you know."

"How foolish," she said. "Is this how rakes get ladies to kiss them, Francis? The ladies must be very stupid, I must say."

"Rakes don't usually kiss ladies," he said, "unless they happen to be their betrotheds, and a roomful of brothers belowstairs are waiting to see that they have done their job thoroughly."

Sophia clucked her tongue and took a step backward.

"We are fortunate, too," he said. "There was a time, you know, Soph, when people used to do it on wedding nights. Flock into the bridal chamber after a decent time, I mean, to view the evidence that the groom had done his job."

"Oh!" Sophia said. "They never did. You are making that up just to shock me. Papa would not like it at all if I told him that you had just told me that."

"By Jove, no," he said, getting to his feet. "He wouldn't, would he? You had better not tell him, Soph. He might forbid the marriage or something like that."

"I don't think you ought to kiss me," she said. "We are not really betrothed after all."

"But your papa granted us all of half an hour," he said. "I think I had better, Soph."

She tilted her face up resolutely and waited.

"You are still puckering." He looked down at her critically. "Ah, that's better," he said when she opened her mouth to make some sharp retort. "Mm."

Sophia never did make the retort.

"You aren't still shaking, are you, Soph?" he said against her ear a few minutes later. He had both arms wrapped about her.

"Of course I am not," she said breathlessly. "Why would I be shaking?"

"I don't know," he said. "But your arms are so tight about my neck that I thought you were afraid of falling."

"Oh," she said, trying to remove her arms but finding herself too closely held to have anywhere else to put them. "No. But what else am I to do with them?"

"Put them back," he advised. "Some poor devil is going to thank me one of these days, you know Soph."

"What?" she said. He was distracting her full concentration by nibbling on her earlobe.

"For teaching you how to kiss," he said. "I must say you are an apt pupil. This is becoming almost as much pleasure as duty."

She bent her arms back at the elbows and shoved hard at his shoulders. "Please do me no favors," she said hotly. "It is certainly no pleasure to me. And if I do not look just kissed to your brothers now, Francis, I never will. Besides, I am going to be embarrassed. And besides again, I don't like kissing and don't intend to do it with anyone else ever again. I want to go back downstairs."

"Some poor devil will never know what he has missed then," Lord Francis said, strolling across the gallery to extinguish the two candles he had lit earlier, and picking up the candlestick again. "I hate to tell you this, Soph, but any decent lady would not allow herself to be touched anywhere but on the closed lips before her wedding night. I suppose that is some consolation for you, though. You will be spared some shock when your wedding night finally does come along."

"I didn't ask you to put your arms about me and pull me so close," she said, on her dignity, descending the stairs beside him, a foot of space between them. "And I certainly did not invite you to do that with your tongue. You ought not have started to kiss me when my mouth was open to speak."

"Ah, Soph," he said, "you should have kept it firmly shut when I was so close."

"And I certainly did not give you permission to do that to my ear," she said severely.

12

Apart from the fact that he had been missing his wife and despising himself for doing so, the few days before her return had been pleasant ones for the Earl of Clifton. There was a good feeling to be had from the approach of a daughter's wedding, he found. He enjoyed the noisy cheerfulness of the duke's family, and it was good to see his mother and aunt and even Olivia's parents. Pleased for their granddaughter's happiness, they had greeted him with warmth and none of the frowns and recriminations he had half expected.

It was good too to see Emma and Clarence and be reminded of the good years of his marriage at Rushton. Clarence had been his friend before he became Olivia's—the two men had gone to school and university together. But they had not seen each other in ten years.

Clarence in fact however was the one guest who somewhat clouded his general feeling of well-being. He had put on some weight about the middle and his blond hair had thinned, though he was by no means bald. But he still had the pleasant good looks that had drawn flirtatious glances from the barmaids of Oxford and more refined glances from the ladies in the London ballrooms. He had seemed impervious to the charms of them all. He was keeping himself for his future bride, he had always said laughingly when teased by his friends.

Clarence had been Olivia's friend even before the breakup of the marriage. He had been her close friend since. Her letters occasionally mentioned him, and Sophia frequently referred to him when talking of home.

And Olivia, he remembered from a certain afternoon in the hidden garden, had become a passionate and experienced lover at some time during the past fourteen years.

The earl tried not to pursue such thoughts. But the thoughts and imaginings pursued him, it seemed, and were not to be resisted during the evening on her return. She had sat with her parents and Emma at tea before mingling more freely with the other guests, and ended up standing alone with Clarence beside the tea tray for all of fifteen minutes. At dinner, she sat with the duke and her father. And in the drawing room afterward, she talked with the duchess and Richard and his wife. He joined her there himself and sat beside her until she was called away to help Claude's wife find some music to play on the pianoforte.

And then she sat on a sofa close to the pianoforte with Clarence and Emma, and stayed there even when Emma got up to play while Claude's wife sang. The two of them were deep in smiling conversation, turned toward each other so that they appeared to have eyes for no one else.

The earl strolled toward the two of them. They both looked up and smiled at him.

"We are reminiscing, Marcus," Clarence said. "It seems only yesterday that Sophia was a child and now she is only a little more than a week from marrying. And looking very happy about it too."

"Yes," the earl said. "She should know what she is about. They have known each other all their lives." Reminiscing about Sophia's childhood and girlhood was something he could not participate in.

"Do you remember the first time they met?" his wife asked, smiling up at him in some amusement. "It was at Rushton when she was just a toddler. All the boys had new balls and three of them would have cheerfully indulged Sophia by sharing with her. But it was Francis's ball she wanted and Francis she wanted to play with."

Clarence chuckled. "I was there at the time," he said. "The first notice he took of his future bride was to pull a gargoyle face and poke out his tongue at her, if I remember correctly."

"A short while before shoving her backward into a patch of only half-dried mud," the earl said. "Her dress was white, was it not, Olivia?"

"Oh yes," she said, "so it was."

"And poor Francis was turned over William's knee for his first spanking concerning Sophia," the earl said.

The other two looked at each other and laughed.

The earl turned away when the noise level rose in the room as Francis and Sophia came back, Sophia looking quite unmistakably rosy about the mouth.

His little girl, the earl thought, as the three brothers went into their usual teasing act and Francis pursed his lips and assured them that jealousy would accomplish nothing and Sophia blushed. She was too young to be mauled about by young Francis. But in nine days' time, she was going to be his bride.

Oh, Sophia, he thought, all the lost years. Years when he had seen her for only brief weeks two or three times a year, though Olivia had never denied her to him when he had asked. Years when he might have watched her growing up and stored away a wealth of memories for his old age and for telling his grandchildren.

His eyes strayed back to his wife, who was laughing with Clarence over something Bertie had just said.

Later that night, he found himself restless as he undressed and made ready for bed. He was unable to think of lying down and addressing himself to sleep. He was not tired. He wandered to the window of his bedchamber and drummed his fingers on the sill. It appeared to have stopped raining outside. Perhaps he could take an early morning ride. But there was a night to live through first.

He thought of going downstairs to the library to find a book. But he did not feel like reading. He would not be able to concentrate.

His wife was in the next room, he thought, stopping abruptly the pacing he had begun. He had felt the emptiness of the room during the previous ten nights, though he had never been into her bedchamber since her arrival at Clifton. But he had felt its emptiness nonetheless. And now she was there again. He could feel her closeness.

Her closeness made him restless. He wanted to talk with her. Only to talk. He wanted her companionship. That was surely what he had missed most through the years. They had been very close friends. They had been each other's second half. He had not been whole in all the years without her.

He wandered through to his dressing room. She was probably asleep already. And even if she were not, she would be outraged if he went into her room. She was at least entitled to the privacy of her bedchamber. But she was his wife and all he wanted to do was talk. She was probably asleep.

He turned the handle of the door between their dressing rooms quietly, not at all decided whether he would open the door. But he did, slowly and indecisively, and stepped into her dressing room. It smelled faintly of her perfume. Olivia's dressing room had always smelled this way. The door into the bedchamber was open. There was a candle burning in there.

She was reclining against her pillows, he saw when he stood in the doorway, a book open in her hands. But she was not reading it; she was looking at him and closing the book and setting it down on the table beside her, next to the candle.

Foolishly, now that he was there and she was not after all asleep, he could think of nothing to say. He stood and looked at her and she looked quietly back, not helping him out by saying anything or ordering him from her room.

"Can Sophia survive the next week?" he asked at last. "She seems excited enough to burst."

"She almost gave in to a fit of terror this afternoon just after our arrival," she said. "Seeing so many family members already gathered here has brought home the reality of it all to her. She had the feeling of being swept helplessly along by events."

"She is not having second thoughts, is she?" he asked. "It can still be stopped, all of it."

"I assured her of that," she said. "I told her that all that matters ultimately are her feelings for Francis and her wish to spend the rest of her life with him. She realized then, of course, that she has loved him all her life. I think she has, too, Marcus, though how she could have done so through their childhood, I do not know. At least she knows that he is not perfect."

There was a silence in the room for several moments. He moved beyond the doorway and came to stand beside her bed. She was wearing no dressing gown, only a thin cotton nightgown, quite low at the bosom. Her hair was shining and loose over her shoulders.

"Yes," he said. "It is important that she knows that. Have we done the right thing, Olivia, in allowing her to marry? I have been feeling something close to panic myself."

"Yes, we have," she said. "I believe they truly love each other, Marcus, and are truly good friends. They have made the decision to marry and we must respect that. She is of marriageable age, after all, though she is young. We cannot live her life for her or ever know if everything we have ever done for her was the right thing. We can only ever do our best. The rest is up to her."

"We deprived her of a family life," he said, seating himself on the edge of the bed.

"Yes," she said. "But we can do nothing to amend what is past, Marcus. And had we remained together just for her sake, perhaps we would have grown to hate each other. Perhaps we would have bickered and quarreled constantly. Would that have been better for her?"

"I suppose not," he said. "Would it have been like that between us?"

"We can never know," she said. "We have exchanged some angry words since my coming here."

"You don't regret your decision, Olivia?" he asked her.

"There is no point in regrets," she said.

"Hm," he said, and he reached out and took a lock of her hair in his hand and spread it over one finger. "Sophia told me that you went to a soirée at Lady Methuen's. Did you enjoy it?"

"I was surprised to find that I knew some people," she said, "even after all this time. Joanna Shackleton was there."

"Ah, yes," he said. "She lives most of the year in town. Her husband is in the government, you know."

"I liked being in London again," she said.

"Did you?" He looked broodingly down at her. "You always did like the excitement of a few weeks there, did you not? You might have gone there over the years, Olivia. I always told you that. I would have stayed away.''

"There was always Sophia," she said. "The country was better for her. Besides, I never had any great wish to go. Rushton has always offered enough social activity for me.''

"I hope you had plenty of new clothes made," he said. "Did you?''

"Far more than I need," she said. "I did not realize that you had written to the dressmaker, Marcus. I suppose you needed to, since the order was to be so large and so hurried. But you need not have given her such strict instructions about what I needed.''

"If I had not," he said, "I would have been fortunate to have found you returning with more than two new frocks and one bonnet. The straw you were wearing this afternoon is very pretty, by the way. It is new?''

"I would neither find nor dream of wearing such a frivolity at Rushton," she said. "But Sophia would not let me out of the milliner's without it and Francis, when goaded by her, assured me that I looked very handsome in it.''

"I would rather say that it looks very handsome on you," he said.

"I was not allowed to pay any of the dressmaker's bill," she said. "I intended to pay at least part, but it seemed you had sent strict instructions about that, too.''

"I must be allowed to dress my women for a family wedding, Olivia," he said.

"Is that what I am?" she said, watching his thumb stroke over the lock of hair across his finger. "One of your women?''

"My daughter's mother," he said.

He watched her swallow, and he lowered his head and kissed the pulse at her throat. She was still watching his hand and her hair across his finger when he raised his head again. He waited for her to say something, to become angry, to order him to leave. She said nothing.

With his free hand he smoothed the hair back from the side of her face and cupped her cheek in his palm. He traced the line of her eyebrow with a light thumb. She closed her eyes and he kissed one and her cheek and her chin. He kissed her mouth, and it trembled beneath the light pressure of his.

He lifted his head and looked down into her open eyes. He could see no anger there, no repugnance, no fear—only a calm acceptance of the moment.

He got slowly to his feet, pulled loose the sash of his dressing gown, and shrugged out of it. He watched her, giving her plenty of time to send him away. Her eyes were on his. He lifted his nightshirt over his head, dropping it beside the dressing gown. Her eyes roamed over him as he watched her. She still had not told him to go away.

She lifted her eyes to his as he drew back the bedclothes and grasped her nightgown at the hem and slid it up over her body. She raised her arms when she realized that he was not going to stop at her waist. He dropped her nightgown on top of his own garments.

It was strange, he thought, that in five years of a perfect marriage they had never been naked together. He had never seen her as he was seeing her now. With his hands and his body he had known her to be beautiful and desirable, and his eyes had confirmed the evidence of his other senses when she was clothed. But their married years had been very decorous. Very close. Very, very loving. But lacking somewhat in physical passion.

She was beautiful beyond description, his thirty-six-year-old estranged wife. His daughter's mother. Livy. She moved over on the bed as he lay down beside her. He did not extinguish the candle.

She was Livy. His eyes told him that in the candlelight, and his hands and his body, too. And yet she was a woman he did not know. His hand at her waist and his mouth on hers told him that she was instantly on fire, that there need be no slow, painstaking efforts to arouse her. She turned onto her side and her palm pushed its way up from his waist to his shoulder. She sucked on his tongue and arched her hips against his. He heard her moaning, as a certain shock in him gave way to instant response.

Livy. My God, Livy.

His hand confirmed his expectation that she was hot and

wet. Desperate for release. Too aroused for foreplay. He held her with one arm and stroked her with light and knowing fingers until she shattered against him. And he held her, crooning to her, unaware of what words, if any, he spoke, as her shudderings gave place to relaxation.

He held her for a few minutes longer before turning her onto her back and coming on top of her, spreading her legs with his knees, and mouthing her while she came awake again.

She was warm, wet, languorous. To be enjoyed at his leisure. He wanted to take her slowly. He wanted always to be where he was at that moment. He wanted it to last forever. There never had been anyone but Livy. There never could be.

He loved her with a slow, deep rhythm, his face in her hair, breathing in the scent of it, his body knowing her again as he had known her as a young man, as a young husband. She was warm and relaxed and comfortable as she had been then. Loving her was an emotional and a physical experience intertwined, inseparable. Loving was the perfect word for what they had always done together in her bed and for what they were doing together now.

And yet he was not in the past after all. He was in the present. And she was different. After a few minutes she was no longer passive. Her hips picked up the rhythm of his loving, circling to his movements, and she lifted her legs from the bed to twine about his. Her shoulders were pressing into the mattress, her breasts lifting to press more intimately against his chest. She was breathing in gasps.

He lifted his head and looked down at her, and she looked back, her lips parted, her eyes heavy with passion. His woman? Yes, his woman to stroke into, to pleasure, to love. His woman to bury himself in, to bring him release. To bring him peace. And love.

Her eyes closed as he changed his rhythm, deepening his penetration of her body. And she could no longer keep the rhythm, but pushed up against him, taut with need.

He watched her, felt her body's response with his own, waited for that indefinable moment when he knew that she would come to him, and lowered his head into her hair again, coming to her at the same moment. And he allowed pure physical reaction to take him beyond the moment and into the world of semiconsciousness beyond the climax. Her body was soft and comfortable beneath his own.

She did not regret it. She *could* not regret it. She had longed for him ever since that afternoon in the hidden garden. She had discovered then how close to starvation she had been for fourteen long years. She might have kept her sexuality unexpressed for the rest of her life, but once having had him again, her hunger gnawed at her like a physical pain, like a warning of imminent death.

She had ached for even a sight of him while in London. She had even cried for him. And she had been unable to sleep earlier, or to read either, though she had been trying to lose herself in a book. She had been too aware of his presence in the very next room, probably asleep. Her need for him had been a throbbing deep in her womb.

She had thought first of all when she had turned her head for surely the twentieth time in an hour and seen him standing silently in the doorway to her dressing room that he must be a product of an over-fertile imagination.

She had wanted him with a sick yearning while they talked and when he sat down on the side of her bed and took a lock of her hair between his fingers.

She did not regret what had happened. Or if she did, it was only the fact that she had been so uncontrolled, so unable the first time to wait even for him to come inside her. She supposed she would feel embarrassed at that memory once the night was over. And he would perhaps laugh at the evidence she had given him of just how much she had missed him.

But the other loving, the one just finished, had been wonderful beyond imagining. He had often used to like to be in her for a long time. He liked the feeling of being physically one with her as well as one in every other way, he had used to tell her, "One body, Liv. It feels good, does it not? Tell me it feels good."

It had always felt good because he was Marc and she loved him and she was doing what a wife does to show her husband that she loves him. Sometimes there had been the beginnings of active pleasure, occasionally even the near completion of pleasure, though always with something just eluding her.

That something was no longer eluding her. And she wondered if he always experienced that pleasure. If so, she could understand why he had liked to be intimate with her so often and why he had always slept so deeply afterward.

It was wonderful. She did not believe her body had ever felt so drained of energy and so relaxed. His weight was heavy on her. Her legs, which she had untwined from his, were spread wide on either side of his. She felt too wonderful to sleep. She would not be able to lift an arm to save her life, she thought with a smile.

And what next? her mind asked, refusing to be stilled as the rest of her body was still. What tomorrow? And what next week—after Sophia's wedding? She tried not to think beyond the wedding.

What would she say if he asked her to stay?

What would she do if he did not?

She tried not to think.

He woke with a start and then lay still again. She waited for him to move. She hoped he would not. She hoped that he would fall back asleep or else lift his head and kiss her.

Marc. Marc. She tried to talk to him with her mind. She was afraid to speak. She did not know what to say. Did what had happened change anything? Everything? Nothing?

He lifted himself off her without looking at her and sat on the edge of the bed, his back to her. Then he got to his feet and crossed the room to look out of the window. The candle had burned itself out.

"You have had a good teacher, Olivia," he said.

"What?" She was not sure she had heard what he had said.

He looked back over his shoulder. The room seemed curiously light. "He has taught you well, whoever it is," he said. "And has obviously given you many lessons."

She reached down for the blankets and pulled them slowly up over herself. She was still not quite sure that she understood.

"Clarence, I suppose?" he said.

Clarence? He was accusing her of having had a lover? And Clarence? Did he not know? Marc and he had been friends for years. But then Clarence had said that she was the only one he had ever told and that he had never done anything to make anyone suspicious.

"You must not be afraid of me, you know, Olivia," he had said to her one evening when he was escorting her home across the park from Emma's.

She had never before thought of being afraid of him. But one gossip of the village had regaled them all quite improperly for part of the evening with tales of an unknown rapist in a town no more than ten miles distant. And she had not really been afraid, of course, only more conscious of the darkness and loneliness of the park.

"Perhaps you wonder why I have never tried to make love to you since Marcus left," he had said. "I suppose you realize that there has been some gossip about us in the village since we do spend a great deal of time together."

"I care nothing for gossip," she had assured him.

"I must tell you something," he had said. "Something I have never told anyone, Olivia, and never thought to tell. But you need to know that you must never fear me. I do not care for women in that way, you see."

She had been stunned. "Do you mean . . . ?"

"Yes, I do," he had said. "And unfortunately it is something one cannot change by a mere effort of will. I am as I am. But no woman or man knows except you. For will-power does enable one to be chaste, you know. I have chosen chastity over the other choice. Are you totally disgusted?"

She had been. Nauseated, too. But he had been her dear friend for several years at that time.

"I am sorry," she had said. "I cannot respond so soon, Clarence. I want not to be shocked. Certainly I want not to be disgusted. I think life must have been hard for you."

"Life is never easy, is it?" he had said. "You know that better than anyone, Olivia. I shall call on you in a few days' time and you shall tell me quite honestly if you can continue to be my friend. And you must not lie to me. I shall know, you see."

No, she supposed Marc did not know.

"You need not think that I am waiting for an answer," he said. "I am not accusing you, Olivia. It would be rather ridiculous to start acting the outraged husband at this late date, would it not? I am glad, in fact, to find that you have been having some pleasure out of life. I imagine that he has been good to you?"

"He is my friend," she said. "My dear friend."

"Ah," he said.

"Lady Mornington was at Lady Methuen's soirée," she said.

"Ah, was she?" he said. "I hope you avoided the embarrassment of coming face to face with her."

"No," she said. "We spoke. She seems a refined lady."

"You expected a vulgar whore?" he said. "She is not. She is my friend." There was a pause. "My dear friend."

She said nothing.

He crossed the bedchamber and stooped down to pick up his nightshirt. He pulled it on and drew his dressing gown over it.

"Well," he said, "must we feel guilt at this night of infidelity to our dear friends, Olivia? I think not, do you? We are after all still married in the eyes of church and state. And sentiment always attaches itself to such occasions as family weddings. I think we can forgive ourselves."

"Yes," she said.

He laughed softly. "At least you can forgive yourself," he said, "even if you are unable to forgive others. Good night, Olivia. Sleep well."

"Yes," she said. "Good night, Marcus."

After he had gone, she got out of bed, drew on her nightgown, and sat on the window seat against which he had stood a few minutes before. A little later she returned to the bed to fetch a blanket to wrap about herself. And she stared out of the window into the darkness until she finally fell asleep a little before dawn.

13

They came seemingly by the dozens during the next week, the wedding guests. There were family—the duke's brother and sister and the former's wife; their children with their spouses and children; two cousins of the earl's and one of the countess's, with their families; and friends of everyone, including the bride and groom.

"I had not realized there were so many rooms at Clifton, Papa," Sophia said to him one afternoon after they had greeted cousins of two generations and a few infants of the third.

"If any more people arrive," he said, putting an arm about her shoulders, "we may have to sweep the cobwebs out of the attics, Sophia, and even set up tents on the parapets. The next time you decide to marry, my girl, remember all that comes along with a wedding, will you?"

The next time you marry. His eyes were twinkling down at her. He was teasing, of course. But she silently resolved that there would never be a next time. She could not do this to Papa again. Besides, she would have no wish to marry once this betrothal was safely in the past.

"Everyone has arrived," she told Francis that evening when several of the younger people had strolled outside.

"And so they have," he said. "I'll wager your papa is glad there are only three more days of this, Soph. One trips over guests wherever one turns. Are you cold?"

"No," she said through chattering teeth. "We cannot wait any longer, Francis. It is going to have to be done tonight. Is it to be by violent quarrel or amicable mutual consent? Either way it must be mutual, I think. I do not want you to seem thoroughly jilted."

"You think we should have a few servants round everyone up and send them to the drawing room?" he said. "There is going to be an almighty squash in there, Soph. And who is to make the announcement? It can hardly be me since honor does not allow me to break a betrothal. You?''

"Me?" Her voice came out a squeak.

"Or perhaps there should be a private meeting with our parents first,'' he said. "Perhaps your papa will make the announcement.''

"Oh,'' she said and unconsciously took a death grip on his arm. "He will be so humiliated. It does not seem fair that the task should be his, does it?''

"And yet it was for his happiness that we undertook this whole charade,'' he said.

"Yes,'' she said doubtfully.

"It looks hopeful, Soph,'' he said. "They have been acting like a couple since we returned from London. They are always together to greet people, and there has been enough of that in the last few days, heaven knows.''

"Yes,'' she said, "but I cannot help thinking that they are doing it just for my sake since I told Papa how I felt, Francis.'' She pulled on his arm. "We must not keep strolling like this, putting it off. We must go back to the house now and ask Mama and Papa and your parents to come to the library.''

"Oh, Lord,'' he said, "I do believe Great-uncle Aubrey and cousins Julius and Bradley and Lord Wheatley have taken possession of the library, Soph, with a brandy decanter and a bottle or three of port.''

"To the blue salon, then,'' she said.

"Aunt Hester and Aunt Leah are exchanging a year's worth of *on dits* in there,'' he said, "with your Great-aunt Clara and cousin Dorothea and half a dozen other ladies as audience.''

"The morning room, then,'' she said.

"The older children have been allowed to spill out of the nursery and into there for the evening, if you remember,'' he said.

"Well, somewhere,'' she said. "There has to be an empty room somewhere, Francis.''

"I have my doubts,'' he said. "But if we summon them

to the middle of the hall, I daresay no one will hear what is being said.''

"Francis!" she said.

"I'll tell you what, Soph," he said, patting her hand. "This evening is entirely the wrong time to do it. Half the men are into their cups and the ladies are into their gossip and a few people out here have stolen into the shadows for a private tête-à-tête and a dozen or so people arrived only today and would not take kindly to having to pack their half-unpacked bags to leave again at dawn. I think perhaps we should leave everyone to an evening's entertainment and tell them tomorrow in the light of day.''

"In the light of day," she said. "Oh, heaven forbid. Francis, it has to be done soon. If we go on like this much longer, we are going to be married.''

"The devil, yes," he said. "We cannot have that, can we? Tomorrow it must be then, Soph, and not a moment later. Married, by Jove. I cannot think of any fate more dreadful, can you?''

"None," she said tartly. "Especially marriage to you. I could think of better ways to be comfortable in hell.''

"Oh, come now," he said, "there is no need for spite, is there, Soph?''

"Well," she said, "you are always saying things about dreadful fates and all that. Do you think our marrying would be any better a fate for me? Do you think I am secretly panting for you? Do you think I am secretly hoping that there will be no way out of this betrothal after all? If the time does not seem right to you tomorrow, Francis, I shall go up on the roof and yell the news out to the whole countryside. How do you like that?''

"I like it very well," he said. "I shall summon everyone out onto the lawn for you, shall I, Soph? The mental image of your standing up there, arms extended, hair streaming in the breeze, is enormously stimulating. I think you would need a larger bosom to carry it off to effect, though.''

"Oh," she said, "so now my bosom is too small, is it?''

"Are you sure you will feel up to discussing such a topic with me once the first flush of your ire has cooled?'' he asked. "I think perhaps it is time I kissed you and took you inside, Soph."

"Don't you come near me," she said.

"A strange command," he said, "when you are clinging to my arm."

She released it.

"Will you be very glad to be rid of me, Soph?" he asked, cupping her face in his hands.

"Yes, very," she said. "Very, very glad."

"You will have no one to quarrel with," he said.

"And no one to insult me," she said.

"And no one to whom to release your venom."

"I won't need to with you gone," she said.

"You are going to miss me," he said.

"True," she said. "Just as I miss the surgeon who pulled one of my teeth last year. Just as I miss the pair of shoes I threw out early this spring because they gave me blisters on all ten toes. Just as . . ."

"Well," he said, "at least we share mutual feelings about being rid of each other. I was afraid that you might miss me in earnest."

"Conceited—mm," she said as he kissed her.

"Mm, yes," he said after a considerable interval of silence. "We share that sentiment too, Soph. Let's do it one more time, shall we? By this time tomorrow, all will be over."

"It cannot be too soon for me," she said. "Mmm."

"Mmm," he said a while later. "I am in total agreement with you, Soph. Shall we go inside before this mood of rare amity is broken by another quarrel?"

"I don't know why you are kissing me anyway," she said. "We do not have to deceive anyone any longer, do we?"

"Sometimes, Soph," he said, "one has to do something purely for oneself."

She looked up at him.

"I could see that you were longing to be kissed," he said. "Ah, that's better. You suddenly look much more yourself."

"You toad!" she said.

* * *

They had spent a great deal of time together since her return from London. But apart from that one night with its bitter ending, they had not been alone together. He had not been to her room again although she had lain awake at night watching the door to her dressing room, expecting him and knowing that he would not come, longing for him and dreading that he would appear.

There were three more days to Sophia's wedding, she told herself on the evening after the last of the guests had arrived. Easy days since there was so much to be done and so many guests to entertain and relatives and friends to spend time with. There would be no chance for them to be alone with each other, and he had shown that he had no further wish to come to her at night. She did not know why he had come that one night. He was missing his mistress, perhaps?

Emma and Clarence were planning to leave the day after the wedding. It was enough that Lord Clifton had entertained such large numbers during the week and more leading up to the nuptials, Emma said. The least they could do was take themselves off without delay once the festivities were over.

"And you will be glad of some peace and quiet and relaxation, Olivia," she said, "after all this excitement."

Yes, she would. But she would not find those things at Clifton. When her friends returned to Rushton, she had decided, she would go with them. There she would begin her battle for inner peace all over again.

She was sitting beside her husband on a sofa in the drawing room, their shoulders almost touching. They were in a group with her parents and the Biddefords and Emma and Clarence. Several guests were in other rooms of the house. Most of the young people had gone outside for a stroll, the rain having finally ceased the day before.

"Yes," her father was saying, continuing a conversation that had been in progress for several minutes. "What you say is quite right, Miss Burnett. One does not need a large number of close family members to achieve contentment in life. We have only one daughter and one granddaughter, though we wished for more of each, did we not, Bridget?

But we have each other and our circle of good friends and we live a blessedly contented life.''

"Friends are the key to contentment," Emma said. "One can choose one's friends, you see, whereas you cannot choose one's family."

"Except one's spouse," the earl said.

"But friendship consists in freedom," Emma said, launching on her favorite theme, "the freedom to give or to withhold affection. That freedom instantly vanishes in marriage. Once one is compelled to friendship, then it no longer is friendship but forced amity. Freedom is killed. Love is killed."

"Not necessarily," Oliver's father said, leaning forward in his chair.

"Olivia," Clarence said with a smile, "I am going to take myself off for a turn about the terrace. If I stay any longer, I will not know who are my friends and who are not or even what friendship is. Would you care to join me?"

She got gratefully to her feet. "That sounds wonderful," she said.

"Would anyone else care for a stroll?" he asked, looking about the group. But everyone else seemed engrossed in the discussion.

Olivia met her husband's eyes and half smiled. "Excuse me?" she said.

"Of course." He inclined his head.

It was a beautiful evening, fresh after the days of rain and cool, too, but not cool enough to necessitate running upstairs for a shawl.

"Emma is in her element," she said, taking Clarence's arm as they stepped out onto the terrace. "She has a totally new audience on whom to unleash her theories."

"I know," he said, grinning. "But I am old audience and thought it time to come outside for fresh air."

"Ah," she said, breathing in the freshness, "it does feel good."

"Things are going well for you, Olivia?" he asked. "I half expected to find the two of you at daggers drawn when I arrived. Instead, I was witness to all of Marcus's impatience to have you home from London, and the sight of the two of you after your return looking like a pair of reunited lovers.''

"He was eager to have Sophia back home," she said. "He has not seen enough of her over the years, Clarence. I always knew from his letters that he loved her. I did not realize until I came here that his love for her equals my own.''

"Will you be staying?" he asked. "You know my opinion about that old quarrel and about your long and unnecessary separation.''

"It was not a quarrel," she said, "and it was not unnecessary. I am going to come home with you and Emma.''

"The day after the wedding? Are you sure, Olivia?''

"I can scarcely wait," she said. "I feel as if I cannot breathe here, Clarence. I want to be home in my own world with my own friends and activities.''

"With Emma and me and the Povises and the Richardsons and everyone else?" he said. "Are we worthy substitutes for Marcus, Olivia? Has he said he wants you to go?''

"He has not said that he wants me to stay either," she said. "It is intolerable being here, Clarence. When I first came, as you know, I thought it would be merely to spend a few days discussing Sophia's future and rejecting Lord Francis's offer. There seemed to be no question of our allowing her to marry. In fact, of course, it was not as simple as that. You warned me, did you not? Neither of us had faced the fact that she is grown up and of marriageable age and that Francis is a perfectly eligible partner for her, even if he has been a little wild since coming down from university. If I had known that this was to happen, I would have written to Marcus telling him that any decision of his would have my support. I would not have come.''

"But you would have come for her wedding," he said.

"Oh," she said. "Yes, I suppose I would have. And we have more or less agreed, Clarence, to come together occasionally after Sophia is married, to visit her or be visited by her. I wish it did not have to be. I am already dreading the next few weeks.''

"Because you will have to go through again what you

went through years ago when Marcus first left?" he asked.

"How will I survive it?" she asked.

"By being proud and stubborn and as strong as any ten other women put together," he said. "And as foolish as twenty."

"What am I to do, then?" she asked. "Go down on my knees to him and beg him to take me back?"

"Perhaps allow him to do that same thing," he said.

She laughed. "I met Lady Mornington in London," she said. "She is not at all lovely, Clarence. And I know that sounds tabbyish, but I do not mean it that way. She seemed like a perfectly sensible, amiable, intelligent woman. She looked like the kind of woman a man would become attached to. They have been together for six years, I believe—longer than he and I were together. I told him I had met her, and he did not deny a thing or try to justify himself. He merely said that she was his dear friend."

"He did not leave you from choice, Olivia," he said. "And fourteen years is a very long time, you know."

"Oh, yes," she said. "I know, Clarence. Believe me, I know." She added on a rush, "We have been together again."

"Have you?" he asked quietly. "Are you sure you should be saying this to me, Olivia?"

"But I have to talk to someone," she said. "I feel so very alone. I cannot talk to Mama. She would only advise me as she has always done to do my duty, whatever that might mean. And I cannot talk to Emma. She would only advise me as she always does to forget about all men and thereby relieve my mind of all stresses and negative emotions."

"And you do not want that advice?" he asked.

"Clarence," she said, "you are my very best friend. Oh, yes, you are. You know you are and have been since Marcus left. I can talk to you about anything on earth and know that you will listen with a sympathetic ear. You will, won't you? We have been together—twice. And it was wonderful and dreadful."

"Dreadful?" he said.

"Afterward," she said, "both times, when I expected

tender words, he had only coldness to offer. As if he had been merely using me, putting me in my place, reminding me that I am still his wife to be so used if he chooses."

"Did you give him tender words?" he asked.

"But he must have known my feelings," she said. "I did nothing to hide them."

"Did you know his feelings?" he asked. "Before he spoke, I mean?"

"But I was wrong," she said. "When he spoke, I knew I had misunderstood entirely. We have been apart too long, Clarence. I do not know him any longer. He is a stranger to me. I think Marc must have died many years ago."

"Perhaps you need to talk to him, Olivia," he said. "Just talk as you are talking to me now. You used to talk to each other constantly, did you not? I used to come upon you out riding or walking together, and you were always so deep in conversation that you both would look thoroughly startled when I hailed you. It happened so many times that it was a private joke I had with myself."

"I would not know how to begin," she said.

"Then begin anywhere," he said. "Begin with the weather. Ideas often flow once the tongue has been set in motion."

"It sounds too simple," she said. "I don't think it could work, Clarence."

"You will not know unless you try," he said. "Why not invite him outside now? We seem to be the last ones out here and it seems to me that we have been outside far longer than I intended to keep you. We will be fortunate not to run into search parties."

"It is late," she said. "Perhaps tomorrow."

"Never put off until tomorrow what can be done today," ne said grinning. "My mother used to say that so often to us children that we used to mouth the words with her if we could just get sufficiently far behind her not to be observed."

She sighed. "You always make life sound so uncomplicated, Clarence," she said. "Perhaps I will do as you suggest. I shall see if he is busy with someone."

The Earl of Clifton was not busy with anyone, it seemed.

He came striding across the hall to meet them as they stepped inside the house, his eyes passing from Clarence to his wife.

"I need to have a word with you, Olivia," he said, taking her arm.

She looked at Clarence and he gave her an encouraging smile.

"I shall see if there is any tea left in the drawing room," he said.

Her husband's hand was firm on her arm. He led her without a word across the hall and opened the door into his private study.

"What is it?" she asked him. "Is something wrong? Sophia?"

There was no light in the study. He closed the door firmly behind them and plunged them into darkness. And he swung her around quite ungently so that she collided hard with his chest, and found her mouth with his own.

The urgency of the kiss had nothing to do with passion or need or love, she realized after the first moment of shock and latent joy. It was a kiss designed to bruise her lips and cut the flesh behind them against her teeth. It was a kiss intended to hurt and insult. She pushed against his shoulders, was wrestled even closer to him, and finally went limp in his arms.

"You will keep away from him while you are in my home," he said at last, his voice tight with fury, "whatever you do at Rushton. My home is full of guests come to celebrate a wedding. Your daughter's and mine. The proprieties will be observed. Strictly observed. Do you understand me?"

She could not see him at all. Her eyes had not even begun to accustom themselves to the darkness.

"Clearly," she said.

"Where were you?" He had her by the wrists.

"Outside."

"Where outside?"

"Outside."

He shook her wrists. "When your mother asked Sophia if you were coming in, Sophia said she had not seen you," he said. "Where were you? In the garden? In the hidden garden?"

She said nothing.

"Answer me." He shook her more roughly.

"I will not," she said.

"You were in the hidden garden," he said and his hold on her wrists loosened. "I'll not have it, Olivia. Not on this property or during this week." The fury had gone from his voice, leaving it flat and expressionless. "At least I did not invite Mary here."

"Lady Mornington?" she said.

"At least I did not invite her here, Olivia," he said. "I think you might have done as much."

"Clarence is my friend," she said.

"Yes," he said, "and Mary is mine."

"Well," she said, "you can be back with her within a week. The guests will doubtless all leave within a day or two of the wedding. I shall be returning home with Clarence and Emma. You need not delay your departure for London."

"I have known peace of mind with her," he said. "She accepts me for who I am."

"Then you are fortunate," she said. "There are not many women who would accept any such thing."

"Olivia," he said. "Stay away from him."

"Why?" she asked. "Are you jealous, Marcus?"

"Envious," he said and there was an edge of anger to his voice again. "I don't have Mary here to dally with."

"I suppose, then," she said, "that I am more fortunate than you. May I leave now?"

He released her wrists and opened the door in silence. She went past him into the hallway and he closed the door quietly behind her, remaining inside the room.

She probably would have told herself the next morning that she had had a sleepless night. Certainly she had tossed and turned for a long, long time and punched her pillows and rearranged the bedclothes and thought of getting up and dressing and going downstairs in search of something to eat or outside in search of air.

But she must have fallen asleep eventually. Otherwise, she would have heard him coming into her dressing room, and seen him coming into her bedchamber and crossing the room to her bed. She would have seen him pulling off his clothes. As it was, she was aware of him only as the bed beside her dipped with his weight.

And then one arm came beneath her and turned her onto her side and his free hand came along her jaw and over her ear and his mouth found hers and explored it warmly and gently. She came fully awake.

He said nothing, only kissed her slowly, almost lazily, touching just her face, her nightgown separating their bodies. ''Easy,'' he murmured to her when desire surged and she arched herself against him. ''Easy.''

And she imposed relaxation on her body and allowed him to lead the way by slow, deliberate, erotic stages until he finally stripped away her nightgown and came onto her and into her and she knew only the frenzy of wanting him, of needing what he was giving her. She pressed her knees to his waist and urged him on to that newly discovered world beyond passion.

''Yes,'' she told him as it happened. ''Yes.''

He sighed against her ear.

She did not try to hold him as he disengaged himself from her and removed his weight from her. She only kept her eyes closed and willed him not to leave her. There was a far worse desolation in being alone after love than in being always alone. She had discovered that on two recent occasions.

Please don't go, she begged him silently. And he slid his arm beneath her neck again and drew her close and pulled the blankets up about them.

''He has taught you passion,'' he said, his voice low against her ear, ''but not control. I'll teach you control and the greater wonder that follows it.''

She thought he would leave then. And she expected to feel fury and the need to order him out of her bed and her room. But she was too tired for anger and too warm and comfortable to want him gone. She willed him not to leave. She burrowed her head into the warm hollow between his shoulder and neck.

Fourteen years without you have taught me passion, she told him silently as she slipped into sleep. *Not Clarence or any other nameless he. Just your long absence from my life, Marc.*

He woke her again in the night and loved her slowly and thoroughly. And remembering his words, she began to learn to hold her desire in check, so that all the meandering paths to glory might be explored and enjoyed, and the glory itself might be the more shatteringly wonderful.

Even then he did not go back to his own room.

14

Sophia slept fitfully through the night. She did not know quite how she was to face the day and the announcement that would have to be made. She wished she had insisted that they do it the evening before despite the reasonableness of Francis's objections. Really, there was no right time to do such a thing. And she wished that she had been blessed with an imagination. She had never thought of what a betrothal and planned wedding would involve beyond bringing her parents together. She had not thought of anything beyond the hope that once together, they would realize that they could not be apart again.

She got up very early and dressed herself and brushed her hair without the services of a maid, intending to go downstairs and outside even though there were heavy clouds that made it look chilly outside.

But she would not do so, she decided suddenly. She would not wait any longer. She *could* not. And why should Francis bear all the embarrassment of confronting both sets of parents when really none of this whole situation was his fault? She would go to her mother, she decided, as she had often gone whenever she was burdened with a problem. She had always liked to go in the early morning, when she could climb into bed beside Mama and curl into her warmth and feel that all the burdens of the world had been lifted off her shoulders and onto Mama's sensible and capable ones.

She could no longer do that, of course. But she would go anyway. Mama would know how best to break the news to Papa and to the duke and duchess. And Mama would be able to advise her on how and when they should make the announcement to all their gathered friends and relatives.

It was not going to be that simple, of course. It was a dreadful thing she had done, despite the purity of her motive, and the consequences were going to be equally dreadful. Indeed, they did not bear thinking of. And it was the effort of not thinking of them that had kept her awake through much of the night, waking from dreams and fighting to remain awake.

But she would go anyway. If there was anyone who could help her it was her mother. Besides, Mama should be the first to know. And perhaps Papa, too, but she did not care to think what Papa would say to her or what he would do. Though it was a baseless fear—Papa had never struck her even when she was a child.

Perhaps she should wait for a more civilized hour, she thought as she stepped outside her room into a deserted corridor and closed the door behind her. Mama was going to be fast asleep. Perhaps she should wait an hour longer. But even an hour was too long to wait—her wedding was supposed to take place two days hence. She walked resolutely and with thumping heart and shaking knees in the direction of her mother's room.

She tapped lightly on the door and opened it slowly and quietly as if afraid to disturb the mother she had come to waken.

"Mama?" she whispered, stepping inside and looking across to the bed from which the curtains were looped back.

And then she stopped abruptly as she found herself staring into her father's eyes. She could not afterward explain to herself how she had the presence of mind to notice details, but she did. Her father's bare arms were about her mother, her head cradled on his arm, her face against his bare chest. Her long fair hair was tousled and covering his arm. Her back was bare. Her father's free hand drew the blankets up about her sleeping mother.

He frowned at Sophia and formed a "Sh!" with his mouth though he made no sound. She backed up until she felt the door handle behind her and then she fled through the door, closing it as quietly as her shaking hands could accomplish. She stood outside the door gulping in air, feeling such a welling of excitement inside that she thought she would surely burst if she had to keep it all to herself.

Cynthia? Cynthia had always been one of her closest friends. But she did not spare Cynthia more than a glancing thought. Her hasty footsteps and overflowing heart took her to another door and she rapped on it a little less lightly than she had tapped on her mother's. Even so she had to repeat the knock.

Lord Francis was wearing breeches when he opened the door. They were all he was wearing. His hair was still disheveled from his pillow. Sophia noticed none of those details.

"What the devil?" he said. "Go away this instant, Soph. Are you mad?"

"Francis," she said, her hands clasped to her bosom, her eyes shining, "guess what? We did it. We did it."

Lord Francis took a step forward, looked to right and left along the still-deserted corridor, grabbed Sophia by one wrist, and hauled her inside his bedchamber. He shut the door firmly.

"We certainly did," he said. "We backed ourselves into a corner. Don't you realize what would happen if you were seen knocking on my door at this hour of the morning, Soph? Your reputation would be in shreds even if you really were within two days of your wedding. There would certainly be no question of calling off the wedding. In one moment I am going to stick my head out there again to make sure there are no watchers at the doors and then you are going to tiptoe all the way back to your room again. Are you this desperate for my body?"

She chuckled and threw her arms about his neck. "They are in bed together and he has his arms about her and she is sleeping with her face against his chest," she said. "We did it, Francis! we did it." And she kissed him smackingly on the cheek.

"Soph, Soph," he said, trying to put her from him, "if there is any attacking to be done, I would prefer to be the instigator, if you don't mind too much. *Who* are in bed together? Oh, your mama and papa, I suppose. And you went walking in on them. Then you can be very thankful that she *was* asleep, my girl. You might just have acquired a permanent blush."

"Do you think they . . . ?" she asked.

"I have no doubt that they . . ." he said. "It usually happens when a man and woman get into bed together, you know, Soph. And I would feel a great deal more comfortable if you were not quite so close to mine, especially in my present state of, ah, dishabille. I am lamentably human, you know."

"Oh," she said, and she jumped away from him and appeared to notice for the first time his naked upper body and his bare feet. She flushed slowly.

"What you see is going to be all yours in two days' time, Soph, if you don't get out of here unnoticed," he said. "In which case it is to be hoped that those blushes mean you like what you see. So they spent the night together, did they?"

"Yes." She clasped her hands before her, and her eyes shone again. "It has worked, Francis. It was all worthwhile after all. Now I will not mind all the embarrassment facing us today. I shall not mind at all, at least for my sake. I shall mind for yours for you have done me a great kindness and I shall never forget it for all that we quarrel dreadfully whenever we are alone together for longer than two minutes. I shall mind the embarrassment to you."

"Look, Soph," he said, "we need to talk a few things over before getting together with our parents. But not here and now, thank you very much. There are limits to my better nature. I'll meet you outside in half an hour. By the fountain. Agreed?"

"Yes," she said. "But I will take all the blame, Francis. It will be worth it now that I know they are together again forever and ever. Oh, you are wonderful."

"You won't think so for much longer if you keep standing there looking like that," he said, striding resolutely back to the door and opening it gingerly. "It is still deserted. Good Lord, I'll wager even the servants are not up yet. Out you go. Now!"

Sophia went, favoring him with a wide and radiant smile as she passed him. Lord Francis in his turn favored the ceiling with an exasperated grimace.

He tried to draw his arm out from beneath her without

disturbing her. God, but she looked beautiful, flushed and disheveled with sleep. And even more beautiful when she opened her eyes and stared upward at him, at first blankly and then with recognition.

"I had better go," he said.

She said nothing.

"I had no right to question the propriety of your behavior last night," he said. "I, of all people. I don't really believe that you would carry on an affair here under the very nose of your mother and mine and a host of other relatives and guests. I'm sorry."

She still said nothing.

"You should understand the way I felt, though," he said. "It is something of a shock to come actually face to face with one's spouse's lover. Not that I blame you, Olivia. It is just strange seeing you again, that is all. My wife and not my wife. Someone I used to know who now has a life I know nothing about. I am sorry about this, too. It is in poor taste, I suppose, even if it is the most lawful bedding that either of us has indulged in in fourteen years."

He smiled when she remained silent, and sat up on the edge of the bed to pull on his nightshirt.

"But it was never your way to forgive, was it?" he said, and he left the room without looking back at her.

He wished this dratted wedding was at an end already and everyone gone home. Including Olivia. He did not doubt that she would leave with Clarence, her friend Emma with them to lend propriety to the journey. He wished she were gone already. He wished that he never need see her again.

His love for her had become a quiet thing over the years, locked away deep inside him, no longer disturbing his day to day living. Now that love had become a pain again, worse even perhaps than it had been at the start. For at the start there had been a great deal of hope—hope that she would forgive him, that she would realize that she could not live without him, that she would see that it was not worth throwing away a life of potential happiness for the sake of one transgression, however bad.

Now there was no hope. Although her manner toward him

in the daytime was amiable, there was a reason for it, an agreement they had come to. And although she had allowed him into her bed and even greeted him there with a passion she had not shown before, her mind was not in accord with her body. She would not speak with him or respond to him or forgive him when passion was satiated.

There was no point in going to bed, he thought when he reached his own dressing room. It must be infernally early, but there was no more sleep to be had. He rang for his valet and peeled off his nightshirt.

And what the devil had Sophia wanted with Livy at this hour of the morning? Some other crisis concerning her wedding, no doubt. They would all be fortunate if the girl did not fall into hysterics long before the ceremony was safely over.

Olivia lay still after pulling the blankets up over her breasts. She stared upward at the canopy.

How he had changed, she thought. She had always been the focus of his world, she, and Sophia after her birth. And Rushton. He had never wanted anyone or anything else. He had often groaned when she had reminded him of some assembly that they were to attend. He had not wanted to attend that Lowry wedding without her. She had urged him to go, thinking that it would be good for him to see his friends again.

And yet now he could lie in her bed, propped on one elbow, and talk about her supposed lover and the tasteless-ness of their making love together just as if it were the most normal thing in the world for a husband and wife to behave so. And the sickening thing was that she knew it was quite normal. Marc had become part of his social world. She had not.

Why had she not denied an involvement with Clarence more vehemently? she wondered. She had told him the night before that Clarence was her friend, but he had misunder-stood or else disbelieved her. She had left it at that. She had felt too upset and too weary to protest something that he should have known without any question at all. If he knew her as she had thought he knew her, he could not even have wondered about her and Clarence.

But Marc belonged to the real world. She was the strange one. What other woman would have urged her man to go alone to London for a wedding and all the parties and drinking and rioting that would be an inevitable part of it? Only a totally credulous innocent.

She longed to be at home. She longed to be away from this and back in the peace of her own home. Except that she knew that that peace would no longer be waiting there for her, but would have to be fought for all over again.

And perhaps never found. For the previous fight had been made possible by the fact that she had considered herself right. What he had done was unforgivable. And though she had forgiven him nonetheless in her heart, she had truly believed that they could never live together again, never restore the trust and the friendship that had bound them so closely together.

She knew now—too late—that she had been wrong in every way. What he had done was not unforgivable. It had been human and everything human was forgivable. And she knew that if only she had had the courage to try, they could have built an even stronger relationship than before, because it would have been based on reality. They would have suffered together and been strengthened together.

She had given away the chance to have her marriage grow. And it was too late now. Oh, it was true that he was treating her with kindness and deference during the daytime, but that was all a charade they had agreed to. And it was true that he had made love to her four times—on three separate occasions—and that they had been wonderful together, far more wonderful than they had ever been during the years of their marriage. But it had been a physical thing only. Sex only.

He had talked about Clarence as if he did not mind if he were her lover. And he had talked about Lady Mornington as if she were an accepted part of his life. Making love with his wife was what had made him feel guilty, not the fact of the existence of a mistress.

He had changed too much and she had changed too little. The gap between them after fourteen years was insurmountable. Only one thing remained unchanged. She still loved him. And her love had become a pain again and would remain so for many weary months. She knew that from experience.

Olivia turned over onto her stomach and buried her face in the pillow where his head had lain.

"How can you be ten minutes late," Lord Francis said, "when you were dressed already, Soph, and all you had to do was come downstairs and out through the door?"

"I went back to my room," she said, "and had a fit of the panics. I thought for a while that I was going to vomit, and I did not want to vomit all over you, Francis. I have the feeling under control now."

"Are you sure?" he asked. "There are two benches here, Soph. We can sit on separate ones if you like."

"And then I was halfway down the stairs," she said, "and remembered that I did not have my cloak and it looked cloudy and raw outside. Actually it is quite warm, is it not?"

"Sit down here," he said. "We have to talk before other people start getting up and wandering out here."

"Yes," she said. "Shall we have breakfast first, Francis, and then ask Mama and Papa and your parents to come to the library? Or shall it be the other way around? Either way, I am sure I shall not be able to eat a bite. I keep thinking of kidneys. Oh, I wish I could think of some other food." Her teeth were chattering.

"Soph," he said, "you don't really think we can do this, do you?"

"I don't want to talk about it," she said. "I just want to do it. I shall have that feeling again if I think."

"The guests are all here," he said, "and the neighbors stirred up to fever pitch. The rector is puffed up with importance and the cook and your father's chef from London are considering giving up sleep for the next two nights in order to get all the baking done. The wedding cake is made and the flowers have been chosen for cutting tomorrow. Your dress is made and your mama's and my clothes. And . . . well, I could go on forever, couldn't I?''

Sophia licked her lips nervously. "You see what I mean?" she said. "We must not think, Francis, or we are going to end up married to each other. We have to do. No one can force us to marry, after all.''

"I think we had better all the same," he said.

She stared at him.

"It would save an awful lot of trouble," he said.

Her jaw dropped inelegantly.

"You would be able to enjoy your breakfast after all, Soph," he said. "And even perhaps have some kidneys.''

"Are you mad?" she said. "Have you gone totally insane? Are we to put up with each other for a lifetime just in order to avoid a little trouble now?''

"In short, yes," he said.

"Francis." She stretched out her hands to him until he took them, and set her head to one side. "I cannot let you do it. Really I cannot. Oh, you are very wonderful. But you would never be able to face life with me. You know that— you spent all of your boyhood fleeing from me. I will take all the blame. Truly, I will. I will make sure that there is not even a whisper of blame put on you. It will be all right, Francis. It will be forgotten. Perhaps you can go away for a year or so until the embarrassment has passed. It will eventually, you know. Perhaps you can go to Italy and see the Sistine Chapel—in Rome.''

Lord Francis sighed. "I had hoped to avoid this," he said. "But I think it is time for a little confession, Soph. Or perhaps not so little, either. I have trapped you.''

"No," she said. "I have trapped you, Francis, by my thoughtlessness. But I shall put all right, you will see.''

"Soph," he said, "I knew from the very start exactly how it would be. I knew that all this would happen—a blind man would have known it. I knew we would find ourselves within a couple of days of the wedding and no reasonable way out of going ahead with it.''

"But you did it anyway," she said, "for Mama's and Papa's sake. How wonderful you are, Francis.''

"I did it to trap you into marriage," he said.

Sophia laughed and then looked at him in incomprehension.

"When I saw you again this spring," he said, "I just couldn't believe that I had done so much running from you when we were younger, Soph. You had changed. By Jove, you had changed. And yet you stuck up your nose whenever I came close and you started to drop all sorts of nasty remarks about rakes and suchlike until I did not know how I was going to get you to take me seriously."

"Nonsense," she said. "You are making this all up just so that I will believe you and you can laugh at me. This is most unkind, you know, especially on this of all mornings. Don't you know that I . . . ."

"Then some ass—was it Hathaway?—suggested this most corkbrained of corkbrained schemes," he said, "and I saw immediately where it could lead. I thought that perhaps my agreeing to it would give you time to realize that I was not the wild libertine you took me for."

"Francis," she said, "be serious, do."

"Well, take it or leave it," he said. "I thought I had better confess, Soph. But however it is, we had better get married. All hell will break loose here if we don't. You have to think no further than my mother."

"I don't want to think at all," she said.

"And your parents are going to start blaming themselves," he said. "They will wonder where they went wrong with you, Soph, and before you know it they will be at each other's throats and leaving each other for the rest of two lifetimes."

"Don't," she said. "I don't want to think."

"Don't, then," he said. "Just marry me."

"I don't want to marry you," she said. "I would rather marry . . ."

"A toad," he said. "I love you, Soph."

"Oh, you do not," she said indignantly. "You are a brazen liar."

"I love you."

"You do not."

"Love you."

"Do not."

"Do."

"Don't. You horrid man. I hate you. I do. I hope you go away this very morning after I have made the announcement, and I hope I never ever see you again."

"You don't, Soph," he said.

"I do."

"Don't."

"Do."

"Do."

"Don—. I hate you, Francis. I hate you. Take your hand away from my face."

"It feels so soft, Soph," he said. "So much softer than my hand."

"I don't want you touching me," she said.

"Don't you?" He moved closer to her on the bench and lowered his head to feather a kiss across her lips.

"Or kissing me," she said.

"Don't you?"

"No."

"It feels so good, though, does it not?" he said. "Like this, Soph? And this? Shall I tell you what I wanted to do with you when you came to my room earlier?"

"No."

"I wanted to do this," he said, kissing her again and running his tongue along her closed lips. "And this." He slid a hand beneath her cloak and cupped one breast lightly in his hand.

"Don't," she said.

"I shan't tell you the rest of what I wanted to do," he said. "I'll show you on our wedding night, Soph. Not tonight or tomorrow night. The next night."

"You are saying that to frighten me," she said. "Don't touch me there, Francis." She set a hand over his, the fabric of her cloak between them. "It makes me feel funny. And don't do that with your tongue. Please."

"Don't you think that perhaps you want me, Soph?" he asked.

"Want you?" she said. "*Want* you? You would just love

for me to say yes, would you not, so that you can ridicule me. Don't, Francis. Don't do that." He was rubbing a thumb over her nipple.

"Marry me," he said. "Tell me you love me, Soph, and that you will marry me. And then on our wedding night you can tell me all the things to stop doing so that I can keep on doing them."

"Francis," she said. "Please. Do you think I don't remember all the times you deceived me years ago?"

"I love you," he said.

She sighed. "Well," she said, "you always won every contest, did you not, Francis? You always made me believe you and then you called me idiot for being so gullible. Why should anything have changed? Why not this time, too? All right, then. I do love you and I will marry you. And now it will serve you right if I do not release you from our betrothal but marry you and plague you for the rest of our lives."

"Plague me, Soph," he said. "And stop pulling away like a frightened rabbit. Let me kiss you properly."

"Frightened?" she said. "Of you? Who do you think you are?"

"Your betrothed," he said. "The man who loves you. The man you love. Let me kiss you properly."

"Francis," she said, setting one hand over his mouth and looking wistfully into his eyes, "do you mean it? Tell me now if you do not. Please? I will not be able to bear it if you kiss me and tell me those things again and then laugh at me and run away from me."

"If I don't mean it, I am playing a pretty dangerous game, aren't I?" he said. "Parson's mousetrap waiting to snap its jaws?"

"Do you really love me, then?" she asked.

"I really do, Soph," he said.

"Really and truly?"

"And that too," he said.

She pulled herself away from his hold suddenly and jumped to her feet. She looked at him with shining eyes.

"I have to go back to the house," she said. "I have to

find Mama and Papa. I have to tell them that we are betrothed.''

''Soph.'' He scratched his head. ''If I were to whisper the word Bedlam, you would not start ripping up at me, would you?''

She looked blankly at him and then chuckled. ''We have this moment become betrothed,'' she said, ''and no one knows.''

''It will be our secret,'' he said. ''Sit down here and let me kiss you properly.''

She sat. ''Will we have to stop quarreling now?'' she asked.

''And lead a dull respectable life forever after?'' he said, horrified. ''Heaven forbid. Let me see now, where was my hand? It was somewhere warm and comfortable. Here?''

''Did you mean it when you said it was small?'' she asked as his hand covered her breast again.

''I have seen many larger,'' he said. ''And, ah, touched a few too.''

''Have you?'' she said tartly. ''Am I to be compared to your—to your pieces of muslin for the rest of my life?''

''Only when I want to start a quarrel,'' he said. ''My hand feels good there, though, does it not? Admit it, Soph.''

''You would love me to do just that, would you not?'' she said. ''You conceited . . .''

He kissed her.

''. . . toad,'' she said.

''Hush, Soph,'' he said. ''I have waited long enough. And you are the loveliest kisser, my love, that it has ever been my privilege to kiss.''

''Oh,'' she said. ''Mm.''

''And you have the loveliest bosom too,'' he said without removing his mouth from hers. ''No answer needed or allowed.''

''Mmm,'' she said.

15

"This cravat is too tight," Lord Francis complained to Claude, pulling at the offending garment and twisting his head from side to side.

"It is your usual size?" his brother asked.

"Of course," Lord Francis said.

"My guess is that it is a quite normal wedding cravat, then," Claude said.

"Eh?"

"Made exactly the same size as all your other cravats," his brother said, "instead of a couple of inches larger to accommodate the swelling of the throat that comes with wedding days. Your shoes are probably going to be too tight too. Now, are they?"

"Ah, I see how it is," Lord Francis said. "I am to be the butt of everyone's wit on the very day when I cannot think up one witticism to hurl in return."

"The cook always puts a dose of poison in the breakfast, too," Claude said. "Just the groom's, of course, not anyone else's. Is your stomach feeling queasy, Frank?"

Lord Francis smoothed the lace at his wrists over the backs of his hands and took one final look at himself in the mirror.

"If I could plan this all over again," he said, "I would choose an unmarried man for my best man, Claude, just as any sensible groom would do. The chances are, he would not be standing there cackling at me. I did not crack one stupid jest when I was your best man."

"You were too busy wondering how long it would take Henrietta's cousin Marianne to fall under your spell during the wedding breakfast," Claude said. "I have been told that she fell under it when we were all still at the church, though I did not notice myself, my attention being otherwise occupied."

"She was too plump for my taste as it turned out," Lord Francis said.

"She was too *eligible* for your tastes," his brother said. "That was the problem, Frank. Her papa all but asked you your intentions, did he not?"

"By Jove," Lord Francis said, "that was it too. It was never safe to flirt with a girl of reputation, was it?"

The two of them were in the dressing room adjoining the bedchamber where Lord Francis had spent the night. It was at the home of a neighbor of the earl's, it not being at all the thing for bride and bridegroom to spend the night before the wedding beneath the same roof or to set eyes on each other before they met at the altar. Claude had ridden over early.

"I am glad you use past tense," Claude said. "You are crying off all women except Sophia for the future, Frank?"

"Good Lord, yes," Lord Francis said. "She would make a road map of my face with her fingernails if I should take it into my head to start looking about me."

"For no other reason?" his brother asked.

Lord Francis thought a moment. "I intend to start setting up my nursery," he said. "It would be too confusing to be setting up more than one. And far too expensive."

"The same old Frank," his brother said. "One never gets a straight answer out of you. It's not that Sophia kept on pursuing you and you just got tired of running? Bertie and Dick and I were talking last night. We were a little worried."

"The chase continued until quite recently," Lord Francis said, pulling on his shoes and wincing. "Until two days ago, in fact. But the direction changed. Have you ever watched a cat deciding in the middle of a wild flight from a dog to stop and face the battle? Almost inevitably the dog takes fright and flees with the cat in hot pursuit. Let us say that I am the cat of the story. Devil take it, but these shoes must be a size too small."

His brother laughed. "Time to go, Frank," he said. "It would not do to keep the bride waiting, you know."

"Soph?" Lord Francis said. "Oh Lord, no. I would never hear the end of it. We would quarrel over it all the way to

Italy. I would far prefer to quarrel over something I knew myself in the right over."

"You aren't intending to spend your married life quarreling, I hope?" Claude said, frowning as his brother passed a hand nervously through his hair and turned to the door.

"I intend to be happy," Lord Francis said. "I shall see to it that I quarrel with Soph every day of our lives, Claude. What was that you said about cooks poisoning breakfasts? Were you serious? I hope my stomach is not going to continue this gurgling when I have it inside the church. It could be a trifle mortifying, don't you agree?"

"The poison loses its effect as soon as you clap eyes on your bride," his brother said.

"Ah." Lord Francis opened the door.

"Hold still one more minute, Sophia," Olivia said, down on her knees in the middle of her daughter's dressing room. "There, it is perfect." She sat back on her heels and looked up. "Oh, you look so very beautiful."

Sophia's wedding dress was of a very pale blue muslin; the silk sash and the embroidery at the neck, short puffed sleeves, and scalloped hem white. The housekeeper, with the assistance of one of the gardeners, had woven a posy of flowers for her hair and a smaller one to wear at her wrist. Altogether she looked exactly what she was—a young and innocent bride.

"Mama," Sophia said, her eyes wide and frightened. "Oh, Mama."

Olivia got to her feet, smiling. "We talked yesterday, Sophia," she said, "for an hour or more. You know exactly what is facing you and appeared very eager—yesterday. But a wedding day, of course, is different. There are so many conflicting emotions to be dealt with, are there not?"

"He says he loves me," Sophia said, her eyes large with tears suddenly. "He has said so over and over again in the past two days. Do you suppose he means it, Mama? One never quite knows with Francis. He always has that annoying twinkle in his eye."

"He must have been saying so for far longer than two days, Sophia," Olivia said. "And of course he must mean it. Why else would he be marrying you? He has been under no pressure, as far as I know, to find himself a bride."

"Maybe there are other reasons," Sophia said. "Maybe he felt himself trapped and decided to be gallant about the whole thing. Though it is quite unlike Francis to be gallant. Oh, Mama, what if he does not love me?"

Olivia took her hands and squeezed them. "Before you panic, Sophia," she said, "look inside yourself. Deep inside. That is where you know the truth. You know whether he loves you or not. Does he?"

Sophia looked down at their hands. "Yes," she said at last. "He does. Mama, he does." She looked up again, her eyes shining. "He loves me and I did not even suspect it until two days ago. I thought he hated me. He always used to say the most lowering things about me and about the possibility of being trapped into marrying me. But he was doing it just to have fun with me, just to goad me. He likes to see me angry. He likes to quarrel with me. He says we are going to quarrel every day for the rest of our lives. He loves me. Oh, Mama, he loves me."

"Sophia?" Olivia smiled and frowned simultaneously at this strange speech. But there was a firm tap on the dressing room door and it opened before she could say more.

"Ah," the Earl of Clifton said, "my two ladies. A haven of sanity in the middle of a madhouse. Rose is weeping already; half the children have escaped from the nursery and are playing some sort of spirited game that necessitates a great deal of running and shouting on the stairs; Claude's wife is trying to herd the children back to the nursery; Wheatley has inexplicably lost his coat; there have been no fewer than three inquiries from the stables about the exact time we want the barouche brought around; and Cynthia is reputedly having the hysterics because as bridesmaid she should be with the bride but instead has to stand still to have her hem turned up because it is too long after all. Need I continue?" He grinned.

"Papa," Sophia said. "Oh, Papa, I am so frightened."

"Well," he said, "perhaps a very little haven of sanity. What is it, Sophia?"

"It has all been so sudden," she said. "Everything has happened so fast. And now it is my wedding day before I have had a chance to think."

"The month has gone fast, has it not?" he said. "But both you and Francis were adamant that it not be delayed any longer, Sophia. Has it not been long enough?"

"But we decided to get married only two days ago," she said.

The earl and his wife exchanged glances.

"It was a pretend betrothal," Sophia said. "A counterfeit passion, Francis called it. To bring the two of you together, to give you a chance to patch up your differences. We were to put an end to everything once we had succeeded. And it worked, did it not? I will never be sorry that we did it because it worked. I was not quite sure until two mornings ago when I went into Mama's room and saw you . . ." She blushed. "Then I was finally sure. But then when I told Francis that we must call everyone together to tell them that there would be no wedding, he said that yes, we must marry because it would be too troublesome to stop all the preparations at such a late date."

"Sophia!" the earl said.

The countess merely looked at her, aghast.

"And he said he loved me," Sophia said quickly. "He said that he had planned it all from the start, that he had known all along how it would be, and that he had always planned to marry me no matter what happened with you. He said he loved me and so we decided to marry after all."

"Sophia!" the earl said again.

"And I love him, too," she continued, the color high in her cheeks. "I always worshiped him when we were younger, but I did not know that I still did so until I started to wake up at nights with my cheeks wet because I had been dreaming of our betrothal ending and of never seeing him again." She was breathless with the speed of her confession. "I would die if I never saw him again."

The earl passed a hand across the back of his neck.

"Perhaps no haven of sanity after all," he said. "I am speechless. I do not know what to say." He looked to his wife for help.

But Sophia had darted between them and had taken an arm of each, being careful not to squash the flowers at the wrist she had passed through her father's arm. "It is all like a fairy tale, is it not?" she said, looking at first one and then the other, her face alight with love and happiness. "You are together again as I have always dreamed of your being and I am about to marry the man I have loved for as far back as I can remember. And he loves me. And we are to marry in the very church where you married. And the sun is shining after all the unsettled weather of the past week or so. And . . . oh, and, and, and." She laughed excitedly.

"Yes, the three of us together again," the earl said, covering her hand with his own. "You are right, Sophia. It is a wonderful day—despite the most hair-raising scheme I have ever heard, you little minx. We are going to be having Francis pacing at the altar if we do not get moving, you know. I have a little gift for you before we leave the room."

She looked up at him expectantly.

"I had them sent especially from London," he said, "since a young lady should graduate from pearls on her wedding day."

He drew a delicate necklet of diamonds from a pocket and clasped it about her neck.

"Happy wedding day, sweetheart," he said, turning her and kissing her on the cheek.

"Oh, Papa," she said, tears in her eyes. "In many ways you will always be my very favorite man."

"You had better say your favorite *father*," he said. "That way you will not create any misunderstandings. And a small gift for you, too, Olivia." He turned his eyes to his wife. "I twisted the arm of your maid and discovered that you would be wearing green today." He looked appreciatively at the rich green of her silk dress and drew an emerald necklace from another pocket. "Do you want to wear that silver chain too?"

She looked at him mutely before fumbling with the catch

of her silver chain and removing it. He replaced it with the emeralds while she bit her lip and leaned her head forward.

"A gift for our daughter's wedding," he said, turning her by the shoulders as he had done with Sophia and kissing her on the lips while their daughter looked on, her eyes shining.

"Thank you." Olivia looked up into his eyes and fingered the emeralds at her throat. "Thank you, Marcus."

The door burst open suddenly without even the courtesy of a knock.

"Sophia," Cynthia said, her eyes as round as saucers, her dark blue dress now indisputably the perfect length. "Everyone else has left and the barouche is at the door and I could have died when I tried on my dress and found that I tripped over the hem whenever I moved and you have managed without me anyway and look even more lovely than I expected and Lord Francis is going to burst with pride when he sees you and . . ."

"And we had better not keep the horses waiting any longer," the earl said firmly. "Or the groom either."

"Oh, Cynthia," Sophia said, taking her father's arm to be led down the stairs, "I have told them. And I am so happy I could burst. And my legs feel like two columns of jelly. I do believe I am going to be sick."

The church was full. Olivia saw that as the Viscount Melville escorted her down the aisle to her seat at the front. It was also looking at its most beautiful, the sunlight glowing through the stained-glass windows, the floral decorations bringing the summertime inside. She was not sure how the church had looked at her own wedding. She had had eyes for nothing and no one except her bridegroom.

Lord Francis, looking very slim and very young and very anxious, was standing with his brother and glancing back to the doorway where Sophia would appear soon with Marc.

Sophia. She felt like crying. Her daughter was about to be married. The sole person she had had to live for for fourteen years. She was to be married. For love. Despite that strange, bizarre story she had told less than an hour before, she was marrying for love.

As she, Olivia, had married for love nineteen years before. In the same church. And suddenly the years rolled back and it was Marc standing there looking pale and nervous and then fixing his eyes on her as she approached with her father. And it was she approaching, feeling that her legs would surely not carry her one inch farther, and then focusing her eyes on the man waiting for her at the altar. Marc. The man she loved. The man she was going to spend the rest of her life loving.

Lord Francis's eyes stilled and lit up suddenly and there was a stir in the church. Olivia, getting to her feet, found herself fighting an ache in her throat and blinking her eyes. And there they were, long before she had won the fight, Sophia's face bright and glowing, seeing no one but Lord Francis. And Marc, looking broad-shouldered and calm and capable. The organ was filling the church with sound.

He sat beside her after giving away their daughter to the man who was about to become her husband. His shoulder touched hers. And she thought quite vividly, distracted from the wedding service for a moment, of what Sophia had told them in her dressing room. She had done it for them. She had betrothed herself to Francis so that they would come together and sort out their differences. And she had seen them together in bed—three mornings before, the last time they had been together—and had concluded with joy that her scheme had worked. Dear naive Sophia.

"I will," Lord Francis said.

Olivia's hand was taken suddenly in a strong clasp, and he placed their joined hands on his thigh.

"I will," Sophia said.

They squeezed each other's hand almost to breaking point. She pressed her shoulder against his arm. Someone was sniveling—doubtless Rose.

"What God has joined together," the rector was saying, "let no man put asunder."

He squeezed her hand even more tightly, if that were possible, looked down into her face, and then laid a large linen handkerchief in her free hand. She dabbed at her eyes with it.

What God has joined together, . . . She clung to his hand
. . . *let no man put asunder.*

He had kissed her at the altar—she could remember the
heat in her cheeks at his kissing her in full view of a churchful
of people. He had checked her steps as they walked down
the aisle together, preventing her from running with the
exuberance of the moment. He had forced her to smile at
all their relatives and friends beaming back at them from
the pews. And then they had stood on the steps outside the
church, shaking hands and being kissed, shaking hands and
being kissed, on and on for what had seemed like an eternity.
She could remember the bells pealing.

And then he had taken her hand and raced with her along
the twisting path of the churchyard to the waiting carriage
before anyone else could get there. And he had drawn the
curtains across the windows of the carriage and taken her
into his arms and kissed and kissed her until the carriage had
stopped outside Clifton and the coachman was coughing
outside the closed door.

Nineteen years ago. And fourteen of the years since lived
apart.

There was a stir and a murmur in the church. A smattering
of laughter. Lord Francis had his hands at Sophia's waist
and she had her face turned up eagerly for his kiss.

Olivia's hand was raised to her husband's lips and held
there for a long moment.

And then somehow they were all outside the church and
Sophia launched herself into first her mother's and then her
father's arms, looking so eager and so happy that Olivia
ached for her innocence. And then Francis was hugging her
and calling her Mama and laughing. The duchess was
weeping into a large handkerchief and uttering incoherencies
about her baby. It was the happiest day of her life, she told
anyone who cared to listen—all her babies were happily
settled.

The church bells pealed out their glad tidings.

And then Olivia's hand was being shaken and her cheek
kissed by a whole host of relatives and houseguests and
neighbors. She and her husband were being congratulated

on having produced such a beautiful bride. She realized that he had one arm tight about her shoulders and she one arm about his waist only when she found that she was shaking people's hands with her left hand.

"Yes," Marc was saying, "we are the most fortunate of parents. Aren't we, Olivia?"

"She has been the joy of our life," she said.

But suddenly there was no one else to greet, though there was still a great deal of noise and laughter and milling about.

"Francis is not as wise as I was," the earl said, looking down at his wife, his eyes twinkling. He still had an arm about her shoulders. He nodded to the roadway beyond the churchyard. "It could take them ten minutes to get away."

Francis and Sophia were in their carriage, but the door was being held open by laughing guests and flowers were being pelted inside and Richard and Claude were actually trying to unharness the horses while their brother's attention was distracted. But Francis had been to a few weddings in his time and participated in active mischief. He poked his head out of the doorway, his face wreathed in a grin, and yelled at the coachman to start and run the rascals down. He closed the door when the carriage was already in motion.

"Ah," the earl said as a hand inside the carriage pulled the curtains across the windows. He turned and smiled down at his wife.

"Oh, Marcus," she said, "can she really be all grown up, then? Is it all over already?"

Sophia was waving tearfully from the window of the carriage later the same afternoon. But there was no one to be seen any longer. The carriage had turned a bend and the house was out of sight. Her husband, she saw when she turned to look, had already settled back against the cushions. He was smiling at her.

"Tears, Soph?" he said. "You are sorry to be leaving your mama and papa?"

"We will not see them for months and months, Francis," she said, blowing her nose and putting her handkerchief away resolutely. "Perhaps not until Christmas."

"Perhaps you should stay with them," he said, "while I go to Italy alone. I can tell you all about it when I return. I'll even tell you if the Sistine Chapel is still in Rome."

She looked at him a little uncertainly. "Perhaps you would prefer to go alone," she said.

He grinned and stretched out a hand to her. "Don't make it this easy for me," he said. "And what are you doing all the way over there? Trying to create a bulge in the side of the carriage? You aren't afraid of me by any chance, are you?"

"Afraid of you?" she said. "Pooh, why should I be afraid of you?"

"Because I am your new husband, perhaps," he said. "Because we are right in the very middle of a wedding."

"We are not," she said. "The wedding is all over. And we are on our way on our wedding journey at last."

"Only the ceremony and the breakfast are over, Soph," he said, lacing his fingers with hers and trying to draw her toward him. "The rest of the wedding—the most important part—is still to come. We are not married until that part is completed, you know."

Her cheeks flamed, and she resisted the pull of his hand.

"Are you afraid?" he asked.

"Afraid?" she said with a brave attempt at scorn. "Of course not, Francis. The very idea."

"Shall I tell you what I am going to do to you tonight?" he said. "Would it make it easier if you knew what was in store?"

"I know," she said quickly. "And I don't want you to say a word. You want to do it only to embarrass me."

"Not a word?" he said. "This sounds distinctly promising. Shall I show you, then, Soph? A sort of rehearsal in the carriage?"

"Don't touch me!" she said.

"Er," he said, "why are you clinging to my hand, Soph, if I am not to touch you?"

"Francis," she said, "don't do this. Let us quarrel tomorrow, shall we? But not today. Today I do not feel up to it."

He chuckled and leaned across the carriage, taking her by surprise by scooping her up into his arms and depositing her on his lap.

"Admit that you are afraid," he said, "and I will have mercy on you, Soph."

"Never," she said. "I have never been afraid of you even when you made me climb that tree because there were wild dogs loose and then went for help so that you could hide in the bushes and bark. I was not afraid."

"Soph," he said, tucking her comfortably against him, "did I do that to you?"

"Yes, you did," she said, burrowing her head against his shoulder. "But I was not afraid, Francis. And I am not afraid now."

"I can't tease you any longer, then," he said. "What a dull journey this is going to be."

"But is it not dreadfully embarrassing?" she said, hiding her face against him. "I think it must be. I shall die of embarrassment."

"Not before I will," he said. "In fact, Soph, I can hardly contain my trembles even now." He shook, convulsively. "I shall be sure to extinguish every light tonight and draw every curtain, including the ones around the bed so that you will not see my blushes. It is the most embarrassing thing ever imagined. We might both not survive it. Indeed . . ."

Sophia punched him sharply on his free shoulder. "Don't make fun of me," she said. "You have no sensibility at all. You are quite horrid and I hate you."

"This is better," he said. "Perhaps I am going to enjoy the journey after all."

"You have done nothing but laugh at me ever since we drove off," she said. "I wish I had not let you talk me into this three days ago. I wish I had held firm. You are horrid, Francis, and I wish heartily I had not married you."

"Kiss me," he said.

"I am not going to kiss you," she said. "Ever. I hate you. I would rather kiss a toad. I would rather kiss a . . ."

"Snake," he said. "Kiss me."

" . . . rat. No."

"Kiss me, Soph," he said softly. "Kiss me, my wife."

"I am, aren't I?" she said.

"Almost, yes." He rubbed his nose against hers. "Kiss me."

She kissed him.

16

After the newlyweds had been waved on their way late in the afternoon, the guests from the neighborhood began to order their carriages brought around and took their leave. The duke and duchess withdrew to their private apartments with their family for an hour's breather, as the duke put it, before dinner and the informal dancing that was to follow it in the drawing room. The other houseguests, too, withdrew to some private and quiet activity, all the excitement of the wedding breakfast at an end.

Olivia abandoned everyone and fled to the hidden garden. It had been such a turmoil of a day, she thought, closing the wooden door gratefully behind her. She desperately needed some peace. And it was there waiting for her, the air inside the rose-draped walls and the surrounding trees of the wood still and heavy with summer, the only sounds the chirping of birds and the droning of unseen insects.

She felt heavy with desolation. Sophia was gone and would be gone for several months. And even when she returned, she would no longer be living at Rushton but in the home of her new husband. There would be only the occasional visit to look forward to.

She sat on her favorite stone in one of the rock gardens and feasted her eyes on the flowers all about her. She breathed in their scents. She felt guilty about being depressed on Sophia's wedding day. Despite the girl's confession of the morning, she had been brilliantly happy and very obviously was deeply in love with Francis. And he with her. They would be happy together. She hoped. Oh, she hoped. It made her nervous to see a bride and groom too deeply in love, especially when the bride was her own daughter.

But it was for herself she felt depressed, Olivia realized. Everything seemed at an end. Her marriage had ended long

190

ago. Now Sophia was gone. And there was Marc to leave all over again the next day. Endings. All endings. No beginnings. And yet she was only thirty-six years old.

No beginnings. Unless . . . But it could not be. Not now. Not at her age. Not when they had tried without success for all those years after Sophia was born until they separated. It would be too ironic. And too bizarre. She had a married daughter who might herself expect to be a mother within a year.

And yet, she thought, clasping her knees and noticing the daisies dotting the lawns, despite a mower's frequent care, it was not impossible. They had been together four times on three different occasions. And she was several days late. She was never late.

She set her forehead on her knees and closed her eyes. She must not begin to panic. It would be foolish when there was no way yet of being in any way certain. Nor must she begin to hope. It would be foolish to invite all the corresponding disappointment when she discovered—as she surely would within the next few days—that it was not so.

She must not begin to hope, she told herself. She must not begin to hope that there would after all be something—*someone*—to fill the emptiness. Some part of him to keep close to herself for a while longer.

She was in the same position, drowsy, almost sleeping when he came. She had been expecting him, she realized when she heard the latch of the door. He would have known where she had come, and he would have come there himself to say good-bye. Tomorrow's farewell would be public. Not that it would not have been better to keep it so, of course, but she had known he would come.

"Olivia," he said when she lifted her head from her knees. He was walking toward her. "They were happy, were they not? We did the right thing not to try to persuade her to cry off after she had told us the truth this morning?"

"They were happy," she said. "I don't believe there can be any doubt of that, Marcus. She glowed. And he was looking at her with every bit as much pride as we were. And with every bit as much love too, I am sure."

"It hurts to lose a daughter, doesn't it?" he said. "Almost as if we really have lost her."

"Rushton will never be her home again," she said. "Or Clifton either."

"And yet," he said, "it feels wrong to be dejected."

"Yes."

"She is happy and all we have ever wanted for her is happiness."

"Yes."

"Olivia," he said, "she did it for us. To bring us together."

"Yes."

"And young Francis saw his chance and agreed to the foolish scheme," he said.

She laid her forehead back against her knees. She felt rather than saw that he came closer and set one foot up on a stone close to her, as he had done on a previous occasion.

"She thought she had succeeded," he said. "She saw us together. She had come into your room for something but only I was awake. She drew what seemed to her the only conclusion."

"Poor Sophia."

"You are still planning to leave with Emma and Clarence tomorrow?" he asked.

"Yes," she said. "I have a craving to get my life back to normal again."

"You would not like to stay awhile?" he asked. "To relax here?"

"I cannot relax here, Marcus," she said.

He said nothing for a while. "Do you have any regrets, Olivia?" he asked. "If you could go back, would you do anything differently? Would you perhaps forgive me—if you could go back?"

She looked up after a long silence. "I forgave you long before you stopped asking," she said. "I knew that you had given in to a momentary weakness and that you were truly sorry. But I could not just continue on as if nothing had happened, Marcus. I did not believe I could love you as dearly as I always had or trust you as implicitly or be as close a friend to you. Everything was spoiled and I did not see how it was to be put right again.''

"And now it is very much too late," he said. "We have grown whole worlds apart with only some appetite and perhaps a little affection left for each other. You have Clarence. It is too late, Olivia. Isn't it?''

She put her head back down again. And he had his Mary. "Yes," she said. "Fourteen years too late. We both made a dreadful mistake, and now it is too late.''

She thought of Lady Mornington, the small rather plain woman who had been his mistress for six years. The woman who had looked sensible and intelligent, an altogether suitable companion for Marc. Yes, it was too late. She had voluntarily given up her rights as his wife and now had no right even to try to burden him with a dilemma. He had known peace with his Mary, he had said.

"Yes, it is too late," she said again.

"He is a good man," he said. "Almost worthy of you, I think. I always wondered why he showed no particular inclination to marry. I did not see that he loved you too. But his devotion has been rewarded. You are happy with him, Olivia?''

She swallowed, tried to frame an answer, and said nothing. He would feel guilty, perhaps, if he knew the truth, guilty about his own liaison. And she no longer wanted him to feel guilt. She had burdened him with more than his fair share years before.

His hand touched the back of her head lightly and briefly. "I wish I could set you free for him, Olivia," he said. "But there would be too much scandal, for the fault would have to appear to be yours.''

"I would not want Sophia to be the daughter of divorced parents," she said.

"No." He lifted his hand. "And I do not want any more bitterness between us, Olivia. There has been enough. We will spend Christmas together, if Sophia and Francis are home from Italy?''

"Perhaps they will go to William and Rose," she said, looking up once again.

"Sophia will want to be with us," he said.

"We must wait and see," she said. "But yes, if she wishes it, Marcus."

He smiled and touched her cheek with the back of his fingers. "Perhaps we will be grandparents before a year has passed," he said.

"Yes." She swallowed.

"I would like that," he said. "To have a child in the family again. It does not seem long since Sophia was a baby, does it?"

"People used to laugh at us and think us very eccentric," she said, smiling, "because we would never leave her in the nursery with her nurse but spent almost all our days with her."

"And nights, too," he said. "The little rascal would never sleep, do you remember? I think I wore a hole in the carpet of the nursery, walking back and forth with her for hours on end."

"You were always good with her," she said. "My energy used to give out and you used to order me off to bed."

"And Nurse was snoring in her bed," he said with a laugh.

"Oh, Marcus," she said, "they were good times."

"Yes," he said, "they were. Perhaps we will be able to recapture some of the pleasure with our grandchildren, Olivia. Though the thought is absurd. You a grandmother? You are only thirty-six years old and look years younger."

She smiled fleetingly.

"Well," he said, "that is all in the future. Perhaps far in the future. Tomorrow you have a long and tedious journey to face. Do you have everything you need, Olivia?"

"I will have Emma and Clarence to keep me company," she said.

"Yes, of course," he said. "And at Rushton? You are comfortable there? Should I increase your allowance?"

"No," she said. "It is already over-generous."

"Well then," he said. "Everything seems to be settled."

"Yes." She smiled at him. "Almost everyone is leaving tomorrow, Marcus? And William and Rose the next day? You will be glad of quietness again."

"I shall leave for London without delay," he said.

Ah, yes. Lady Mornington. Olivia found herself fighting tears.

"It will be time for me too to get my life back to normal," he said.

Yes. She held her smile.

He set one hand on her shoulder and squeezed it tightly enough to hurt. "I am sorry for what has happened here between us, Olivia," he said. "Sorry if you found it distressing or distasteful. I ought not to have forced myself on you merely because you are still legally my wife."

"You did not use force," she said. "But I am sorry, too. It feels almost like being unfaithful, does it not?"

He squeezed her shoulder again and turned to walk back across the small garden. She watched him go. He stopped with his hand on the latch of the door and looked back over his shoulder.

"Olivia," he said, "I did love you, you know."

Did. *I did love you.* She stared at the door long after he had gone and long after tears had blurred her vision.

Did. Past tense. All over and gone. All endings. It was too late for them now. Very much too late. It was what he had said and what she had agreed to. Doors closing everywhere. None opening.

She dared not hope for the one glorious beginning that might yet compensate for all the other endings.

She dared not hope.

And yet she could not stop herself from hoping.

He had avoided Clarence as much as he possibly could during his stay. They had once been the best of friends. And he could still not see any reason for not liking the man. He was amiable, courteous, always willing to fall in with whatever activity suited other people. But how could they still be friends?

Was it possible, the Earl of Clifton wondered, to be friendly with the lover of the wife one still loved? And yet he could not blame either her for taking a lover or him for loving her. She had chosen wisely and well. Clarence had always been devoted to her. He could see that now, looking back. And faithful too. They had been friends for longer than the fourteen years. And lovers for probably many years. He did not know for sure. They must always have been very discreet. He had never heard a whisper of scandal concerning them.

He had been avoiding Clarence. But seeing him strolling alone from the direction of the stables, he paused and then redirected his steps so that they would meet.

"You have been out riding?" he asked.

"No, no," Clarence said. "Just checking for myself to see that my horses will be ready for the journey tomorrow. Most of the people at the house seem to be resting."

"It was good of you to come so far," the earl said. "I appreciate it, Clarence."

"How could I resist an invitation to Sophia's wedding?" Clarence said. "I have always thought of her as a type of niece."

"It has been good for Olivia to have you and Emma here," the earl said. "And it will make my mind easier to know that she will have your company for the return journey."

"We will be making an early start," Clarence said.

"Clarence." The earl spoke impulsively. They both stopped walking. "Look after her."

"I shall fight off any highwaymen with two guns blazing," Clarence said with a grin. "And Emma will send them fleeing with her tongue. Have no fear."

"That is not what I meant," the earl said. "I meant look after her for the rest of your life."

Clarence's eyebrows rose. "What?" he said.

"I don't think we need to keep up this civilized pretense," the earl said. "I may not have lived with her for many years, Clarence, and I may have had other women while she has had another man, but I still care for her, you know. I want her to be happy."

Clarence pursed his lips. "This other man being me?" he asked. "Is that what Olivia has told you, Marcus?"

"I am sorry I mentioned it," the earl said, "since I seem to have caused you some embarrassment. I suppose it is difficult to discuss openly such a matter with the husband of your mistress and your former friend to boot. I just . . . Well, never mind.''

"What has she told you?'' Clarence asked. "How long we have been lovers? How frequently we indulge our amours? Where? What degree of satisfaction . . .''

Lord Clifton's fist caught him a left hook to the chin at that moment and he fell awkwardly. The earl stood, feet apart, his fists clenched, waiting for the fight he fully expected. Clarence propped himself on one elbow and felt his jaw gingerly.

"I don't believe it is quite dislocated,'' he said. "You might have warned me to defend myself, Marcus.''

The earl's shoulders slumped suddenly and he reached down a hand to help his former friend to his feet.

"Devil take it, Clarence,'' he said. "Forgive me, will you?''

"You are a fool,'' Clarence said, accepting the offered hand and getting to his feet, still feeling his jaw. "You still love her, don't you? And yet you are going to let her go home tomorrow—with me.''

"I'll not impose myself where I am not wanted,'' the earl said. "I never did, Clarence, and I have not changed. I will not interfere with her freedom, either, despite that facer I just planted you. I just want to make sure that you will be good to her. But then there is nothing I can do to ensure that, is there?''

"Olivia is very dear to me,'' Clarence said, "and I will do all in my power to be good to her, as you put it, Marcus. More than that I cannot say. I don't know what she has said to you. But you are a fool for all that. If I had ever had the sort of happy and secure relationship that the two of you used to have, I would have fought heaven and earth to keep it. And public opinion and the law of the land, too, if necessary,'' he added quietly.

"Well,'' the earl said, "we had better return to the house. My guests are going to have regained their energy soon and will be ready to resume the festivities. Do you think my daughter made a good match? Olivia and I are pleased despite

early misgivings. Young Sutton has been something of a
hellion since coming down from university. But he appears
to care for Sophia.''

They walked back to the house together.

Claude and Richard and their wives and children were also
leaving early the following morning. The terrace before the
house seemed crowded with carriages and even more
crowded with people. There was noise and laughter and the
shrieks of children. And tears.

"Olivia, my dear,'' the duchess said, folding her friend
in her arms when she was able to tear herself away from
her children and grandchildren for a moment, "how
wonderful to have seen you again and to have this connection
of marriage between our two families. We must not let it
go so long again. Perhaps within nine months we will share
a grandchild.''

Olivia hugged her in return while the duke was shaking
Emma heartily by the hand and assuring her that he had been
charmed to have had a chance to converse with such a
sensible lady. Clarence and Marcus were taking their leave
of Francis's brothers and their families.

And there were her mother and father to hug and kiss, and
more tears to be shed.

The horses were snorting and stamping in the chill morning
air. The coachmen were stamping their feet and were very
obviously eager to be on their way. Servants and trunks were
already loaded into the accompanying carriages.

The duke hugged Olivia. "It has been wonderful to see
you again and in such good looks, Olivia," he said. "I hope
it will not be so long until the next time, my dear.''

The children were inside the carriages with Richard's wife.
Claude was handing in his own wife. Emma was already
seated in their carriage, and Clarence waiting beside the door.
Marcus was shaking Richard's hand.

Olivia felt panic clutch at her stomach. She turned hastily
and reached out a hand for Clarence's.

"Olivia," a voice said from behind her and she turned
back again. "Have a good journey.''

His hand closed about hers, warm and firm. Such a strange formal gesture. Such formal words. She had expected him all the night before, although she had known it would have made no sense at all for him to come. Not after their words in the hidden garden. But she had expected him. She had wanted him desperately. She had even got out of bed at some time during the night, determined to go to him herself. But she had got no farther than the door into her dressing room. As soon as all his guests had left, including herself, he was to return to London. To Lady Mornington.

"Yes," she said. "Thank you."

"Good-bye, then," he said.

"Good-bye, Marcus."

There was a moment when perhaps they swayed a little toward each other. Perhaps not. Perhaps it had been in her imagination. And then his hold on her hand shifted so that he could help her into the carriage. Clarence came in behind her and seated himself opposite. Both he and Emma studied the formal garden beyond the far window.

"Good-bye," he said again, and he stood back so that a footman could close the door firmly.

The coachman must already have been in his place. The carriage began to move almost immediately. She looked at Marcus once through the window and felt panic grab at her again. She clenched her hands hard in her lap so that she would not throw the door open and hurl herself from the carriage.

Good-bye, Marc. She leaned back against the cushions, closed her eyes, and fought the sharp pain in her throat.

"Olivia," Emma said. "Why are you being so foolish? For a lady of remarkable good sense, you have always been most foolish in your marriage. What on earth are you doing here with Clarence and me?"

"Not now, Emma," Clarence said. "Your timing is disastrous. Change places with me, if you please?"

A few moments later Olivia found her hand in her friend's reassuring large one.

"I hope that it is not your favorite coat, Clarence," she said, her voice ominously calm. "It is going to be soaked."

"I shall squeeze out the excess moisture when you are finished," he said, "and it will be as good as new again."

She laughed shakily. And then she turned her head, buried her face against his sleeve, and cried and cried.

"Oh, dear," Emma said. "Is there nothing we can do, Clarence? Would it help if we turned back? I always feel so helpless when it comes to affairs of the heart."

"We could converse about the weather," he said. "That would help, I believe, Emma. That topic invariably leads on to others."

The Duke and Duchess of Weymouth left early the following morning. The Earl of Clifton was on the road for London just one hour later. He could not have stayed longer at Clifton if his life had depended upon it, he thought.

He had gone to the hidden garden after she had left the day before, and sat for an hour or more on the stone where she had always liked to sit. But although the sun shone and the birds sang and the flowers bloomed, there was no peace to be had there. She was gone. Her absence from the garden—and from his life—was like a tangible thing.

He had been horribly reminded of what his life had been like for a year and more after he had left her.

During the night, unable to sleep, he had wandered into her bedchamber, sat down on her side of the bed, and laid a hand on her pillow. But she was gone. Irrevocably gone. He had counted the months to Christmas—almost five. An eternity. Would Sophia and Francis be back by then or would they extend their travels on the Continent? And would she come even if they were home? Would there perhaps be some excuse for not coming? Winter weather? Bad roads?

He had wondered if he would ever see her again.

And finally and foolishly, he had lain down on her bed, his head on her pillow, and slept.

He was going to spend the rest of the summer and the autumn and winter in London, he had decided. Perhaps he would go to Brighton for a week or two if the weather remained warm. It did not matter where he went as long as he did not have to remain in Clifton.

He had a visit to make in London, one that he would really rather not have made at all. But it had been no casual acquaintance. It had lasted for six years. And Mary was his friend. No more than that, in fact. But he had to end the whole relationship. Because she had been such a close friend, somehow the relationship now seemed adulterous to him.

Perhaps it was foolish to end a good friendship when he might possibly never even see Olivia again. End it he must, though. But he could not just drop her without a word. He had to explain to her. She would understand. She knew that he loved Olivia, just as he knew that she still grieved for her dead husband.

Life might be altogether less complicated, he thought, if he loved Mary instead of his wife. If she really were his mistress.

17

He had three letters from her before he saw her again.

The first came two weeks after his arrival in London. It had been to Clifton Court first. It was a short, strange letter, and left him wondering what her motive had been in writing it. Why had she not simply told him face to face?

"I want you to know," she had written, "that Clarence is not my lover and never has been. I have never had any lover but you. Clarence is my friend, as you have always known and as I told you. He is my friend. There has never been even a suggestion of anything else between us."

That was all, apart from a polite inquiry after his health and the expressed hope that they would hear from Sophia soon.

Was it true? the earl asked himself. But of course it was true if Livy said it. There could be no doubt about that.

Did she want him back? Was she trying to clear the path for his return? Was that why she had written? It was his immediate and first hope. Or perhaps it was just that Clarence had complained to her and embarrassed her and she thought it time to clear up the misunderstanding.

Or perhaps she wished to remind him once more that the responsibility for the breakup of their marriage was entirely his. She had remained faithful, if unforgiving.

But not entirely unforgiving. She had told him that she had forgiven him even before he had stopped asking. But she had considered it impossible to continue with their marriage. All had been spoiled, she had said. And it was far too late for them anyway to try to pick up the threads of a relationship that had lapsed fourteen years before. She had said that too.

No, there was no room for hope. No point in writing back to her to tell the truth of his relationship with Mary. For though he had never lain with Mary, he had lain with other women. He put the letter away with all the other letters he had received from her over the years, most of them concerning some problem with Sophia or some estate business. Never anything personal. But he had kept them all anyway.

The second letter came soon before Christmas. Sophia and Francis had still not returned from Italy. They were to spend the holiday in Naples, they had written. They expected to be home by spring. The earl had written to his wife that he hoped she would accept the invitation to spend Christmas with William and Rose and their family. He could assure her that Rose was particularly eager to see her now that there was the connection of marriage between their families.

She wrote back to say that she would be unable to go. She had already made her excuses to Rose, she had said. She was recovering from a chill and did not feel it wise to travel. Besides, she had other commitments for the holiday. She wished him a happy Christmas.

He wrote again, asking about her health, but she did not reply. He considered going to her but did not do so. She had made it plain as she possibly could without being openly offensive that she did not wish to see him again and would do so only when it became necessary for the sake of their daughter's happiness. She would not thank him for arriving on her doorstep to express his anxiety over a long-cured chill.

He spent Christmas with the duke and duchess's family and several other houseguests and felt lonelier than he had ever felt in his life.

The third letter came early in April, just after Sophia and Francis had returned from the Continent and taken up temporary residence in London. Sophia had known, of course, from letters that had reached her from home, that they were still living apart, but it was evident that she had not given up hope. Perhaps Mama would come to London for part of the Season, she had suggested. She could even stay with them if she wished, instead of with Papa. The four of them could go about together.

She had written to persuade her mother to come. And he had written to tell her that Sophia was glowing with health and happiness and young Francis was still doting on her. But it would mean a great deal, he had written, if she would consent to spend a few weeks in town so that they could all be together on a few occasions.

She could not come, she wrote back. He let the letter fall into his lap and read no more for a while. So much for a hope that he had always known to be unreasonable. And so much for a promise she had made to spend some time with him when Sophia should return.

She was made of marble, he thought with a wave of unaccustomed anger against her. She was quite implacable in her contempt of him and what he stood for. She would not come. So. He would never see her again. He might as well drown himself in liquor and go on a tour of all of London's whorehouses that night. He might as well . . . He picked up the letter wearily and read on.

"It is not a recurrence of the chill," she wrote. "There never was a chill. I could not bring myself to tell you the real reason. I find it difficult now. But you have a right to know. I should have told you a long time ago. I will be delivering a child some time this month. Of course, a journey to London is out of the question.

"I would like to see Sophia if she would care to come here and miss the beginning of the Season. Will she be embarrassed to have a sister or brother so much younger than herself, I wonder? You need not feel obliged to come, Marcus. Nor need you feel guilty. I want this child more than I have wanted anything for a long, long while. And I have been in good health. I shall inform you of the event as soon as my confinement is over."

The Earl of Clifton got to his feet with such haste that his chair crashed to the floor behind him.

The air felt good. After three days of rain, the sun was shining again and there was the smell of fresh vegetation. Spring had come late. There were still some daffodils blooming, and the tulips and the other late-spring flowers were coming into their own. The trees had all budded into new leaf.

It felt good to be strolling outside in her favorite part of the garden beside the house. It had always been called the rose arbor, though at present it was filled with spring flowers. The roses would not bloom until later.

She sat down slowly on a wrought-iron seat. She felt as if she had just walked five miles instead of the short distance from the house. The baby had dropped, although there were still two weeks to the expected birth date. It was a little easier to breathe, but it was difficult to walk. And difficult to sit, too, she thought ruefully.

Indeed, she had been feeling quite out of sorts all day. Hot and restless with alternating spells of listlessness and nervous energy. She could not recall having felt quite so huge and heavy with Sophia. But of course, that had been almost nineteen years before. It was not surprising that she did not remember. And she was also nineteen years older than she had been then.

Would Sophia come? she wondered. And perhaps Francis too? She hoped so. She wanted to see them. She wanted to assure herself that what Marc had written about them was true. And she wanted Sophia close to her again. She had been almost nine months without any family. An unborn baby, she thought, spreading one hand over her bulk, did not quite qualify as family capable of keeping her company.

It was going to be a boy, Mrs. Oliver, the housekeeper had predicted. She could always tell from the way it carried. And she claimed she was almost always right.

Olivia hoped Sophia would come.

And she hoped that Marc would not come. She could not bear to see him. Not now. She needed tranquility in her life for the next few weeks. She hoped he would not feel obliged to come.

She could hear the sound of horses far down the drive. It sounded like more than one. Clarence usually rode over. Perhaps it was Emma, she thought, or the rector's wife. She had promised to call one afternoon during the week. Perhaps it was Sophia. But no. Her letter would not have reached London more than a day or two before. There would have been no time for Sophia to come.

It was a curricle, she saw as the vehicle came into sight. She stood up to watch it. Whom did she know with a curricle? There was no one in the neighborhood. It must be someone come from a distance.

Marc?

But no, it could not be Marc. There would not have been the time for arrangements to be made for a journey and the journey accomplished.

She drew her shawl closer about her shoulders and spread both hands protectively over her unborn baby.

It was Marc. She knew it long before she could see the driver clearly and despite the improbability that it was he. Her thudding heart and the blood pounding at her temples told her that it was he. But she could neither run to him nor away from him. She stood quite still.

It was Marc. And he had seen her. He was signaling to a couple of grooms who had appeared at the gateway of the stableyard to see who was approaching. He jumped down from the high seat, leaving both curricle and horses to their care.

It was Marc. Her baby moved violently inside her. He had flung his hat onto the seat of the curricle. She had forgotten his silvering hair. She had forgotten how attractive it looked.

She was standing in the middle of the rose arbor, a woolen shawl drawn over a flimsy, loose-fitting dress. She was enormous with child and quite pale and quite impossibly beautiful. He did not even look behind him to see if the two grooms he had signaled were coming to take his horses. He strode toward her.

"Livy," he said, reaching out his hands to take the hands she had stretched out to him. "My God. Oh, my God." Her hands were cold. He squeezed them tightly.

"Marc," she said, "why did you come? Oh, why? I have been hoping and hoping that you would not."

"Have you?" he said, and he could feel his jaw tightening. "You did not think I would be interested in the birth of my own child? You did not think I would consider it important enough that I need be informed before now?"

"Yes," she said, "I knew you would be interested. It

might be a son. Perhaps you will have an heir long after you must have given up all hope of having one.''

''And perhaps it will be a daughter,'' he said. ''Either way it will be a child of my own body. And of yours. You had no right to keep it from me this long. No right at all.'' All the shock and anxiety and love that had sustained him on his journey were converted suddenly and unexpectedly to anger. He had committed one wrong long ago in the past, and ever since she had made him into a monster of depravity and insensitivity.

She withdrew her hands. He had come because of the baby. Of course. It would be his only reason for coming. She had known that. It was why she had not wanted him to come. And yes, it had been spiteful to make those remarks about a son and heir. He would love the child if it were a girl, just as he had loved Sophia. He would want to share the child as he had shared Sophia. But it was her child. This time she had done all the suffering alone.

''This is my child,'' she said. ''All mine. You shall have no part of this child. You have not been here.''

''I was there at the start,'' he said harshly. ''I will not satisfy you, you see, by suspecting you with someone else. No child can be yours alone, Livy. The child is ours. And I would have been here ever since the start if you had only said the word. You know that.''

''No, I do not,'' she cried. ''You could not wait to return to London and your whore.''

''Mary is not a whore,'' he said, ''and never was my mistress either. And you know you are being unfair. I wanted you to stay longer, if you will recall. Or have you forgotten that detail? Does it not fit your image of me as a compulsive womanizer and therefore must be suppressed from your memory?''

''I don't want to argue with you,'' she said, turning away from him. ''I don't want you here.''

''What is it?'' he asked when she stopped abruptly.

''Nothing,'' she said, taking a deep breath. ''The baby moved. It is low and awkward.''

He reached out and touched her shoulder. She was heavy

and awkward with his child. He felt an ache at the back of his throat. "How have you been, Livy?" he asked. "Has it been a difficult confinement?"

"Because I am thirty-seven years old?" she asked him. "No, I am still capable of bearing, Marcus. I must return to the house. I need to sit down in a proper chair."

She was being deliberately nasty and spiteful. She realized that, but she could not seem to help herself. It was either that or cast herself into his arms weeping. She would not show him that she needed him, that she had longed for him every moment of every day and night since she had returned from Clifton the summer before. He had come because of the baby. He had left Lady Mornington so that he might have a new child to go back and boast about. Had he told the truth about her? She frowned.

"Let me help you," he said.

His arm was so much firmer than Clarence's. So much easier to lean on. But the distance to the house suddenly seemed a formidable one.

"What is it?" he asked when she stopped.

"More movement," she said. "I need to get back to the house. I have not been feeling well today."

"And you have no one to insist that you stay indoors when you are feeling so?" he asked. "You will have me from now on."

"There are two weeks to go," she said. "Sophia was late. Perhaps this child will be too. It could be a month. You will miss part of the Season if you stay. There will be no need to do so. I shall let you know immediately."

"You might as well save your breath for the walk," he said. "This is my home too, if you will remember, Livy. This is where I plan to be living for some time to come."

"I don't want you here," she said.

"Don't you?" he said. "Too bad."

"I was hoping that Sophia would come," she said.

"I sent a note around," he said, "but I did not wait long enough for a reply. I had the sudden and strange urge to visit my wife. For all I know they may be on my heels. What is it?" She had stopped walking again and was drawing a deep breath instead of setting a foot on the bottom step leading up to the house.

"I think," she said, "that this baby is not going to wait another two weeks. I think it is going to be born much sooner than that."

There were more servants than usual in the hall, all of them curious to see the master they had either never seen or not seen for many years. The front doors were open. There were certainly enough servants present to answer the earl's roar for attention. Soon one was scurrying for My Lady's maid, another for Mrs. Oliver, and a third for the doctor. The remaining ones gawked as My Lord swept his very pregnant wife up into his arms as if she weighed no more than a feather and half ran up the stairs with her.

She could not lie down. The pains were more severe and more frightening when she tried to lie down and rest between times. She should try to lie on her side, her maid told her. She should bring her knees up to cushion the pain, Mrs. Oliver advised. She should pile the pillows beneath her head so that she was not so flat, the doctor said.

They might all go hang, the earl said, and leave his wife to do what was most comfortable for her. And no, damn it, he would not leave the room. His wife was about to have his child and he would damned well stay in the room if he damned well pleased.

He apologized to the ladies for his language when his wife relaxed after a particularly lengthy contraction, but refused to change his mind.

"Lean against me, Livy," he said, "when the pain comes again. Perhaps it will help."

And so when her indrawn breath signaled the onslaught of another bout of pain, he got behind her at the side of the bed and stood firm while she pressed back against him and arched her head back onto his shoulder.

"It helps?" he asked when she relaxed again.

"Yes," she said.

Her maid had disappeared. The doctor and Mrs. Oliver

were deep in low conversation at the other side of the room—probably some conspiracy to get rid of him, the earl thought.

"Livy," he said. "I came because of you, you know. Not because of the baby."

She was sitting upright again, her head dropped forward. Her eyes were closed.

"The child was begotten in love," he said. "At least on my part. I love you. I always have and I always will. About that at least, I have always remained steadfast."

She lifted her head and drew a deep breath and he took her against him again and stood firm as she grappled with her pain. She stayed against him when it had passed.

"I have never been as much of a womanizer as you seem to think," he said. "There was someone for a year after you made it clear that there could be no reconciliation between us. And a few since for brief spells. And there was Mary for six years—my friend, as Clarence has been yours, Livy. But I broke off with her immediately after Sophia's wedding, nevertheless. I knew there could be no one but you, even if you would never have me back."

"Marc," she said, "you do not need to say these things."

"Yes, I do," he said. "I know you have a low opinion of me, Livy. But you must have consoled yourself while Sophia grew up with the knowledge that my fall from grace came several years after her conception and birth. I think you need to know that this child too is not the child of a total degenerate."

"Marc," she said. But she drew in a sharp breath and pressed her head back into his shoulder. "Oh," she said when it was finally over. "It hurts. It hurts, Marc."

"Oh, God," he said. "If only I could do this for you."

She laughed softly.

"I love you, Livy," he said. "For the child's sake I want you to know that. I have always loved you. And I have been faithful to you since its conception. It broke my heart when you left last summer and I have longed for you every day since. I want you to know that for the child's sake, not to make you feel uncomfortable."

"Uncomfortable," she said. "It is so hot in here. Open a window, Marc."

"They are all open," he said. He raised his voice. "A cool cloth, Mrs. Oliver. Hand it to me. Her ladyship is feeling uncomfortably warm."

It was a long labor. The doctor took himself off to sleep in another room in the house some time after dark. Some time after midnight, the countess's maid replaced Mrs. Oliver at her vigil. The earl refused to leave. If he moved from the bedside in order to wet the cloth afresh or sip some water, his wife would cry out in panic for him when another wave of pain assaulted her. She had become dependent upon the warmth and firmness of his body at her back.

Daylight came before she finally felt the urge to push and her maid went flying off to rouse the doctor.

"Take my strength, Livy," her husband murmured against her hot temple during an ever-shortening interval between pains. "I wish I could give it all to you, darling."

"Marc," she said. "Marc. Ahhh!"

He held her by the shoulders, willing his strength to flow into her.

He had paced belowstairs during the long hours of her delivery of Sophia. The time had been endless, and he had seen in her face afterward that the birthing had not been easy for her. But he had had no idea of what a woman must suffer to bring a man's child into the world. He would have died for her if he could, to save her one more moment of pain. But he could do nothing for her but stand and hold her and bathe her face between pains and remember the pleasure it had given him to plunge his seed into her.

Even after the doctor came back to the bedchamber and persuaded her to lie down at last and position herself for the birthing, it was not over and not easy. It terrified Marc to see her use more energy, at the end of hours and hours of the weakening pains than he had ever used during a hard day's work.

My God, he thought, as he helped Mrs. Oliver for surely the dozenth time to lift her shoulders from the bed as she bore down to release herself of her burden. My God!

Both the housekeeper and the doctor had given up long before trying to make him leave as any proper husband would do. He had been an improper husband for long enough, he thought. Why change now?

And then she bore down and did not stop, only letting out her breath with a whoosh two or three times before gasping it in again. And he watched in wonder and awe as his son was born. He was sobbing, he realized as he lowered his wife back to her pillows, and he did not care who saw it.

"We have a son, Livy," he said. "A son."

And the baby was crying and being set, all blood streaked, on his mother's breast as Mrs. Oliver wiped at his back with a cloth.

"Oh," Olivia said. "Oh." She touched him, smoothed a hand over his head, touched his cheek with light fingers. "Look at him, Marc. Oh, look at him."

And then Mrs. Oliver was taking the baby away to clean him and the doctor was coughing and suggesting that his lordship leave the room while he finished with her ladyship.

The earl straightened up and dried his eyes with a handkerchief. But she turned her head and smiled radiantly up at him before he could turn away.

"We have a son, Marc," she said, reaching up one weak hand, which he took in a firm grasp. "We have a son."

He raised her hand to his lips and laid it against his cheek. "Thank you, Livy," he said. "I love you."

The doctor coughed again.

18

Everything looked remarkably the same after almost fifteen years. It was true that downstairs she had made some changes. The draperies and carpets and some of the furniture had been changed. He remembered her writing for permission and funds to make the changes. But the park he was looking at through a window was much the same. There had never been formal gardens at Rushton; only the kitchen gardens and the greenhouses behind the house and the rose arbor to the west. The room behind him, his bedchamber, had not been changed at all. Some of the belongings he had left behind were still in the drawers.

He had slept for five hours and bathed and shaved and felt much refreshed, though he was still feeling somewhat light-headed at the knowledge that he had a son. Just three days before, he had not even known that Livy was with child. And now he had a son. And he was at Rushton again, looking out at the familiar park, his wife and child in the next room, presumably asleep since he had left instructions that he was to be called when she awoke.

Had she named the child yet? he wondered. What would she name him? Jonathan? That was the name they had picked for a boy before Sophia had been born. But that was a long time ago. It was still nearly impossible to believe that he was almost forty-one, Livy thirty-seven, that they had been estranged for close to fifteen years, had been together briefly the summer before, and now had a newborn son. A son born that very morning.

He had been absently watching the approach of a vehicle along the driveway. It gradually revealed itself to be a traveling carriage belonging to Lord Francis Sutton. They had had his note, he thought with some relief, turning away from the window and hurrying to the door. And they had traveled at a pace almost as furious as his.

He met them outside the house. Francis, vaulting out of the carriage even before the steps were lowered, flashed him a grin over his shoulder.

"Here she comes," he said as Sophia hurried into his arms, was lowered to the ground, and raced toward her father. "If I had allowed her to run instead of riding in the carriage, she would have run. Wouldn't you, Soph?"

"Papa," she cried, her face flushed and anxious. "Is it true? I could not believe it, though Francis said that there could be no doubt about it since you have such neat handwriting and the words were as clear as day. Is Mama with child? *Is* she? And *where* is she?"

"It's true, Sophia," he said. And he folded her tightly in his arms and felt his tears flowing again quite unexpectedly. "You have a brother, born this morning. I was with her."

She went very still in his arms. "I have a brother," she said. "I have a brother?" She tore herself from his arms, whirled about and launched herself at her husband. "Francis, I have a *brother.*"

"I heard you the first time, Soph," he said, swinging her once around. "But it bears repeating twice more, I must confess. A little less volume, though, sweetheart."

"I have a brother," she said once more, releasing her death grip on his neck and beaming first at him and then at her father. "And Mama? Is she well? Where is she? I want to see her. And I want to see the baby."

"Congratulations, sir," Francis said, extending his right hand. "If I did not have enough brothers to plague me, now I have a brother-in-law too. But at least this one is younger than I."

"What is his name?" Sophia asked, linking one arm through her husband's and one through her father's and drawing them up the steps to the house. "I can't wait to see him. And Mama."

"He is still nameless, I believe," the earl said. "And as for seeing them, Sophia, they are possibly still asleep and I would not want them woken. Your mother had a hard time. Go upstairs to freshen up and I shall have refreshments sent to the morning room. In the meantime, I will go up and see and come for you in ten minutes' time if they are awake—or if your mother is, at least. Good enough?''

''Not nearly,'' she said. ''But I know that tone of voice too well to try to defy it, and I know Francis will take your part if I try to insist on seeing Mama without further delay. He has developed into a tyrant, Papa. I am a mere shadow of my former self.''

''Which is about as great a bouncer as you have ever told, Soph,'' her husband said, taking her firmly by the hand and leading her up the stairs. ''If you are a shadow of your former self, I would hate to have met the original. I have never found Amazonian wenches very appealing. Ten minutes it will be, sir.''

Olivia was awake, the baby asleep beside her, a fist curled beneath one fat cheek. He had his father's dark hair. She felt deliciously lethargic after a sleep of several hours. She stretched her toes and felt her almost flat stomach with satisfaction.

She wondered when he would come. She could send for him, but she wanted him to come without being summoned. She wanted him to come because he wanted to come. To see his son, she thought. To see his heir. He would come to see the baby.

But no, she would not indulge in thoughts even tinged with bitterness. He had said wonderful things to her the night before, things she had longed to hear the previous summer, things that she wanted to hear again. Perhaps he had said them to comfort her during her labor. But she had believed them then, and she wished to believe them now.

She wished he would come. She turned her head to the door and it opened as if in answer to her thoughts. She watched him come inside and close the door quietly behind him. He was wearing clean clothes and he had shaved. His hair had that soft look it always had when freshly washed.

''You may leave us, Matilda, if you please,'' she told her maid.

''Livy,'' he said, leaning across their son to kiss her cheek.

She noticed that his eyes looked only at her, not at the baby. "Have you slept? Are you feeling better?"

"I feel wonderful," she said. "I have never felt better in my life."

"Liar." He smiled at her.

And then he looked down at their child and the look of tenderness on his face made her want to cry.

"Is he not beautiful?" she said.

"No," he said, smiling. "We will have to add a new word to the dictionary, Livy. There is no adequate word that I can think of. What have you named him?"

"*We* have named him Jonathan," she said. "Unless you have changed your mind since last we thought we might have a son."

"Jonathan," he said, touching one knuckle to his son's soft cheek.

"I was listening to you last night," she said, "although I could not respond a great deal. I heard everything, Marc."

"Good," he said. "Then I need not repeat it all."

"Would you?" she said. "If I had not heard? It was not just that I was in pain and needed comforting?"

"Shall I start now?" he asked. "With I love you? I can talk on that theme for an hour or so, if you wish." He sat on the edge of the bed, careful not to disturb the baby, and turned to look down at her.

"Marc." She lifted a hand and laid it on his arm. He covered it with his own hand. "I was dreadfully wrong, was I not? Only things can be spoiled beyond repair. Not relationships. We could have repaired ours, couldn't we? It could have been as strong as ever. We could have been happy again, couldn't we?"

"Only if we had both been committed to being so," he said.

"And I was not," she said. "I would not allow for your humanity, Marc. I wanted you perfect or not at all. And so I emptied my life of all that might have given it meaning—except for Sophia. I did a dreadful thing. I destroyed the rare chance of a life of happiness. And I did terrible things to you, too. You have not been entirely happy through the years, have you?"

"Don't kill yourself with remorse, Livy," he said. "Guilt can eat away at you and destroy the future as well as the past. I know. I lived with guilt for years until someone persuaded me that divine forgiveness has to be accompanied by forgiveness of self. You told me last summer that you had forgiven me. Have you?"

"Yes," she said.

"Then forgive yourself too," he said. "Mine was the greater sin, Livy."

"All the lost years," she said sadly, tears in her eyes.

"We have lived through them," he said. "And they are gone. All we really have is the present and as much of the future as has been allotted us. And at present, I am with my wife and my son and I am feeling almost entirely happy. I will be totally happy if my wife can assure me that the three of us will be together for the future too."

"Marc," she said, "I never for a moment stopped loving you. I never did. And last summer—I loved you so very much. When you said he had taught me passion, it was of yourself you spoke. I had never got over missing you or wanting you."

"Don't upset yourself," he said, drying a spilled-over tear with his thumb. "We were both living under a misunderstanding last summer, and both nobly freeing the other for what we thought a deeper attachment. But last summer, we loved, Livy. Whichever of those lovings started Jonathan was a loving indeed."

"It was the one in the hidden garden," she said. "The first one. I already suspected the truth before I left Clifton."

He smiled. "I am glad it was that one," he said.

"You cannot know," she said, "how I hoped and hoped and tried not to hope at all."

"Livy," he said, "tell me in words what I think I am hearing but am too afraid to be quite sure of. Are we together again? Are you taking me back? Are we going to bring up Jonathan together? Are we going to piece together an old spoiled relationship and make something perfect of it again?"

She took his hand, which had been stroking the hair from her face, and brought his palm against her mouth. She felt hot tears squeeze their way past her closed eyelids.

"I have wasted so many weary years," she said. "I don't want to waste another moment, Marc. Stay with me forever."

"And ever," he said, leaning carefully over her and kissing her mouth. "Is our son and heir trying to break up a tender moment?"

The baby was fussing and squirming. He suddenly contorted his face, opened his mouth wide, and yelled out his need for food and attention.

"My other man needs me," she said, turning and slipping her hands beneath the baby and lifting him. His crying did not abate. "He needs a dry nappy and my breast in that order. Marc?"

He laughed down at her.

"It is either you or Matilda," she said. "I don't think I have the strength yet." She laughed back at him.

"I don't think male hands were made for this task," he said, crossing the room to fetch a clean nappy. "You never made me do this for Sophia, Livy."

"Then it is high time you learned," she said. "I must say I am rather out of practice myself. Let us see what we can accomplish together."

They had done a great deal of laughing and cooing, and the baby a great deal of crying before the clean nappy was successfully, if somewhat inexpertly, in place and Olivia, propped against a bank of pillows, stopped the crying with her breast.

"Oh," she said, looking down in wonder at her baby and smoothing one hand over the soft down of his dark hair, "I remember this feeling. Oh, Marc, I am a mother again when I thought only to have the comfort of being a grandmother. How wonderful!"

"Oh, Lord," he said. "I am not much of a father, am I? Sophia is here, Livy, and Francis. She was all ready to come roaring in here, bringing all the dust of travel with her, but I ordered her to freshen up and have some tea and Francis hauled her away. I promised to be back for her within ten minutes. That must be well over half an hour ago."

"Sophia is here?" she said. "Oh, what a glorious day this

is turning into. I shall see her, as soon as this hungry little babe has finished sucking. Will you go and tell her that, Marc?''

"Yes," he said, taking his seat on the bed again close to his newfound family and gazing down at them as if he would never have his fill. "In just a moment, Livy. How I envy my son."

She looked up at him and laughed softly. "Your turn will come," she said, "if you will but give me a couple of months."

"I'll wait," he said. "But my love does not depend on just that for nourishment, Liv. I have what I want most in the world right now at this moment—my wife with our son at the breast right before my eyes, and our daughter under the same roof. What greater happiness could there possibly be?''

She smiled at him the dreamy smile of a woman suckling a baby.

Sophia closed the door to her mother's bedchamber a little more hastily than she had opened it. She turned a blushing face to her husband.

"We cannot go in," she said, "and I am very glad that it was I who peeped and not you, Francis."

"Good Lord," he said, "what is going on in there? She has just given birth, has she not?''

"She is nursing the baby," she said. "And Papa is sitting on the bed watching. And neither of them looked embarrassed." Her color flamed even higher.

He placed one hand beneath her chin and raised it. "What a strange combination of boldness and prudery you are, Soph," he said. "What is she supposed to do—hide away in the darkest corner of the nursery and blindfold the baby?''

"No," she said, "but I would have thought she would at least be embarrassed."

He tutted. "All those things we do in the dark," he said, "and that draw such satisfying sounds of pleasure from you, Soph, would cover you with confusion if I could just persuade you to leave a candle burning one of these times, would they not? And yet nothing different would be happening. I could describe your body to you in the minutest detail, you know. Do you think your father does not know what your mother's breasts look like—and feel like and taste like for that matter?''

"Don't," she said. "You are trying to make me uncomfortable, as usual. He has dark hair, Francis.''

"The baby?" he said. "Nice change of subject, Soph.''

"And Papa was sitting close," she said. "And they were smiling at each other. Not at the baby, but at each other. What do you think that means, Francis?''

"It means that they were smiling at each other, I suppose," he said. "But you are fit to bursting with some other interpretation, I can see. You tell me, then.''

"They are together again, that is what," she said. "And how could they not be? You see, it must have happened last year, Francis. It must have, if she has had a child. But they were too stubborn then to admit that they could not live without each other. But now the baby has brought them together and they will stay together and live happily ever after. That is the way it is, I will wager.''

"Wagering is not ladylike, Soph," he said, "and I would not wager against such a theory anyway. It sounds altogether likely. We had better find something to amuse ourselves with while we wait for the heir to Clifton to finish his port and cigars. Could I interest you in a little sport in our rooms? That inn bed last night must be where the spare coals for the fire are stored.''

"Francis!" she said.

"I know," he said, sighing, "it is broad daylight. But we can pretend we are in China, Soph. I imagine it must be dark down there.''

"I would blush all the way to my toes," she said.

"I know," he said. "That is what I want to see. Well, if it is not to be that, we must go off somewhere and have our daily quarrel. We have not had it today and the day has been dreadfully dull.''

"It has not!" she said indignantly. "Do you call arriving in Rushton and seeing Papa again and finding that his note really meant what it said and discovering that Mama had already had the baby and that I am a sister and you a brother-in-law—do you call that all dull?''

Lord Francis yawned loudly, steering his wife in the direction of their rooms.

''I see how it is,'' she said hotly. ''My family means nothing at all to you. You have always had brothers, and now you have sisters-in-law and nephews and nieces. You do not know what it is like to grow up alone, with even one's parents living apart. You do not know what it is like to long and long for a brother or a sister. You think all this is dull?''

''It begins to get more interesting,'' he said, closing the door of their sitting room behind them.

''And now it seems that at least Mama and Papa are back together again,'' she said, ''something I have dreamed of for years and years and something we schemed to bring about last year. Now it has happened, and you call it dull, Francis? Or beginning to get more interesting?''

''Very much more interesting,'' he said, taking her face between his hands and running his thumbs across her lips.

''And don't think you can kiss me now and all will be well,'' she said. ''You have done that every day of our married life and I have always been foolish enough to give in to you. But this is my family you are calling dull. My mama and papa and brother. It is me you are calling dull. Stop it!''

He was feathering kisses on her mouth.

''This is all very, very, very interesting,'' he said.

''Stop it!''

''Fascinating.''

''Don't.''

''Indescribably gloriously wonderful.''

''Don't start doing that with your tongue,'' she said.

''Why not?''

''Because it always weakens me,'' she said severely. ''I want an apology from you.''

''You have it,'' he said. ''Abject, servile, groveling apologies, Soph.''

''You make a mockery of everything,'' she said, her arms creeping up about his neck.

"No, I don't," he said. "One thing I don't make a mockery of, Soph. Two. My feelings for you and what is inside you. We had better not break the news right away, by the way."

"Why not?" she said. "I cannot wait."

"They might find it a little bewildering," he said. "All on the same day becoming parents and learning that in six months' time they are to be grandparents. We had better wait a day or two at least."

"My brother is going to be an uncle in six months' time," she said. "I wonder what his name is, Francis."

"Do you think you could wonder in a supine position?" he asked. "I think you are going to have to get over this maidenly aversion to daylight, you know, Soph. And I'll tell you why. I have every intention of doing what your papa is doing now, when you are doing what your mama is doing now."

"You would not," she said. "I would die of mortification."

" 'Here lies Lady Sophia Sutton,' " he said, " 'who passed from his life, at the age of nineteen years, of mortification when her husband gazed at her naked breast with an infant attached.' Do you think it would make a suitably affecting epitaph? Churchyard viewers would weep pailfuls when they passed by it, don't you think?"

Sophia giggled.

"Ooh," he said. "Not good. Not good at all, Soph. You are supposed to be clawing at my eyes by now so that you would not notice that I have walked you through to your bed-chamber and am laying you back on your bed. Let me think of something quickly to revive this quarrel."

"You do not really mean to, do you?" she asked as her head touched the pillow.

"Look at your naked breast in naked daylight, or make love to you at a time when I don't first have to search for you in the darkness?" he said. "Both, actually, Soph."

"Just kiss me," she said, stretching up her arms to him. "That will be enough for now, Francis. Doubtless Papa will be coming for us soon."

"Don't worry about it," he said. "I have locked all the doors. We can tiptoe along to your mother's room again in half an hour's time and nobody will be any the wiser about what we have been up to. Now, let's see if I have been making love to a woman all these months or to a crocodile or worse."

"Don't be horrid," she said. "Don't look!"

"Mm," he said. "It is all woman so far. Of course, one never knows what the next inch of fabric removed might reveal. This is most interesting. I am sorry I ever called the day dull, Soph."

"Oh," she said. "I shall die. Don't look so deliberately, Francis, and with that odious twinkle in your eye. I would like to blacken it for you. I really would. You are the most horrid man I have ever known. I should never have married you. I should have married a toad before considering marrying you. I should have . . ."

"Eels, snakes, rats buffaloes, elephants," he said. "I would not advise elephants, though, Soph. Too heavy. Especially when you start swelling as you will soon. Mmm. All woman after all, my love. And sure enough, blushing all the way down to the toenails. I love every rosy inch of you, you know, and shall proceed without further ado to prove it to you."

"I hate you," she said. "I really do."

He grinned at her. "Enough quarreling for one day," he said. "Time to kiss and make up, Soph. Tell me that you love me." And he lowered his head to hers.

"Mm," she told him.

"Good enough," he said.